It had been a c

CW01502245

The Millionaire's First Love

They never thought they'd see each other again… Their reunion is intense, sensual, special.

But their past still stands between them… Can these couples work through their differences and accept their rich rewards?

Mary Lynn Baxter and Fayrene Preston present two poignant reunion stories

Dear Reader,

A very hot summer welcome to Desire!

We aim to send your temperature soaring this month starting with the wonderfully exotic **Seduced by the Sheikh** featuring *Sleeping with the Sultan*—the last instalment of Alexandra Sellers's THE SULTANS—and *Hide-and-Sheikh* by Gail Dayton.

The Millionaire's First Love brings together *The Millionaire Comes Home* by Mary Lynn Baxter and the final THE BARONS OF TEXAS novel with the last of the Baron sisters to be hit by love—*The Barons of Texas: Kit* by Fayrene Preston.

Protecting the innocent is the theme of our final volume this month, **Her Personal Protector**, where you'll find Dixie Browning's *Rocky and the Senator's Daughter* and *Night Wind's Woman* from Sheri WhiteFeather.

They're great summer reading!

The Editors

The Millionaire's First Love

MARY LYNN BAXTER
FAYRENE PRESTON

SILHOUETTE®
DESIRE™

*Silhouette, Silhouette Desire and Colophon
are registered trademarks of Harlequin Books S.A.,
used under licence.*

*First published in Great Britain 2002
Silhouette Books, Eton House, 18-24 Paradise Road,
Richmond, Surrey TW9 1SR*

THE MILLIONAIRE'S FIRST LOVE
© Harlequin Books S.A. 2002

The publisher acknowledges the copyright holders of the
individual works as follows:

The Millionaire Comes Home © Mary Lynn Baxter 2001
The Barons of Texas: Kit © Fayrene Preston 2001

ISBN 0 373 04757 6

51-0802

*Printed and bound in Spain
by Litografia Rosés S.A., Barcelona*

THE MILLIONAIRE COMES HOME

by
Mary Lynn Baxter

MARY LYNN BAXTER

A native Texan, Mary Lynn Baxter knew instinctively
that books would occupy an important part of her life.
Always an avid reader, she became a school librarian,
then a bookstore owner, before writing her first novel.

Now Mary Lynn Baxter is an award-winning author
who has written more than thirty novels, many of which
have appeared on the *USA Today* list.

One

He wondered if she still lived here.

Denton Hardesty scoffed at his thoughts of his old girlfriend as he braked his BMW at the first and only stoplight in Ruby, Texas. He couldn't believe he'd been born in this one-horse town and lived here until he'd left for college. But Ruby had been his parents' home; he'd had no choice.

Thank heavens he had a choice now. Dallas, the city *he* called home, was a far cry from this quaint little tourist town with its bed-and-breakfast lodgings, antique and gift shops. Too quiet to suit him. As soon as he finished his meeting with his prospective client, regardless of whether a deal was cemented, he would hit the road again, back to Big D.

When he heard a truck honk from behind Denton realized he'd been camped at the light. Muttering under his breath, he shoved down on the accelerator only to have the engine sputter, then quit completely.

A few choice words escaped his lips as he watched the truck swerve around him, a killer look on the driver's face. So, all of Ruby wasn't that laid-back. With dark amusement, Denton found that somewhat comforting as he restarted the BMW. It died on him again directly in front of a service station, the old-fashioned kind where a sign said owner/ mechanic on duty—only in Small Town, USA.

The owner came out immediately, wiping his greasy hands on an equally greasy rag. He smiled, showing off crooked teeth stained with tobacco. "Howdy, need some help?"

Denton figured that went without saying but refrained from stating the obvious, keeping his impatience on a short leash. "My engine's giving me trouble. Mind if I leave it here until the dealership can come get it?"

"Don't mind atall, only how 'bout I take a look at it?"

Denton eyed the tall, lanky man with suspicion. "You know something about foreign cars?"

"Use to work on 'em, especially these." The man nodded toward the sleek black vehicle.

Somehow Denton believed him, even though it seemed unlikely anyone who knew how to work on BMWs would be stuck running a one-man station. But stranger things had happened, he reminded himself ruefully.

"Maybe it's just something minor, and I can have you on your way real soon," the attendant pointed out. "If not, you can call the dealer and nothing will be lost."

Except my valuable time, Denton thought, irritated beyond measure. Curbing his impatience, he made a gesture and said, "Be my guest. See what you can do."

"By the way, my name's Raymond."

"Denton Hardesty."

Raymond stuck out his grimy hand. Then, as if seeing the look on Denton's face, jerked it back and gave a sheepish smile. "Sorry, it's still a bit greasy."

"No problem," Denton muttered, clearly distracted.

"You just passing through?" Raymond asked, his head cocked to one side.

Denton wasn't about to indulge in small talk, not when he had much bigger fish to fry. Besides, for a spring day it was hotter than hell, and he didn't want to be wet with sweat when he met with his client. "Yeah, you might say that."

For once Raymond didn't comment.

"Is there someplace cool where I can get a cup of coffee while I wait?" Denton asked.

Raymond nodded toward a bed-and-breakfast. "Across the street."

"Thanks," Denton said, turning and heading in that direction. The first thing about the two-story colonial style mansion that caught his attention was the lovely grounds: manicured lawns, landscaped flower beds, lilacs and big oak trees, and annual beds that flanked the walkway and proudly lined the front of the porch.

The colors of the mixed annuals were so vivid they were almost blinding. Even though he hadn't set foot on the property, he could smell the lilacs. They offered their ethereal scent and exquisite blossoms to all the passersby. Lucky souls, he thought, remembering the lilacs in his own front yard when he was a youngster.

As he approached the sidewalk, his gaze settled on the porch. Country calm, he reminded himself, a gentle breeze acting as a coolant to his damp skin. Great if you could stand it…. He could tolerate this setting maybe a day, two max, then he'd be climbing the walls. He preferred the sound of horns and car doors slamming. Also, it was imperative he hear the sound of human voices as opposed to the chirp of birds.

Yet, he might have felt differently if he and Grace had…

Ah, to hell with those thoughts. While his memories of living here were for the most part good, Denton couldn't imagine ever doing so again under any circumstances.

When his dad had been transferred out of state the summer of his junior year in college, he hadn't been happy. He'd admit that. He hadn't wanted to leave Grace even though what had happened between them had scared the hell out of him. However, his parents were not about to leave him behind. Once they moved, the unthinkable had happened. His dad had fallen victim to a stroke, something else that had torn him in two.

Suddenly forcing his mind off that dark period and back on more pleasant thoughts, Denton's gaze swept his surroundings. Up close he could see the house needed some repairs, especially the porch, though the state of disrepair didn't dilute any of its charm. What a perfect place for guests to gather for nonsensical conversation and summer breezes.

A wicker swing and settee, along with several

creaky rockers, provided a Norman Rockwell type setting familiar to porches across the South. The only things missing from the ideal picture were platters of watermelon and pitchers of lemonade that would provide wholesome refreshments for the guests. It was a safe bet both would most likely appear later on in the day.

Thinking of lemonade made him thirsty. But the thought didn't last long, knowing what he really needed was another stiff cup of coffee which never failed to give him the extra push he needed to get through his hectic days and nights. He still had a long way to go before this day was over. And the way it had started out didn't bode well.

Maybe the owner would be obliging this late, sunny morning and provide him with that much-needed kick. After slapping at a bee buzzing around his head, Denton lifted the old-fashioned door knocker and let it go.

Grace Simmons hummed to herself as she finished putting away the last of the clean breakfast dishes. She paused in her actions and peered out the back window at the grounds of Grace House. As always, her breath instantly caught and held.

Tulips, her favorite sign of spring, blended together to form a tapestry of natural beauty nothing could ever surpass.

Hers.

This was all hers. And the bank's, she corrected mentally. But such wouldn't always be the case, she reaffirmed with conviction. One day she'd get it paid off, then she'd be the proud owner of this graceful old house. She'd bought it for a song, but in order to make it habitable, then fulfill her dream of turning it into a profitable bed-and-breakfast, she'd had to borrow an additional healthy sum of money.

Still, she paid her banker each month with a cheerful heart, knowing what she wanted to do would work and eventually pay its own way. And while the profit margin remained ever so slim, she was able to keep herself and the home afloat and pay the bank. For the time being that was all that was important.

Extra money for more repairs to the old home would come. She didn't know when or from what source, but she wasn't worried about it. In fact, she didn't worry period. Not anymore. She had learned long ago what worrying did to her, and she could no longer allow herself that indulgence, especially since she ran a business in which other people depended on her.

And she thrived on the never-ending challenge of providing her guests with the cleanest rooms, the loveliest ambiance and the best breakfast she could, at an affordable cost.

As a result her house stayed at full occupancy year-round. However, at present she had one room not booked—a rare occurrence. Yet she wasn't concerned. The right person would show up, and the room would be waiting.

A smile brightened Grace's face as her eyes fastened on a bluebird perched on a limb, grooming himself. Spying on a wild creature was such a small thing, but she had learned, the hard way, it was the small things that made life worth living.

So what if she was a woman alone in a couples' world? So what if she was often lonely, especially in her big bed at night? So what if she wished for what was apparently not going to happen—a happy marriage and children?

So what?

After all she'd been through, she could accept that and be glad for the peace and tranquility that now shaped and dominated her life. Besides, her life was too full to dwell on past mistakes and future longings. At thirty-two she had wasted enough time on something that had brought her heartache rather than joy. At present she was only concentrating on the joy.

Living and working in Ruby, Texas, did just that.

Thinking of work made Grace realize she had too much to do to stand and gaze outdoors, even if it was candy for the soul. She would put her grounds up against anyone else's in town, though she could only take credit for the flowers. Those she did plant and maintain, a full-time job in itself. Because of her part-time helper, Connie Foley, Grace was able to create her miracles outdoors, which she knew brought pleasure to her guests.

Maybe later she would cut some of the tulips for the sunroom, definitely before afternoon snack time, a fun ritual that only two of her present occupants would take advantage of—the elderly couple who were honeymooning. A wider smile forced her dimple deeper in her right cheek as she thought about Ed and Zelma Brenner. In their seventies, and giddily in love, they were a hoot. After both had married someone else, borne children, then widowed, they met on a cruise and married five days later.

On their way to a planned honeymoon at a cottage on Lake Austin, the couple had driven through Ruby. They never made it any farther. According to Ed, the minute they saw Grace House, they had been enchanted and chose to stay there. Hence, Grace had been honored with their presence for over two weeks now. Each day she grew more fond of them. If her parents hadn't died in a freak auto accident when she was in college, she wondered if they would have turned out like Ed and Zelma. She liked to think so, since the thought was somehow comforting.

Her other guest, however, was cut from a far different bolt of cloth. Ralph Kennedy was a well-known children's author who sought complete solitude for the purpose of penning his stories. Here he had apparently found his niche because he'd been a guest for more than four weeks. His brief appearance at breakfast was about all she ever saw of him except on rare occasions when she'd catch him strolling through the grounds. She suspected he was trying to work through a story problem. Despite the fact that he wasn't her usual outgoing boarder, rather weird to be exact, she had no complaints. He paid his weekly bill and seemed content. That was all that mattered.

Deciding it was time to get back to her chores, Grace grabbed a dust cloth out of the cabinet. Opting to keep on her apron, which she loved to wear in spite of its being out of vogue, she made her way out of the large, bright kitchen and headed toward the garden room. It was her favorite room in the entire house, a hard choice to make as the rest of the old dwelling had other bragging rights. The polished hardwood floors, which made no attempt to soak up the sounds of hard-soled shoes, were magnificent. Another favorite was the exquisitely gorgeous Waterford chandelier that hung in the foyer.

She gave a cursory glance to the arched doorways and beveled glass of the front door, to the antique furnishings as she went into the garden room that was a prime environment for lush plants. Grace had seen to it that the room was much more than that since the living room flowed into it, providing an informal but lush setting in which to relax over breakfast with a newspaper or good book or to sip afternoon tea.

Grace had wanted the room to seem drenched in light. So she had painted the walls a pearly white, keeping the furniture to a minimum and dispensing with drapes altogether. She had achieved her goal, the space becoming a charming blend of yellows and greens, mixed with seasoned wicker, plump cushions and pillows and a myriad of flowering bushes and plants.

On one wall she'd painted an ivy-covered trellis. Even in the dead of winter the garden room gave one the feeling of being constantly bathed in greenery and light.

She had just begun dusting the glass-topped coffee table when the doorbell chimed. Stuffing her cloth into her apron pocket, she hurried to open the door, only to cling to the doorknob for support.

Grace would have recognized him anywhere, regardless of the fourteen years since she'd seen him. Denton Hardesty, a ghost from the past.

It was obvious from the stunned look on his face that he hadn't expected to see her, either, as his mouth was slightly open while his green eyes narrowed.

"Grace," he finally muttered, his tone hoarse as if he had a sore throat.

"Hello, Denton," she responded, staring at the man who, one starlit night, took her virginity and her heart with him.

Two

Somehow Grace managed to derail that traumatic thought and force herself to behave as though Denton Hardesty were a stranger, someone she'd never known. But that wasn't easy, as she was more than a little overwhelmed and flustered by his showing up on her doorstep out of the blue. Holding on to her fractured composure was even more difficult because her senses had leaped at the sight of him.

Dear Lord, that would never do.

"What on earth are you doing here?" she finally asked, the silence having built to an almost thundering roar, at least to her. Maybe it was the sound of her heart beating. Absurd. She no longer gave a fig about him.

"I could ask you the same thing."

"I live here," she said simply, feeling her chin jut slightly and her spine stiffen.

As if he picked up on the slight edge of defiance in her posture, he sighed. "I was wondering if you'd ever left."

"Again, what brings you back to Ruby?"

His sigh deepened. "So that's the way it's going to be?"

For a second Grace was confused. "Excuse me?"

"I can't say that I blame you for not inviting me in."

Grace flushed, realizing that she hadn't budged so much as an inch since she'd opened the door. In fact, she seemed to be guarding the door as if he was an intruder who might force himself inside. In a way that was exactly what he was. However, she had no intention of letting him know that her senses still hadn't quite settled, that his unexpected presence had definitely thrown her for a curve.

"Of course you may come in."

His head leaned to one side. "Are you sure?"

"Certainly," she said, swallowing her irritation at his assumption that she gave a damn one way or the other. She'd best be careful. He'd always had the uncanny ability to read her heart. But that was then, when she was just a teenager. Now she was an adult and he didn't know beans about her.

Finally she stepped back and gestured with one hand. "Welcome to Grace House."

He pulled up short. "You mean this is your place?"

"Yes." Again her tone held a note of defiance, this time with an edge of acid.

Denton chuckled. "I see you haven't lost that sharp tongue."

"Some things never change," she said, more breathlessly than she intended.

"In some cases that's not bad."

It wasn't so much what he said as the way he said it that set off a warning inside her. That raspy note in his voice was just as much a turn-on now as back then. What had she done to deserve this cruel twist of fate? She'd never expected to lay eyes on her first love again.

And why now, when she was lonelier than she'd ever been?

"I'm impressed."

Grace forced herself back to the moment, though what she really wanted to do was tell him to leave, to go back where he came from and not disrupt her life one more second.

Instead she made her way into the garden room and watched as he strode to the long expanse of windows before turning and facing her again.

"Would you like a glass of iced tea?" she asked. "Or would you rather have coffee?"

"Both, actually."

A spontaneous laugh erupted before she could control it. "That's not a problem."

He answered with a smile that hit her like a sledgehammer. He was still too good-looking for words, even if the added grooves of maturity made him appear older than his thirty-four years, two years her senior.

Too, there was an uptightness, a restlessness that she didn't remember. But it had been so long since that summer evening after her last year in high school, when she'd been so madly in love with him, she couldn't be expected to remember every detail about him. Nor did she want to.

Liar.

Right now she was standing there like an idiot, soaking up every detail about him. His hair, while still brown, was now dusted with silver. Not a bad thing, she noted, since the silver highlighted his tanned skin and green eyes that were surrounded by such thick lashes they appeared darker and sootier than they actually were.

As for his over-six-foot frame, he hadn't added an ounce of fat to it. At one time he'd had washboard abs, and since his knit shirt hugged him in all the right places, she knew that hadn't changed. Nor had his long legs and powerful thighs. When her gaze reached that part of his anatomy, and she saw the slight bulge behind his zipper, she averted her eyes back to his face. Those perfect white teeth hadn't changed, either. Or that smile. Both had always been high-wattage and still were.

Not fair.

Here she was, aging, gathering wrinkles in all the wrong places. So what? It didn't matter whether the years had been kind to her or not. Except that it did. Granted, Denton was just passing through, but it was important to her that she at least didn't look like the wrath of God, for heaven's sake.

Then it hit her she was still wearing her apron.

Feeling her cheeks flood with color, she reached for the sash at the back and jerked it.

"Don't."

Her head jolted up. "Don't what?"

"Take it off."

Her hands stilled, and when she opened her mouth to speak, nothing came out.

"It's…different."

Grace rolled her eyes. "Right."

"No, I'm serious."

"What you are is 'seriously' making fun."

"Somehow it suits you."

"You don't have a clue what suits me," Grace snapped, then mentally kicked herself.

"True," he said, his mouth slightly downturned. "But I know what I like, and I like your apron."

"Fine. But I don't." She jerked it off and headed toward the kitchen. "I'll get the drinks and be right back."

"Need any help?" he called to her back.

She didn't so much as slow down. "No, thanks."

By the time she had a tray filled with both iced tea and coffee, her hands were shaking. It was a miracle she had glasswear of any kind left. Just get through this, she told herself. Be polite, make small talk, then get rid of him. Send him back from whence he came.

Blowing out a deep breath, Grace planted a smile on her face and went back into the garden room. Denton had taken a seat in one of the wicker chairs. When he saw her, however, he rose and reached for the tray.

She shook her head, then set it down on the coffee table in front of the settee. "Your choice?"

"Coffee," he said, reaching for it on his own.

She chose a glass of iced tea. For a moment they each sipped in silence, though for Grace that silence still had undertones of booming thunder.

"This is really yours?"

"You sound like that's not possible."

"Hey, that's not it at all. It's just that I'm impressed."

"Impressed, huh?"

"Yeah, impressed. This is a grand old house, and apparently you've made a success of operating it as a bed-and-breakfast. To me that's impressive."

"I'd like to think so. I know that I love every minute of being an innkeeper, so to speak."

"You would. It fits your personality to a T."

Again she wanted to tell him he didn't know jack about her personality, but she refrained. She was already in water over her head. Why purposely drown herself?

"Did you buy the old place?"

"I'm buying it. Right now the bank and I are partners."

He chuckled. "I hear you."

"One of these days, though, it'll be mine free and clear."

"You're that busy?"

"Ruby's grown, despite the fact that it maintains its status as a quiet country town. Being so close to Austin has given us the tourist boost we needed to grow our economy."

"I noticed several antique stores as I drove down main street. Ruby never had anything like that before."

"Again, it's the boom going on in Austin that's responsible."

He looked around for a moment, then faced her again, his eyes probing. If only he didn't have that certain way of staring at a woman as if she was the only person on the face of the earth. Denton could rival Richard Gere when it came to that feat. At one time she'd loved that. Now she hated it.

"You look great, Grace. Have I told you that?"

A warmth spread through her, which she promptly ignored. "No, but that's okay. I'd rather talk about you."

"I'm sure you're curious."

"Let's just say I know you're not passing through for old time's sake."

Did he flush or had she imagined that?

"You're right," he said, reaching for his coffee and taking a drink. "I'm here to see a client."

"In Ruby?" She didn't bother to mask her astonishment.

"A quirk of fate. What can I say?"

"Whatever," she said, hearing that breathlessness in her tone again and wishing she could get her act together.

He set his cup down, then crossed an ankle over the other knee. "I'm an investment broker in Dallas, have been for several years now."

"That's nice."

He chuckled. "'How boring' is what you're really saying."

"I wish you'd stop trying to second-guess me," she said, trying to control her edginess but failing miserably.

"I was always pretty good at doing that, if you'll remember."

His voice had dropped to a husky pitch, and his eyes were so intent on her lips that she felt a rush of color to her face while all the air seemed to have been sucked out of the room. "Look—"

"Sorry. I didn't mean to go down that road. It's

just that I never expected to see you again, especially not here in Ruby.''

''Just because you hauled it—''

His lips thinned. ''You're right to be pissed.''

''Look, Denton, I'm not pissed, okay? Let's just leave the past where it is. Buried.''

''So my car just broke down. How's that for a mundane topic of conversation?''

Ignoring his hint of sarcasm, she asked, ''Where?''

''At the station across the street.'' Denton went on to explain what was going on.

''Ah, Raymond's in charge.'' Her lips quirked in a smile. ''No doubt he's proudly displaying that BMW for all the town to see.''

''Reckon?''

They both laughed at Denton's choice of words. Then, realizing how chummy that sounded, Grace sobered. ''What if he can't fix it?''

''The dealership in Austin will have a loaner car here in no time.''

My, my, how nice, she almost said in a snippy tone, but didn't. Obviously, he was making money hand over fist. She wondered which rancher in Ruby had the kind of big dollars it would take to invest with him? She wasn't about to ask, for several reasons, the main one being she wanted to get rid of him. The longer this indulgence stretched itself, the more dangerous it became to her peace of mind, especially with his gaze seemingly fixed on her breasts.

In spite of her efforts to the contrary, the color lingered in her face. ''You're welcome to wait here,'' she said, glancing away.

''Are you sure?''

His husky tone drew her back. "I even have a vacant room," she quipped.

"I just might take you up on that."

Her jaw went slack. "I didn't—"

"I know you didn't mean it, but I do."

"We both know that's not going to happen."

Both of his eyebrows shot up. "I wouldn't bet on it."

"Are you married?" she asked bluntly, more for herself than for him. She was desperate to steer things back on course after she'd opened her mouth again when she shouldn't have. But no way was he going to remain in Ruby. The thought of him sleeping in her place as a guest was ludicrous and she wouldn't let it happen.

"Not anymore," he said in answer to her question.

"Ah, so there was a Mrs. Denton Hardesty?"

"*Was* is the correct word."

"Not an amiable parting, huh?"

"Not hardly."

"Sorry."

"Me, too. I hate failing at anything. But nothing about our relationship was right from the beginning. Thank goodness there were no children."

She wanted to amen that but didn't.

"What about you? I don't see a ring on your finger."

"There hasn't been one."

He raised his eyebrows again. "I find that hard to believe."

"That I'm an old maid?"

Denton made a snorting sound as his gaze roamed hotly and blatantly over her. "You know better than that."

She turned away, her heart in her throat, feeling the inability to handle much more of this togetherness. "Let's just say I'm happy with my life the way it is."

"There's nothing wrong with that."

A silence fell between them during which she made a conscious effort not to meet his eyes.

It was then his cell phone rang. Grace tried to ignore what he was saying by concentrating on what she was going to serve for snack time. The Brenners would be back shortly, and on rare occasions even Ralph was known to appear for the afternoon goodies.

Only after Denton shoved his cell back into its clip did she face him again.

"I've been stood up, at least for today."

"Oh?"

"My client had an unexpected emergency to deal with. That was his housekeeper."

Relief almost made her giddy. "I guess you'll have to come back to Ruby another time."

Their eyes met and held for the longest time.

"I have a better idea. I'll take that vacant room and hang around."

Three

Panic paralyzed her.

Stay. He didn't mean that, not for a minute. He was just jerking her chain again. That had to be the case. It just had to. She almost laughed at the very idea.

In an unsteady tone, she voiced her thoughts. "You're really joking."

His eyes took on a warm, lazy cast as they swept over her. "Is that your way of saying I'm not welcome?"

She swallowed, quelling the urge to slug him. He was baiting her, and she didn't have a clue why. After all, he'd been the one who'd walked out on her. If anyone had an ax to grind, it was she.

"Of course, you're welcome. It's just that—"

"It's just what?" he pressed.

"I can't imagine why you'd want to stay here." There, she'd said it. She'd been as blunt as she knew how to be. If that didn't do the trick then nothing would.

"Can't you?"

Denton's tone suddenly matched his eyes, adding to her confusion. Was he flirting with her? Suddenly the feelings of acute sexual awareness that hung between them was overridden by a sense of outrage. How dare he think he could just show up on her doorstep and behave in such a brazen manner? She had to call a halt to such madness right now. She wasn't about to let him back inside her life only to have him walk out again.

"No, I can't," she said through tight lips. "You don't belong here anymore."

A flash of anger darkened his eyes. Yet, when he spoke his tone was even. "Is a room available?"

Say no. Tell him that you made a mistake and that it's promised. She couldn't lie, and even if she did, he wouldn't believe her. "Yes."

"Good. I'll take it."

"For how long?"

Several heartbeats of silence followed during which Grace forced herself not to bite a hole in her lower lip.

"Couple days max."

"Fine."

A smile of sorts suddenly lightened his features. "I promise not to be any trouble."

"You'll be treated like all my other guests," she said as nonchalantly as possible.

"Fair enough."

Their gazes met again, and only by sheer force of will was Grace able finally to turn away.

"Yo, we're back."

Grace almost wilted visibly with relief at the timely arrival of the Brenners. "In the garden room," she called out.

When the elderly couple walked in and saw Denton, they pulled up short. "Sorry," Zelma said. "Are we interrupting anything?"

Grace smiled. "Of course not."

She introduced them, then watched as Denton smiled and shook their hands.

If ever two people appeared mismatched, it was Ed and Zelma. Ed was short and robust while Zelma was tall and thin. Though both were in their late seventies, they were full of boundless energy. Grace dreaded the day they left Ruby. She would miss them terribly, though they had already promised to return countless times.

"You're going to love your stay here, Mr. Hardesty," Zelma said, taking a seat across from Grace.

"I bet you're right about that," Denton said, smiling at Zelma.

Grace groaned inwardly as she watched him mesmerize the old lady. As a young man, he'd had plenty of charm. As a grown-up, he had perfected it and knew how to use it to his advantage.

With Ed and Zelma he was welcome to go all-out, to turn it on full blast if that would make him happy. As far as she was concerned, he was wasting his time. She planned to avoid him the entire length of his stay.

"Just wait till you taste her cooking," Ed was saying. "It's the best this side of heaven."

Zelma made an unladylike noise, though there was a twinkle in her eye as her gaze landed on her husband. "Are you saying I can't please you?"

"How would I know, honey bun? You haven't ever tried."

"Uh, right," Zelma said with a blush. "Well, are you ever in for a surprise."

He cut her a look. "I bet you can't cook."

"How'd you guess?"

They all chuckled, then Ed turned to Denton and asked, "You just passing through, young man?"

Grace looked on in silence as Denton explained about his vehicle. She tried not to concentrate on him, but it was hard. He was so easy to stare at she had to force her gaze away.

"Lucky man to have trouble in such an ideal spot," Ed responded. "We're both from Houston, but we're thinking about pulling up stakes and moving here."

Grace stared at them in amazement. "You are?"

"We're talking about it," Zelma said, sounding less enthusiastic.

Ed rested his gaze on Denton. "You couldn't ask for life any easier. It's sure nice not to hear the constant sounds of engines and horns. Instead you hear chirping birds and prattling insects."

"That's not Mr. Hardesty's cup of tea," Grace said without thought. "I'm sure he'll be bored with all that serenity."

Denton rested his intense gaze on her which made her want to squirm, but she didn't.

"I'm counting on you to see that doesn't happen," he said in an easy drawl, in contrast to her rather sharp one.

Ed and Zelma exchanged looks before bouncing their gazes between Grace and Denton as if picking up on the undercurrents in the room.

Deciding it was time to call a halt to this little chat, Grace stood. "Kitchen duty calls."

"I wish you'd let me help," Zelma said.

Grace shook her head. "Not a chance."

"Point me toward my room before you go, will you?" Denton asked, facing Grace.

"Now that I can do," Zelma said, claiming Denton's attention. "You just follow me."

"Thanks," Grace murmured, relieved she was spared being alone with Denton again. Her nerves were far too frayed to push her luck.

Ed shuffled toward them. "Wait for me."

Several minutes later Zelma walked back into the kitchen.

"What did he say?" Grace asked.

"He thanked me, then said he was going across the street to check on his car."

Grace merely nodded, her hands busy placing the fresh fruit on the tray.

"So what's with you two?" Zelma asked, a slight twitter in her tone.

Grace's head popped up. "I don't know what you're talking about."

"Now, honey, you can't fool this old fuddy-duddy. I know when electricity's crackling between two people."

"You're imagining things."

Zelma eyed her carefully. "I don't think so, but for now I'll mind my own business. But when you're ready to talk, I'm ready to listen." She paused with a wink. "I'll meet you back in the garden room."

Grace sagged against the counter, her heart beating far too hard and fast against her chest.

* * *

"It won't be long now, Mr. Hardesty, and I'll have you up and running."

Denton put his sunglasses on, then stared at the mechanic. "So you think you found the problem?"

"I know I have. It's just taking a tad longer than I thought to fix it."

"No problem. You take all the time you need."

Raymond gave him a puzzled look. "You mean you ain't in no hurry?"

"That's exactly what I mean."

Raymond rubbed his slightly grizzled chin. "Whatever you say."

Denton slapped a couple of bills in Raymond's hand then turned and headed back across the street.

A few minutes later he was opening the door to his room when a man strode by without so much as a nod. Strange-looking dude, Denton thought, comparing the stranger to someone out of a *Star Wars* movie. He was tall and thin to the point of gauntness. A hank of dark hair hung over his left eye.

He certainly didn't appear as if he belonged at Grace House, but then neither did he, Denton reminded himself scathingly.

Once he was in his room, he walked to the window and peered out at the front lawn. Though glorious beauty filled his vision, he failed to appreciate it, reaching into his pocket and pulling out a roll of antacids. After popping one in his mouth and chewing it, he released a deep sigh, then turned and stared at the antique four-poster bed with a step stool enabling a person to climb aboard. He smiled with no humor.

What the hell was he doing here? Had he lost his mind?

Yes.

No doubt about it: he'd taken complete leave of all his faculties. And why? Grace. It didn't take anyone with smarts to figure that out. Still, his actions made no sense.

Granted, when she'd opened the door, he'd felt as if he'd been hit upside the head with a crowbar. For some unknown reason, he'd assumed she hadn't hung around Ruby, either—that she'd flown the coop long ago. So much for that assumption. She'd not only remained but she'd gone into business here and apparently was very successful in her endeavor, which made him glad for her.

What a looker she'd turned into. Oh, she'd always been pretty, especially at eighteen, blessed with a natural beauty that few women could claim but all envied. That naturalness had stayed with her; only now it was enhanced by maturity and a hint of makeup.

Little else about her had changed, though, especially that delightful dimple. That had always captivated him and still did. He'd found himself wanting to dip his tongue in it the way he'd done so many times in the past.

A frown marred his face at the same time his loins stirred. Suddenly he fought the urge to grab another antacid, turn and get the hell out of there as fast as his legs could carry him. Yet he didn't move a muscle. It was as though his thoughts had him welded to the spot.

And that apron. He couldn't forget about that. He hadn't been making fun when he'd called attention to it, either. He'd been intrigued. And delighted. How quaint. How *uncitified*. But again, only someone with Grace's whimsical beauty and charm could pull it off.

The thought of any of his women friends donning an apron was so ludicrous he almost laughed out loud.

For his own peace of mind he wished Grace were married with 2.3 children and sported wrinkles and a little more fat. Instead she had remained thin, but not too thin, because her breasts seemed to fill her knit shirt to his standard of perfection.

Of course, her hair had changed. She now wore it in a short style that was a little edgy, a little messy. However, its color remained intact, the light-brown locks with blond streaks still contrasting sensationally with her dark eyes and luscious thick lashes.

She oozed a natural sexuality that he'd bet she wasn't even aware of. When he was in the room with her, he found it difficult to breathe. He was sure other men had been affected the same way.

So why had she been content to stagnate here where obviously there were no available men? No wonder she wasn't married. Suddenly he felt a small pinch of gladness at the thought, which was absurd since he was only passing through.

No matter. After he had walked out of her life the way he had, he was surprised she'd let him in the door. Maybe he'd been just as much a passing fancy for her as she'd been for him. Again it didn't matter. He had sworn off women, at least those with marriage in mind.

One wife, followed by a nasty divorce, was enough for him.

Yet he realized now more than ever that he'd never forgotten Grace or that night of passion they'd shared. He'd been nuts about her and hadn't wanted to leave her. He remembered that all too clearly. However, nothing had worked out according to either of their plans.

But that was then and this was now. He was no longer the horny college student who thought he'd die if he couldn't make her his, thinking he was in love. Lust. That was the emotion that had driven him. Love hadn't had anything to do with it, or so he'd convinced himself, having felt rotten at the outcome of their relationship.

"Damn," he muttered, reaching for another antacid.

This time there was no relief for the sour taste in his mouth and in his stomach. All he had to do was walk out of the room, tell Grace he couldn't stay, and that would be that. His life would be back on track once again, back to Dallas, back to his job.

And back to his nightmares about the plane crash that had brought him sleepless nights and restless days. Why had he been the only one spared that fateful day? He had walked away from the scattered debris and the mangled bodies of his best friend and the pilot.

It had been nearly a year since a malfunction in the engine had sent the small plane to the ground. Would the dark end of that bright spring day haunt him forever?

As if his body had suddenly become detached from his mind, Denton reached for his cell phone and punched in the number of his firm in Dallas.

Four

"See you later, dearie."

"I'm counting on that," Grace said, mustering up a sincere smile for Zelma.

Zelma winked, then whispered in a conspiratorial tone, "I'm going to join the old man for a late siesta."

This time Grace grinned openly. "Works for me."

Zelma's attractive features sobered. "You really ought to think about—"

"Don't you dare say it. Don't you dare think it."

"Oops, looks like I stepped in over my head again."

"Close to it," Grace countered, though her smile was back intact.

"It's just that you're so lovely, it's a shame—"

"Zelma!"

"I'm gone. I'm gone."

Once Grace was alone, she took a deep breath. She

knew Zelma meant well, that she wanted her to find and experience the kind of love that she and Ed shared. And while Grace appreciated that, she couldn't let Zelma think for one second that Denton might be the one.

A shiver darted through her. She had no intention of trekking down that rocky road again, though Zelma knew nothing of her and Denton's past and never would. Even so, she wasn't about to stand for Zelma's matchmaking, even if it was from the heart.

Grace glanced at the clock and saw that it was later than usual. But then, snack time had been later. Now, with the exception of Denton, the guests had all exited the garden room after having devoured the snack.

Since he'd returned from the gas station, he hadn't left his room. Most of the time he'd been on the phone. Because his room was the closest to the living areas, all had heard the sounds of his muffled voice. Although she couldn't decipher the exact words of his conversation and certainly didn't try, she had gotten the gist of them, anyway—all hell seemed to have broken loose in his office. No wonder he popped antacids as if they were going out of style.

What a dreadful way of life. Still, that was his choice, and he seemed to thrive on pressure. That was why she expected him to renege on his stay and leave at any time, regardless of his client and regardless of the status of his vehicle. She crossed her fingers that would be the case. Having him underfoot for even one night was not good. Seeing him again had affected her much more than she cared to admit. Her mind's eye suddenly conjured up the whipcord leanness of his body at the same time her senses smelled the slightly musky odor that was exclusively his.

And when he looked at her in that certain way, her entire body tingled. Stop it! she told herself. Stop adding fuel to an already smoldering fire. Those memories were not welcome. Besides, she could feel the anxiety building inside her, and she couldn't afford to let that happen. She'd been doing so well. No way was Denton Hardesty going to undermine that.

Suddenly unable to stand her idle hands, Grace scooped up the remains of snack time and almost ran into the kitchen. Keeping her momentum, she grabbed a bowl out of the cabinet, then crossed to the pantry where she latched on to a box of coffee cake mix, rationalizing that something different would be an extra attraction for tomorrow's breakfast. That way she could get ahead and keep her mind and hands occupied at the same time.

She was stirring the batter as if it was the enemy when she looked up and watched Zelma walk back in. "I thought you were taking a nap." Grace grinned. "Or something."

Zelma's mouth turned down. "Ed's snoring. What does that tell you?"

Grace's grin spread. "That you struck out."

"What's that you're whipping up on?" Zelma asked.

"Coffee cake."

"Ah, more fat for these hips."

"Pooh. You don't have an ounce of fat on you."

"Well, Ed does, but he's working on it."

"Think he'll forgive me for throwing temptation in his wake?"

"He won't forgive you if you don't."

They both chuckled, then Zelma said, "I came to see if you wanted to go dancing with us."

"Dancing?"

"Yeah, in Austin. We accidentally stumbled on a place that caters to old folks like us. Last week, though, there were several singles that joined in. So how about it?"

"Thanks, but I'll pass. It's been a long day."

Zelma eyed her curiously. "Are you sure?"

"I'm sure."

"Ah, come on and go. It'll do you good to shake a leg."

Both women turned and watched as Ed strolled in. Grace frowned, thinking something was not quite right about him, but she couldn't say what. For starters his color wasn't good; he looked almost pasty. She wondered if Zelma had picked up on that. Should she express her concern? No. It could just be her imagination which meant she would set off an alarm for nothing. But what if it wasn't?

"Ed, are you okay?" Grace asked.

"Yeah, honey," Zelma said, frowning in his direction. "You look—"

"I'm fine, sweetheart," Ed interrupted. He winked at Grace. "You're feeding me too good. That's the problem."

Still not convinced, but deciding to let the matter drop, Grace smiled. "So you two go ahead and shake all the legs you want. I'm heading for the bathtub."

"We'll see you later, then, hon," Ed said, taking Zelma's arm and steering her out.

Grace watched as they left the room, then turned her attention back to the cake batter, noticing that it had lumped on her. She began stirring it harder than ever.

"Why didn't you take them up on their offer?"

Grace's hands stilled, but her pulse didn't. It spiked to an all-time high. She raised her head. He was standing just inside the kitchen, looking and smelling much more appetizing than the cake batter in front of her. He had on a white knit shirt and a pair of casual slacks that left no doubt as to the strength of his muscles.

Judging from the dampness of his hair, he'd apparently just showered, which should have made him appear more rested. It didn't. It was obvious that he was tired, the grooves cutting deeper than ever into his eyes and mouth.

"I didn't want to dance, that's why," she finally said, dragging her gaze off him.

"It sounds like fun."

"I'm sure they'd let you tag along," she said for lack of anything better to say.

His lips quirked as he stepped closer. "I don't think so."

"Are you hungry?" she forced herself to ask. She had to dispel the sudden burgeoning tension.

"No, thanks."

"Just tired, huh?"

"Is it that obvious?"

"To me it is."

"Maybe that's because you know me so well."

Her eyes flared. "I don't know you at all."

"I haven't changed that much."

"Oh, please," she muttered, feeling as if she just stepped off into quicksand, and it was about to suck her under. But then that was the effect he'd always had on her from the first day she'd met him. Apparently, the years hadn't changed that, much to her chagrin.

"I like your kitchen."

His mentioning such a mundane thing was like being thrown a lifeline. She brightened and said, "Since I love to cook, I wanted it to be special."

And it was, with the large airy windows that went from ceiling to floor, letting in warmth and light and greenery from the outside. One seemed to be embraced the instant one walked in. Another attraction were the updated countertops and the polished hardwood cabinets.

"It feels like you've brought the outside in," Denton said, plopping down on the bar stool in front of her.

It was all Grace could do not to flinch visibly as his body seemed to envelop her. Unable to meet his direct gaze, she took a quivering breath, then pretended to stare outside. "I take that as a real compliment because that's exactly what I strove to do."

"So you decorated the house?"

His question drew her back around. "Most of it. Couldn't afford to hire anyone." Afraid she might sound as if she was whining, she added hastily, "But I wanted the responsibility, loved every minute of making this old place come back alive after sitting vacant for several years." She paused. "I'm not through, though, not by a long shot. There's so much else I want to do that needs to be done."

"I have faith in you," he said in a low tone.

Had that been his breath she felt caress her cheek? Swallowing against the clamoring going on inside her, she asked, "Sure you aren't hungry?"

"Depends."

"On what?"

"What you have to offer."

She expelled a shaky breath but it did little to relieve the pressure inside her. He was deliberately toying with her emotions. But if she hit him with that accusation, he'd deny it. Or would he?

God, what an intolerable situation. Drawing back, she said, in what she hoped was a perfectly normal but standoffish tone, "I have some cold cuts, salad—"

"Thanks but no thanks," he said abruptly.

She watched as he reached in his pocket and pulled out his pack of antacids.

"That's obviously your diet of choice."

His lips thinned as he rubbed the back of his neck in a gesture of frustration. "It gets the job done."

"I hope the job's worth it," she said, holding on to her normal tone, though it was hard, especially when she wanted to reach out and touch those grooves in his forehead, soothe them away. Then, realizing where her thoughts had wandered, she shut them down.

"It is." His tone was definitely clipped.

"Did I hit an exposed nerve?"

He scowled. "So you obviously don't like pressure. Well, I do. Otherwise, I'd be bored."

"Good luck."

His eyes narrowed. "What does that mean?"

"On convincing yourself."

A smile of sorts softened his lips. "You don't pull any punches, do you? Okay, so things aren't going so well right now. I'll admit that."

"The boss is not happy you're here." It was a statement of fact.

Denton's laugh was humorless. "That's putting it mildly."

She didn't dare ask him when he was leaving. She didn't want him to go, but she was afraid for him to stay. And why that was so, she dared not ask herself. Having him in front of her, within touching distance but not touching him, was playing havoc with her emotions, a complication she didn't need or deserve.

"So, is making more money your goal?"

He almost smiled again. "That and making partner in the firm."

"I guess that makes Mummy and Daddy proud." She had purposely avoided asking about his parents, whom she partly blamed for their breakup. They had never liked her, never thought she was good enough for their son. However, she couldn't blame then totally. Denton could have bucked them, but he hadn't. He'd gone right along with his dad's wishes. Then his dad had had a stroke, which had further complicated matters.

"Sarcasm doesn't become you," he said, drawing her back to the moment at hand.

"Is that on the horizon? Becoming partner, I mean?" she said, deliberately changing the subject.

"It'd better be. If I nail this client, then I feel I'm a shoo-in."

"Then I hope it happens."

He delved into her eyes. "You don't mean that."

She flushed, stirring harder. "You're doing it again."

"What?" he asked in a innocent tone.

Innocent, hell. He'd never been innocent. "Assuming you can read my mind."

"What are you making?" he asked, his tone having dropped to a sultry pitch deep in the danger zone.

''Uh, a cake,'' she responded, clearly thrown off-kilter by his unexpected change in subject.

He chuckled suddenly, and his eyes heated.

Her system went haywire. ''What's…so funny?''

''You've got a glob of batter on your face.''

Before she could respond, a finger reached out and scooped it off. Then, without removing his hot gaze, he deliberately licked his finger, making a sucking noise.

The bottom dropped out of her stomach.

Five

He should've kept his hands to himself, dammit. He didn't know what had possessed him. Yes, he did. That same old lust, smoldering deep in his gut had spurred him into action. Too, she'd looked so delightful with that glob of batter on her cheek, almost dead center on the dimple, that he couldn't resist touching her.

No excuse.

That gesture was bad enough, but to deliberately lick the goo off his finger had earned him a swift kick in the butt. For a second he'd even been tempted to kiss her. However, his sound senses had come to his rescue, taunting him with the realization that actions good or bad had consequences. He'd pulled back.

His mood darkening, Denton strode to the bedside table and stared at his cell phone. He ought to call Dallas, more specifically his boss Todd Joseph. But not right now, he argued. He wasn't in the mood to intentionally put himself in front of a firing squad.

At the moment he was feeling more vulnerable, more exposed than he had since the crash. Not a good feeling.

Maybe seeing his client today and sealing a deal would help him regain some of his perspective and sanity. For some reason, both seemed to have deserted him, or he would never have stayed the night here when he'd had plenty of other choices.

Grace.

She was the reason he hadn't left. It was as simple as that. Only it apparently wasn't that simple or his gut wouldn't be twisted in a knot or his mouth as dry as a pine knot. When she had opened that door yesterday, he'd been suckered in again like days of old. He'd thought about her all night, and even now at dawn thirty, he couldn't stop thinking about her.

Nothing had happened, for God's sake, he kept telling himself, sounding like a damn broken record, or rather a teenager in heat.

He *hadn't* kissed her. He'd only touched her and very briefly at that. He was making it a much bigger deal than it was. At this rate he'd be a candidate for the rubber room if he were to get mixed up with Grace again.

It was obvious from her reaction to his touch that they were on the same page. Her eyes had widened, and she had flinched as if he'd struck her. However, he was barely conscious of her reaction, since he was so busy trying to control and mask his own turbulent emotions.

He'd experienced an instant tightening behind his zipper, and his breath had jammed in his throat.

"You don't care who you hurt, do you?" she'd said in a tight, quavering voice, her troubled eyes meeting his.

"Grace, I—"

"I don't want you to say anything. Just know that I'm not the innocent I once was and that I can see you for who and what you are."

That time he'd flinched, her words having cut to the core, because he knew what she said was the truth even though he hated to admit that even to himself.

"I never meant to—"

Again she'd stopped him in a voice that was colder than chips of ice. "Let it be, Denton. Now, if you don't mind, I'd like to finish the cake."

In other words, go take a hike was what she'd told him. And while he'd thought about calling her hand and pushing his luck, he hadn't. She'd already made him feel like pond scum. Why stick around and beg for more?

He had left and gone to his room where he'd worked on several reports until the wee hours of the morning, having thought to grab his briefcase out of the trunk when he'd checked on his BMW. He hadn't even bothered to climb on the big bed. Instead he'd taken a couple of catnaps on the chaise lounge.

That was why he felt as if he'd been drawn and quartered this morning, though he suspected his exhaustion was as much mental as physical. After a hot shower, he'd feel better, more like facing the day and the responsibilities that it would bring.

Forget her.

Once he left town that would be easy enough to do. And once he was back home on his own turf, everything would shift back in sync. He'd forget all about this trip down memory lane. Most of all he'd forget about Grace, forget her infectious smile, the delectable curve of her breasts, the ''come hither'' sway of her hips. What he wouldn't forget, however, were her lips, how that lower one was fuller, how it protruded just enough to make him want to take it in his own and suck it.

Denton groaned as a shaft of heat surged through him, so intense that it almost buckled his knees. He took several deep breaths, then practically fell onto the chaise and closed his eyes.

No relief.

Grace had managed to invade his space to the extent that she was imprinted on his brain. Déjà vu. That was what this was all about, the memory of their last time together suddenly burning a destructive trail through his memory.

They had begun dating toward the end of her senior year in high school, his second year at Stanford. He'd come home for the summer to work and take some classes at the University of Texas.

He had met Grace at a friend's party. From the beginning he'd been smitten. He'd taken her home from the shindig, and that was it. He couldn't leave her alone. They had been together every evening, despite the fact that his parents objected, thinking he was getting much too serious about someone whom they saw as a threat to their son's bright future.

Denton ignored their pleas, knowing he couldn't leave her alone even if he'd wanted to. Still, he'd kept his head, knowing his limits—until that night. Since he was returning to Stanford the following day, he had taken her on a picnic to his parents' farm so they could have complete privacy.

It had been a lovely spring day much like yesterday. They had consumed a lot of food and drink and had fallen asleep on the blanket.

He had been the first to awaken, watching as the sun slowly turned its reign of power over to the moon. He had nuzzled her awake with his tongue, first in her ear, then her cheek, and finally her mouth.

A pleasurable moan had escaped through her lips as she'd opened her eyes and pulled his face closer. "Don't leave tomorrow," she whispered. "Please."

"God, I don't want to," he said, his tone filled with agony. "I can't stand the thought of not seeing you for weeks."

"Then don't go."

"My parents would kill me."

He dipped his tongue in her mouth and for a moment tongues sparred gently. Then his hands found and kneaded her breasts before unbuttoning her blouse. She didn't have on a bra, which didn't surprise him since she knew how much he loved to touch her breasts.

After tweaking both nipples, he leaned over and began sucking them.

She squirmed, her hand reaching for his crotch where she rubbed up and down, something she'd done on numerous occasions without him losing control. Instead he would use his tongue and lips to full advantage, confident he brought her complete and intense satisfaction, not worrying about himself until later.

But that evening it was especially difficult to hold himself in check, maybe because he knew he wasn't going to see her for a while. Or maybe it was because he wanted her so desperately.

"Make love to me," she whispered, her voice raspy and pleading.

"Grace, you know I want to, that I'm dying to be inside you."

"Then what's stopping you?"

"You know." He frowned. "What if you got pregnant?"

"I won't."

"How can you be so sure?"

"I'm taking the Pill."

He sucked in his breath and stared hard at her. "Since when?"

"Since long enough for them to take effect."

"Grace, I—"

"Shh, I don't want a lecture, I want you."

It was then that she snuck her hand down in his running shorts and surrounded him. Within seconds they were both naked, his lips and hands all over her. Only after he feared he would explode in her hand did he ease inside her, instantly hitting a barrier.

Cursing, he tried to pull out, but she clung to him.

"It's…okay," Grace said breathlessly. "It'll be all right. I want you so…much."

He thrust into her then, crushing her against him….

At first Denton wasn't sure what was ringing, his head or his phone. Nonetheless, his eyes popped open and he bounded off the chaise as if he'd been shot. Following several hard-won breaths, he realized it was his cell.

He grabbed it like a lifeline, sweat pouring off him. Gritting his teeth, he flipped the lid. "Hardesty."

"Your ass had better be headed this way."

"Good morning to you, too."

"Don't you 'good morning' me," Todd snapped.

If Denton hadn't had such a hard-on, literally, he would've laughed. In his mind's eye, he could see his friend and soon-to-be partner in his chair with his feet propped on his desk, chomping down on that unlit cigar stuck in one corner of his mouth. A disgusting habit, Denton never failed to tell him every chance he got. No matter—Todd continued to cram it between his lips.

"Chomp a little harder on that cigar," Denton advised. "That'll take some of the pressure off."

"What the hell's going on?"

"I'm seeing my client today."

"You should've come back yesterday, then gone back."

"That's crazy. Besides, my car is out of commission."

"Well, all hell's breaking loose here."

"The money we're going to get from this deal will glue things back together real quick."

"If you nail it."

"Oh, I'll nail it, all right. Look, I'll see you this evening."

"You damn well better."

With that Todd slammed down the receiver. If it had been anyone else, Denton would've been livid. But Todd, like him, marched to his own drummer. You either tolerated him or you didn't. Denton chose to tolerate him, as he was one intelligent cookie and knew more about investments and the stock market than the Japanese.

Hanging with Todd, despite his idiosyncrasies, would make him a rich man before he was forty if he made partner, which he was determined to do. That was why he had to get the hell away from Grace. She was messing with his mind, and he couldn't allow that.

Still sweating, he headed for the bathroom as his cell rang again. He was tempted not to answer it, thinking it was probably Todd calling back to further harass him. But he couldn't take a chance. He had several deals pending.

He answered it, only then to halt in his tracks and stifle a curse.

Did she look as bad as she felt?

Probably worse, she told herself. But what could she expect when she hadn't closed her eyes the entire night? She did indeed look worse than she felt, though she'd tried to mask the dark circles under her eyes with a stick of concealer, a product she rarely used. Extra blush and lipstick had given her little satisfaction.

At least her outfit was presentable. She'd chosen a pair of khaki capri pants that molded her slender frame and a pink knit top that did the same. Right in step with spring, she told herself sarcastically, wondering why she cared how she looked.

After this morning she would never see him again.

A tight squeeze inside her chest took her breath. If only he hadn't touched her. If only he hadn't looked at her with such smoldering desire. And when he'd blatantly licked his finger, heat had pooled between her legs, something she hadn't experienced in years. When he had walked out of the kitchen, she'd felt wrung out and still did.

But it would all be over shortly. She didn't look for him to appear at breakfast, which would be a blessing. She would have to face him when he tried to pay her, only she had no intention of charging him, even though she could use the money.

She just wanted him out of her life before she did something stupid and let him kiss her, or worse. Once he was gone, the sexual longings he'd aroused in her would go dormant again, the way she wanted them. Until then, she'd just have to endure the moistness between her legs and her distended nipples.

She had prepared most of the breakfast and set the table when he walked in, looking as if he'd fought the same bear she had. Good. Misery loved company. Too, he deserved whatever he got for opening that sealed can of worms.

Yet, she fought the urge to run to him and fling her arms around him. Just one more time.

"Mornin'," he said into the silence, avoiding her gaze.

Grace nodded. "Are you joining us for breakfast?" she asked without preamble. Of course he wasn't. But as hostess she had to ask.

"As a matter of fact, I am."

She gave a start. "But I thought—"

"Me, too, only there's been a change of plans."

"Oh." The tiny word was barely audible.

This time his gaze met hers directly. "I need to stay a few more days. Do you mind?"

Six

In a hunter-green T-shirt and casual khaki slacks, his dark hair once again damp and slightly mussed, he looked big, sleek and undeniably sexy. And totally out of place in *her* kitchen, in *her* life. That was why he had to leave. She couldn't allow him to stay and continue to disrupt her routine.

After her sleepless night, she hadn't as yet gotten her act together. Hence breakfast was going to be a few minutes late, and that didn't sit well with her. Not only was she a stickler for time but for perfection. With Denton around, nothing was on schedule. Certainly nothing was perfect.

"Well?"

"I don't think that's a good idea."

"Why not?"

Her temper rose. "Don't treat me like I'm an imbecile."

He blew out a breath, and his eyes narrowed. "That's not what I intended, and you know it."

"I don't know any such thing."

"Okay, so I was out of line. I'm sorry."

Maybe he was sorry, but that didn't change anything. However, unless she was prepared to have an all-out verbal slinging match with him, which she was not, she'd best take hold of her fractured emotions and handle this volatile situation as best she could.

"Look, there are other places—"

"Is the room spoken for?" he interrupted.

That was when she noticed his exhaustion. His eyes were bloodshot and his lips were stretched in a thin line. When he'd first walked in, his sexual charisma had overpowered her, and that was all she'd noticed. Now she realized he must've had a night comparable to hers. Only she didn't kid herself that his restlessness pertained to her, but to Dallas and his job.

So why didn't he just go back there?

"Grace, answer me."

Her brain buzzed while she stalled for time. "Er, no, it's not."

"Then I'd like to have it for at least several more days."

Oh, dear Lord, no. She'd be a fool to let him stay any longer. "Why?" she asked, then colored, having realized that was none of her business. She would never have asked another guest that question. But Denton wasn't just another guest, she reminded herself. He was an unwelcome memory from her past.

"My prospective client's still out of town, won't be back for several more days."

"You don't have to return to Dallas?" Again she was treading on unprofessional ground, but she didn't care. If he minded, then he could leave, which is what she wanted. Didn't she?

He walked toward her, not stopping until he reached the stove where she stood preparing breakfast. He placed an arm on the countertop as though to brace himself. She felt his eyes probing, but she dared not look at him. Besides, she was suddenly mesmerized by his hands, by the coarse dark hair that dusted his skin.

"I should get back to the office, only I'm not," he said in a raspy tone.

She didn't respond right off, still too conscious of him, his nearness suffocating in its intensity.

"Grace, I'm not going to hurt you."

At those softly spoken words, her head whipped up, and their gazes slammed together. It was as if she'd been hit by an electric shock. She knew that he'd felt it, too, as he released an unsteady breath and stepped back.

"You'll never get that chance again, Denton. Trust me on that."

He flushed. "I deserve your contempt and more."

"Look, I have to get breakfast."

"So do I get the room or not?"

Still she hesitated.

"Do you want me to beg?"

"Of course not," she muttered tersely. "And you wouldn't, either."

"Don't count on it."

A shiver darted through her. What kind of game was he playing? More to the point, why was she letting him play it?

"Yes or no."

"You sure you wouldn't rather I call another B&B?"

"I'm positive," he said, his eyes probing once again.

"Oh, all right," she said ungraciously.

"Did it hurt that badly?"

A smile was now toying with his lips which lessened the tension considerably. She even took a clear breath as she once again busied her hands with placing the biscuits on an oven tray. Thank goodness she'd already prepared the scrambled eggs, gravy and grits. They were in the warmer, waiting to be served. The fruit cups were also filled and in the frig.

"No, I guess it didn't," she finally admitted, though she couldn't quite muster a smile.

"Is there anything I could do to help?" he asked.

"Like what?"

A genuine smile broke through his lips. "Hey, I can cook."

"As in popping TV dinners in the micro," she responded, hating the way her pulse reacted to that smile.

"I can fix beans and corn bread. Does that count?"

"Not this morning."

He chuckled. "Well, I could—"

"Cut some flowers for the table."

"You got it," he said, suddenly sounding like a youngster who was eager to please.

Not good. Not good at all, at least not for her peace of mind, she told herself, all the while raking herself over the coals for giving in to his demand to board him for several more days. Later, she knew she'd really be in a state. Now, however, it was imperative she act as if he were just another guest, no one special.

Holding a sigh in check, Grace reached into a nearby drawer. "Here's a pair of scissors, and the vase is in the top of that cabinet."

"Any particular brand you want?"

Her lips twitched at his terminology. "It's your call."

He stared at her a moment longer then turned and strode out the French doors, an added bounce to his steps. Grace, on the other hand, leaned against the counter, feeling limp like all the air had been let out of her body.

She'd lost her mind. That was all there was to it. She should've told him to get lost. Instead, she'd committed the unpardonable—she'd let her heart overrule her head, one more time.

Grace fought the sudden urge to untie her apron and take flight herself. If he wouldn't go, then she would. That thought was absurd, of course. Still, the urge refused to go away, and she felt tears festering behind her eyes.

She didn't want them to wander down that old familiar path; she didn't want to feel this disturbing softening towards him. She wanted only to remember how badly he'd hurt her, how he'd crushed her heart into tiny pieces that had never quite mended despite the passing years.

Yet here he was back in her life, back in her house, for heaven's sake. But not in her bed. Never that. If he so much as tried to touch her again, she'd—

"Who's that good-looking specimen messing in the flower garden?"

Zelma's presence was a heartfelt relief to her battered thoughts. "Denton Hardesty." She forced her tone to remain generic.

"Ah, the man I met yesterday."

Grace nodded.

"So he's still here." A flat statement of fact.

"For a few more days."

"Mmm."

"Zip up your mind, my friend."

Zelma laughed. "Whatever you say. Ah, here comes that sweet husband of mine."

"Good morning," Ed said, leaning over and kissing Grace on the cheek. "How's my other girl?"

Grace smiled, glad to see that Ed seemed to be feeling much better. "I'm about to serve you something to eat." She paused. "How was your outing last night?"

Before either could answer, Ralph Kennedy ambled into the kitchen. "Am I too early?" he asked, looking his usual uncomfortable self.

"You're just right," Grace said. "Go ahead and take your seat in the dining room."

What a strange person, she thought again as she smiled in at him, hoping to put him at ease. She had thought her hearty morning meals would have put some meat on his gaunt frame by now, but so far they hadn't. If anything, he appeared more skeletal than when he first came. This morning his glasses were perched on the bridge of his nose indicating he had already been hard at work.

Denton chose that moment to walk in with a vase filled with an incredible array of tulips.

"Oh, Mr. Hardesty, how gorgeous."

He turned on his high-wattage smile on Zelma. "Make that Denton, ma'am."

"As long as you call us Zelma and Ed."

Grace formally introduced Ralph to Denton before they all took their place at the table. Grace began serving immediately, finding that her hands were quite steady despite the fact that she sensed rather than saw Denton's eyes track her every move.

All in all, breakfast turned out to be a fun time. Denton held court and all seemed to enjoy his anecdotes, even Ralph, which surprised Grace. She didn't recall ever having heard him laugh.

Soon, however, the meal was completed and everyone left the dining room with the exception of Denton. She was back in the kitchen at the sink when she sensed he'd joined her. She swung around.

"Need some help with the dishes?" he asked.

She picked up on the note of uncertainty in his tone, realizing he was at loose ends and didn't know what to do with time on his hands. But that was his problem, not hers. He should've taken that into consideration when he decided to remain in town. If he thought she was going to entertain him, he was in for a rude awakening.

"No, thanks. My part-time help will be here shortly."

"I could pitch in till then."

She expelled a sigh, then muttered, "Go sightseeing."

"That's a nice way of saying get lost, right?"

She flushed but didn't flinch.

He stepped forward, his gaze trapping hers, then in a low, tortured voice he whispered, "I dreamed about us making love last night."

Grace was bone tired, but, like the night before, sleep eluded her. She'd had a hot bath and a warm glass of milk. Neither had taken the edge off her nerves. Maybe she should go talk to Zelma. Her eyes went to the clock on the table next to her chaise lounge. Ten o'clock.

By her usual standards that was early, but with her exhaustion being at such a high level, ten was late. She hated to disturb Zelma. Anyway, what could she tell her? Nothing. She wasn't about to divulge her past with Denton, so what would be the point?

For one thing she couldn't stand to be alone with her thoughts. Denton and only Denton filled her mind to capacity. After he had told her he'd dreamed about them making love, her body had gone into instant meltdown and hadn't recovered.

"Go away and leave me alone," she'd said, lashing back at him.

"Dammit, Grace, you just don't get it, do you?"

"I don't want to get it."

"I stayed because I thought—"

"Thought what? That we might just play footsie in bed again?"

His face went white. "I just thought—" He broke off and rubbed the back of his neck in a frustrated gesture. "Oh, hell, I don't know what I thought."

"You didn't think."

"Do you hate me that much?"

"Yes," she lied.

He sucked in a harsh breath. "Then I guess that says it all."

Before she could come up with a suitable come-back, he turned and marched out of the room.

Now as she sat alone in her room, Grace wished she could recall those bitter words, tone them down a bit. Okay, so she'd like to make love to him again, too.

Just the thought sent a fiery warmth spreading through her body. It had been a long time since she'd been with a man. And when she had, it hadn't been a pleasant experience.

Only Denton had brought her the sexual satisfaction she craved. And since she couldn't have him, she'd decided to do without.

Then Denton had waltzed back into her life. And if she so chose, she could have him back in her bed. But at what price? One she wasn't willing to pay.

Holding on to that thought, Grace switched off the lamp and made her way back to bed.

At first she wasn't sure what awakened her. Her eyes suddenly opened wide. Then she heard the noise again. A scream. A bloodcurdling scream, at that. It sounded like Zelma.

With her heart pounding out of her chest, Grace tossed back the sheet and ran out of the room into the hallway. Denton, with only a pair of running shorts on, met her there.

"What the hell?" he asked.

"Screams coming from Ed and Zelma's room."

Together they ran down the hall as another scream rent the air.

Grace reached the door first and thrust it open, then pulled up short, causing Denton to slam into her. Following a muttered curse, he righted her with hands on both her arms. She was hardly aware of the contact as her eyes were filled with the image in front of her. Zelma was cradling Ed's seemingly lifeless body in her arms, rocking back and forth.

"I...I think he's gone," she whispered, focusing tear-stained eyes on Grace.

Seven

"**I** can't believe he's not gone."

"Hey," Denton said to Zelma, holding her against his side and squeezing her thin body for a moment. "He's going to pull out of this. I won't pretend it's not serious, because it is. However, he's a determined man, and that makes a difference. Anyway, he's not about to give up and leave you to run the streets of that big city alone."

"Oh, Denton, I can't thank you and Grace enough. I don't—" Zelma's voice cracked, and she couldn't go on.

"Shh, don't get yourself all worked up again." Denton smiled down at her before gently pushing her away. "You'll be in the bed next to him if you don't buck up."

"He'd have another attack if that happened," Zelma said with a semblance of a smile.

Grace looked on, thinking how wonderful, how like a rock Denton had been throughout this entire ordeal. Had it just been three hours ago that Zelma's frantic cry had jerked the entire B&B awake? It seemed as if she'd been up several days without sleep. Her eyes felt filled with sand.

Denton wasn't faring much better, appearing equally as weary. But he didn't let on for a second that he might be running out of energy or confidence. She didn't know what she would've done if he hadn't been there. Oh, she would have coped; she would not have had any choice. However, it wouldn't have been easy, given her past problems and Zelma's hysteria.

As they waited for the doctors to return to the hospital waiting room and update them on Ed's condition, Grace uncurled her legs, stood and stretched. For some reason she chose that second to look at Denton. He was watching her, his eyes on her jutting breasts, breasts that were bra free.

Instantly Grace felt her nipples tighten and thrust against the thin fabric of her blouse. She knew that Denton saw them, too, as heat suddenly leaped into his eyes, darkening them. For a second she couldn't move, heat surging through her own body as their gazes met and held.

She deliberately jerked her eyes off him and back to Zelma who was standing with her back to them, facing the lit parking lot outside. Purposely, Grace walked up next to Zelma and placed her arm around her.

"Oh, Gracie, I'm so frightened."

"I wish you'd let me call your kids."

"If he's not really better, then we will," Zelma said. "I promise. But they all live so far away."

"Like Denton said, he's going to make it."

"You're right, he is."

All eyes whipped around and faced the small and rather rotund doctor who was smiling at them. "He had a heart attack for sure, though the damage to his heart muscle is minimal."

"Oh, Doctor, praise the Lord," Zelma cried.

"We're going to keep him overnight, of course, and part of tomorrow, and run some more tests to see just how much blockage he has. Then you can take him home."

"Thank you so much, Doctor," Denton said, stepping forward and shaking his hand."

"Mrs. Brenner, you may see him now."

Once Zelma had left, the tiny waiting room in the cardiac unit fell silent as a tomb. Grace wrapped both arms around herself to keep herself from shaking. She couldn't lose it now, not when the crisis was past. Thank God Ed hadn't died and was going to actually get well.

"Are you okay?"

Denton's low, raspy voice brought her around to face him. "No," she said honestly.

"Didn't think so."

"How 'bout you?"

"Don't worry about me. I deal with one crisis or another every day, though someone's life doesn't hang in the balance. But you'd think it did, the way some of my clients carry on."

Grace shuddered visibly. "I'd hate that."

"Sometimes I do."

"Then why don't you do something else?"

An eyebrow shot up. "How did we get onto me?

It's you who looks like you're going to drop any minute.''

Grace gnawed at her lower lip and when she spoke,
her voice wasn't quite steady. ''I haven't slept much
lately.''

''Me, neither.''

For another long moment their eyes met and held.

''Grace,'' he muttered, stepping forward.

''Hey, you two, Ed's asking for you. Follow me.''

The unexpected sound of Zelma's voice shattered
the spell, though Grace continued to shake on the inside, fighting off the crazy feeling that Denton had
just kissed her.

She shivered again.

His BMW was repaired, washed and polished until
it shone like new money and was waiting to be
driven. Standing at the window the following morning, Denton could see it. It was almost as if it was
beckoning him.

So why didn't he walk outside, jump in it and haul
it back to Dallas?

The bottom line was that he was enjoying the relaxed atmosphere, the chance to slow down and smell
the roses, the main rose being Grace, even though
plucking that rose was off-limits. But he needed this
time. He'd earned it.

Still, in his gut he knew he had no business what-
soever lollygagging around Ruby any longer. It was
a given that Grace didn't want him here, though he
knew she wasn't as immune to him as she'd like to
be. He'd seen matching fire in her eyes when she'd
caught his gaze locked on her jutting nipples.

But looking was as far as he would ever get. He

might as well accept that and move on. And since Ed was out of immediate danger, he wasn't needed here.

But he was needed in the office. He should return to Dallas, then drive back to meet his client. Simple solution.

Hell, driving was no big deal. He put thousands of miles on a vehicle each year since his clients were spread all over the country. What was a big deal was his absence from the office. He didn't know how much longer Todd was going to humor him before he went on the warpath. He did that often when he didn't get his way.

Denton hadn't called and told him he'd decided to cool his heels and take a few days of his vacation, something he'd never done since he started with the firm years ago. He'd often thought his penchant for work had helped bring about the demise of his marriage.

Once he and Marsha had split up, he'd rarely thought of her, a fact he considered odd. It was almost as if that time in his life had been a dream rather than a reality. They simply hadn't had enough in common, or spent enough time together, which was his fault. He'd felt that he had to get ahead, make it big. His parents had drilled success into him, stressing that money was the measuring stick for one's success.

He no longer thought that, yet he hadn't been able to get off the fast track. Until now. And he had Grace to thank for such a remarkable about-face, though he couldn't share that with her. Right now, if he even looked at her, she seemed to panic, not visibly, but he could see it in her eyes, in the way she froze up.

Her reaction was his fault, too. He would give anything to right that old wrong, but he didn't know how.

He wanted her, in his arms, in his bed. He wouldn't deny his need, not even to her. There was something about her, about them, that was explosive. He couldn't explain it, but he didn't see it ever changing, not after all this time.

He was as infatuated as if the years had never passed. Watching her work in the kitchen, watching her do anything, made him want her just one more time.

However, he wasn't looking for a serious relationship. Not now, not ever. Hell, he was too big a mess to take on the responsibility of someone else. Since the plane crash, he'd done some crazy things. Remaining in Ruby for no reason other than desire was probably the craziest yet.

A harsh sigh escaped Denton as he massaged his neck where tight ridges of muscles didn't want to give.

Making love to Grace would do the trick, bring relief to his aching muscles and his manhood. Then what? She wasn't the one-night-stand kind of woman. And if he ever made love to her again, he doubted he could walk. That thought alone jarred him to the core.

So the answer was to keep his zipper zipped and his head on straight.

"Give it a rest," Denton spat, the sound of his voice bouncing off the walls.

God, everything was so quiet, a novelty for him, certainly something he wasn't used to. Right now the solitude was what his battered senses needed. With that thought in mind, he made his way out of his room and into the kitchen.

Empty.

Where was Grace? He'd missed breakfast, which

was not important. He was used to drinking his morning meal, his gaze targeting the coffee urn, then making a beeline for it.

He had just poured himself a full mug when he saw Grace through the window, traipsing toward the vegetable garden. How fresh and lovely she looked this bright spring morning, dressed in a purple T-shirt, white walking shorts and white tennis shoes with no socks. But it was the straw hat perched on top of her head just right that made him chuckle out loud.

The women he knew wouldn't be caught dead in a hat. Hell, they wouldn't be caught dead working in a garden. Of any kind. He watched, fascinated, as she pulled a pair of gloves out of her pocket, put them on, then dropped to her knees.

By God, she was going to weed the garden.

Not without his help, she wasn't, he told himself, making his way to the door as fast as he could.

"Hey, Z, I'm so glad you called," Grace said. "I was afraid to call you for fear of disturbing Ed."

"He's doing great, honey. We talked to all the kids."

"Talked them out of coming, I'll bet," Grace said.

"Of course, we did. We're coming home in the morning."

Grace felt a warm feeling flood through her when Zelma referred to the B&B as home. What a compliment to her. "Does he have to behave himself?"

Zelma laughed. "He can't dance the jitterbug right off, but he can dance."

Jitterbug. Grace rolled her eyes, thinking she'd have trouble jitterbugging, and she was eons younger. She bet Denton could. Suddenly her face lost its animation. She didn't want to start her morning off thinking about *him*.

But she might as well have as Zelma's next question concerned him.

"So how's our knight in shining armor?"

If she only knew. "I haven't seen him."

"Oh? Well, when you do, tell him again how much we appreciate him and what he did. You, too, but that goes without saying."

"I'll tell him."

There was a short pause, then Zelma said, "You wouldn't consider giving him a hug for me, would you?"

"Zelma," Grace muttered, "don't push your luck, okay?"

"All right, my dear. Oops, gotta go. The doctor just came in. I'll talk to you later."

Once the receiver was back in place, Grace peered at the clock. With the Brenners' absence and Denton having no interest in breakfast, she'd prepared a tray and taken it to Ralph's room, a gesture he seemed to appreciate as he was trying desperately to finish his novel on time.

Now she had extra time of her own and didn't know what to do with it. She did know, however, that she had to keep busy or she'd go nuts. Having Denton under her roof continued to unnerve her.

Okay, so she still hadn't gotten over him, dammit. Okay, so he had the power to turn her bones to butter when he looked at her. Okay, so he didn't even have to look at her; he just had to walk into the same room.

She was smitten. Still.

But that would change, she told herself. Thank God she no longer loved him. Her fixation was loneliness and lust. But those were a disastrous combination. Hopefully this time her recovery period would be much shorter. Her heart knew they had no future, that he merely wanted to make love to her, then walk away like before.

They were from two different worlds, and that wasn't going to change. Nor did she want it to. She couldn't survive in the city and he couldn't survive in the country. But their differences went much deeper than locale.

She had known the boy. She didn't know the man.

"Grrrrh!" she muttered, suddenly feeling claustrophobic, knowing she had to get out of the house.

A few minutes later she headed for the garden. She was halfway there when she sensed she was being watched. She didn't know how or why. She would have to credit her gut instinct.

Denton. It was him. Her instinct was on high alert.

Unable to stop her heart from racing, she bent down and attacked the weeds without mercy, not even looking up when she saw him leave the house and stride toward her.

"I know you won't refuse my help *this* morning."

Eight

He strolled into the garden where she'd been weeding, and without waiting for her permission to help, he dropped to his knees and began jerking out the weeds right alongside her. Her breathing had become so erratic she feared he could hear it.

"Do you always do just what you want?" she finally said into the building silence.

He turned and cut her a lopsided smile, sweat already dotting his forehead and upper lip. "If I think it's necessary."

"And you thought this was necessary, huh?"

"Yep, since there's more weeds than flowers." His grin widened. "Besides, you have no idea how long it's been since I've had my hands in dirt."

This time she chuckled. She couldn't help herself. "I bet if your colleagues back in the office could see you now they would think you'd lost it."

"Probably, but then what they don't know won't hurt them. Right?"

"Uh, right."

"How 'bout the vegetables?" He angled his head in the direction of the adjacent vegetable patch. "They're in as bad a shape. Or worse."

Grace pushed back her hat and wiped at her forehead. That was when she realized he was watching her again, his eyes piercing. And still he was so close—almost shoulder to shoulder close.

"Did I tell you how great you look in that hat?"

Her face flooded with color, but she hoped he wouldn't notice. Or if he did, he'd think it was the heat rather than his huskily spoken compliment. "Are you making fun?" Her voice quavered slightly.

"No, I mean it. It makes you look—" he broke off and smiled "—I don't know. Younger maybe, like a girl." Then he flapped a dirty hand in the air. "Hell, I don't know. I just like it. It's kind of like your apron—it's just you."

"Quaint."

"Why are you always putting yourself down?"

"I'm not," she snapped, jerking out as much dirt as weeds. "I think this town and I are just jokes to you, something you can and will chuckle about when you get back to your highfalutin office."

"I don't think so."

"I hope not," she said, "because my life, including cooking and gardening, brings me the greatest of pleasure."

"Hey, again, you don't have to convince me. I'm on your side. If I had an outlet like this maybe I—"

"Wouldn't be continually eating antacids like candy."

He didn't so much as flinch at her directness. In fact, he smiled, which made her heart turn over. "Can't argue with the truth."

As if she'd really given him food for thought, they worked in silence until Grace had to stand; her legs were beginning to cramp from being in one position for so long. While Denton hadn't looked the least uncomfortable, he was sweating profusely despite the fact the near-temperature was only in the low eighties. The bad guy was the humidity. It was high today, rare for the hill country.

Denton also stood, wiped the sweat off his face with a handkerchief from his back pocket, then asked, "Shall we hit the veggies next?"

"Are you serious?"

"Sure. Why not?"

"Look, I really appreciate your help, but—"

"Hey, lighten up, okay? I don't have anything else to do. But even if I did, I'd want to help."

"You always did have a green thumb. I'd forgotten until now."

"Me, too," he said in a low voice tinged with regret.

"Well, if you're serious, let's get to it," Grace said, that breathlessness back in her voice. But as long as he was sharing her space, nothing about her would be normal. Everything would be out of sync. She might as well accept that and deal with it.

Thirty minutes later, that task was also completed. By then neither had a clean or dry stitch on them. But Grace was thrilled that both gardens were back in perfect working order, only it was more obvious than ever how critically she needed to replenish the vegetables.

She voiced her thought. "I think I'll make a quick run to the nursery."

"I'll drive you," Denton said eagerly.

"That's not necessary."

He expelled a harsh breath. "How 'bout not arguing for once. Think that's possible?"

Curbing her anger at his high-handedness, she said, "I guess so."

His eyes twinkled. "Ah, we're making progress."

Grace realized she needed to lighten up, for her own sake if nothing else. After all, she'd let him stay, which meant she'd made the choice and had to pay the consequence. But she honestly hadn't known he would become her shadow. And while that was heady stuff, it was also dangerous. No way, she vowed again, could she let him back inside her heart.

"Why don't you drive my SUV?" she said.

"Come on, let's go."

Closed up in the vehicle with him, she became more aware of him than in the garden. Maybe it was the close confines. Or maybe she could better smell the distinctive odor of his cologne mixed with the sweat from his body. They made a potent cocktail.

She smothered a sigh and gritted her teeth. Get over it, she told herself. He would be leaving soon. This was all just a lark to him. When the pressure from Dallas become too great and he became too bored with all this "quaintness," he'd hit the road back to the city and not look back.

"Where is this place?" he asked.

His question jerked her out of her thoughts. "We're going to Mantooth nursery. It's been on Sycamore Street forever."

"A teacher and her husband owned it. Flora and Abe Mantooth, right?"

"Yep. She taught while her husband ran the nursery, only he's dead now."

"I had her for math."

"We all did."

"So she must be older than dirt."

Grace smiled. "Pretty close to it, I'm sure."

"You don't smile often enough," he said, cutting her a quick gaze. "Or is it just around me? After all, I barged in on you and messed up your playhouse."

"I don't think you want to go there."

He sighed. "No, I guess not. Anyway, here we are. I'd forgotten how easy it is to get around in a small town."

"Kind of nice, isn't it?" She stole a glance at him, a glance he unexpectedly returned. Their eyes held for a heartbeat.

"Yeah, it is," he said finally, an unreadable look in those green eyes.

"Ah, here comes Ms. Flora." Grace unbuckled her seat belt, breaking the tension. "She recognizes my vehicle."

"Regular customer, huh?"

"She needs the business."

They got out then and met the old woman halfway. Although she was almost painfully thin from hard work, and her face was severely wrinkled from years in the sun, her smile was bright and targeted on Grace.

"I was hoping you'd come today. I just got a shipment of new tomato plants."

"Oh, great." Grace turned to Denton, then back to Flora. "You recognize him?"

Flora peered hard at Denton, then chuckled. "Why you're Denton Hardesty, one of my most obnoxious students."

"That's right, ma'am," Denton drawled, extending a hand.

"Forget the handshake, boy," Flora said, "I want a hug."

Denton laughed good-naturedly as she gave him a bear hug before letting him go. "My, but it's good to see you. You were always a nice-looking boy, but you've made a downright handsome man."

"Why, thank you, ma'am," Denton drawled again, turning and winking at Grace.

That gesture sent her pulse skyrocketing. Careful, she warned herself afresh. You're letting his charm suck you in again. Remember he has no sticking power.

"So has business picked up any?" Grace asked in a rushed tone.

Denton cast her another look, but didn't say anything.

"No, it hasn't," Flora responded, her tone bleak. "But that new nursery out on the highway is mopping up."

"Maybe if you advertised," Grace suggested, angry that the people in town were deserting Flora.

"Can't afford it, honey. I'm doing good just to hang on." Suddenly her eyes filled with tears. "For Fred more than me. He would roll over in his grave, God rest his soul, if he thought I was thinking about closing this place."

"Is that what you want, Mrs. Mantooth?" Denton asked.

"Heavens, no. I love selling my plants and flowers.

Why, without any kids or close family, I don't know what I'd do. Grace knows what I mean, don't you, honey?''

''Unfortunately, I do, Flora,'' Grace said, feeling Denton's eyes on her at the same time her face suffused with color. She refused to look back at him for fear she'd see pity in his eyes—the last thing she wanted.

''I'd like to help,'' he said into the small silence.

Flora's jaw went slack. ''You would?''

''Yes, ma'am.''

''Pooh, son, stop that 'ma'am' stuff. I don't remember you being so polite when I was trying to teach you to add and subtract.''

Denton's lips twitched and so did Grace's. Flora was in one of her salty moods today, which was good for both of them. Since Denton had strolled into the garden, he hadn't popped one antacid.

''All right, Flora, so the new kid on the block has come in and threatened your livelihood. Tell me what you need to keep up with the competition.''

''Look around, sonny. There's not much I don't need.''

Flora was right, Grace thought. The nursery was in a sad state. The greenhouses were practically falling down, and the plant and vegetable stands were so rickety they could topple at any moment. The building that served as an office and housed inside products was in even worse shape. It needed major repairs, especially the roof. When it rained, customers had to dodge buckets.

''So let me do some checking, and I'll get back to you,'' Denton said, rubbing his jaw while his gaze surveyed the premises.

Flora squinted her eyes at him. "Are you serious?"

"You bet."

"But you don't even live here anymore." She angled her head. "Why do you care?"

"I can't have anyone messing with my favorite teacher," Denton said lightly. "That's why."

"Hogwash," Flora said, though it was obvious she was pleased.

And relieved, Grace noted, watching as some of the years seemed to have dropped off her face, leaving her looking less weary and frightened. Bless Denton. This was a side of him she'd never seen, but then that wasn't surprising. Again, she'd known the boy not the man. Still, she'd never thought he'd be this thoughtful which proved how much a stranger he really was.

"Hogwash, huh?" Denton pitched his head back and laughed. "If we had said that in your class, we would've been sent to the office."

"But not before getting your mouth washed out with soap," Flora added with a grin.

"How old are you, Flora?" Denton asked.

"Eighty-one," she declared without offense.

"Damn," Denton muttered, turning to Grace. "They don't make 'em like her anymore."

"Oh, yes they do," Flora chimed in. "Grace'll be working until she drops."

"Flora!" Grace cried.

"Well, you will."

Denton laughed again which severed the good-natured argument.

"Look," Grace said, "I need to pick out my stuff and get back to the house. I have work to do."

Flora snorted but immediately began helping Grace

choose the very best variety of vegetables and plants. Once they were back in the SUV, Grace turned to Denton and said, "Thanks."

"For what?"

"You know. She's barely hanging on."

"That's obvious. I'll need you to put me in touch with some contractors and her banker so I can give her some operating money."

"I can't believe you're doing all this."

His gaze left the road and rested on her for a long second. "I've always had a secret passion to dig in the dirt, to work with plants, but there never seemed time for either. So…" He let his voice trail off.

"You just shoved that passion on the back burner," Grace said, finishing the sentence for him.

"That's the long and short of it."

"Maybe if you had indulged yourself, you wouldn't pop so many stomach pills."

"That's why I'm staying in Ruby."

She gave a start, dumbfounded that he admitted the fast track had gotten to him.

"Shocked, aren't you?" There was a teasing note in his voice.

"Yes," she said bluntly.

"So will you teach me how to relax?"

Loaded question. "Denton—"

"Forget I said that," he muttered gruffly.

He was turning into the drive, which saved her from having to respond. Maybe he'd leave her alone to finish her work in the garden. All this togetherness was beginning to get to her. Her body was a bundle of nerves.

No such luck. As before, he began working by her

side. Only after all the vegetable plants were in the ground did they stop.

"I appreciate all your help," she said at last, an uncertain note in her voice. On the one hand, she felt grateful; on the other, she felt annoyed. She hadn't wanted his help. She had wanted him to leave her alone.

Liar, a little voice taunted.

"I enjoyed the hell out of it," he responded. "Later I'll come back and work some more."

She decided not to argue, resigned to the fact that it was easier to give in than to fight him. On some things, that is, she corrected mentally. "Let's go in, and I'll pour us some tea."

They remained silent even after each had taken several sips out of glasses filled with apricot-flavored tea, her concoction, a specialty of the house.

"Man, this is good stuff."

"Thanks," she responded, that old suffocating feeling returning, especially since he had ambled around the bar and was now standing next to her.

"Know what?"

She swallowed, his husky-toned voice having drawn her eyes up to his. "What?"

"You have dirt on your lip."

Before she could say anything, he reached out and removed it with the tip of a finger.

"Don't," she whispered, a feeling of raw hunger surging through her. "That's becoming a habit."

"What?" he asked again, his tone having dropped to a huskier pitch.

"Touching…me."

Nine

"I...know," he whispered, his head inching lower. "Only, I can't stop myself."

"Denton..." Her voice was an aching plea, a plea for what she no longer knew. His nearness, his touch, were driving her wild.

"I love it when you say my name like that."

His lips were so close now she could feel his breath, taste his breath, *taste him.*

"We...shouldn't."

"Yes, we should."

She tried to turn her head, but his thumb, trailing a hot line across her trembling lower lip, prevented that move.

"Grace..."

It was her name, whispered with such agonized longing, that was her undoing, that made her throw caution to the wind and part her lips in anticipation.

He groaned, his hands digging savagely into her shoulders as he sank his mouth onto hers. Her breath caught in her throat as his lips seemed to sear hers with their heat while his tongue thrust its way inside and meshed with hers.

Her legs turned to water, and if he hadn't been holding on to her so tightly, they would've buckled under her.

He moaned, deepening the kiss at the same time he pressed the entire length of her lithe body into his. Instantly she felt his hardness stir against her lower abdomen, firing up the memory of that night long ago when nothing had been between them.

Only flesh against flesh.

She hadn't wanted this to happen, but now that he was ravishing her mouth, she was powerless to stop him, the heat from his lips, from his body, affecting every quivering nerve in hers.

She'd tried to tell herself that her mind could win over her body, that she was immune to him, but she knew now how wrong she'd been, how badly she had miscalculated. Both still remembered. Both still craved him, especially her *flesh*. How could that have happened? How could she have not seen this assault coming?

"Grace, Grace," he murmured, continuing to drain the sweet nectar from her lips.

She should be strong. She should stop him *now*. Instead, her breasts swelled, her nipples pebbled and her legs parted of their own violation to his seeking hand that had found its way there, probing, feeling, making her wet.

"I want you. Let's go to my room."

His gutturally spoken words were the catalyst that

brought her to her senses. With a superhuman effort, she jerked out of his arms. For a second thereafter they stared at each other, their breaths coming in gasps.

She had come so close…

Shivering uncontrollably, Grace wrapped her arms around herself and fought back the threat of tears. She wanted to disappear on the spot. Perhaps in another minute she would have capitulated, let him make love to her right here in the kitchen, writhing on the floor.

"Grace, it's okay," he said at last, though he didn't look or sound convinced of that. His voice had the rough edge of sandpaper. And he was pale, as if all the blood had been drained from his body.

"No, it's not," she said, fighting for a decent breath.

His gaze was intense. "I would never have done anything you didn't want to."

"I don't believe you."

"Yes, you do," he countered in a low, soft voice.

He was right. She knew he would never have forced himself on her. It was she who was the problem. In that moment of hot passion, she would've let him do anything he wanted and that was what galled her, what mortified her. But she couldn't tell him that. She had no intention of humiliating herself any further.

"Please, just leave me alone," she said, forcing her gaze off him and gnawing at her lower lip.

"You…we didn't do anything wrong, Grace. I wanted you and you wanted me. There's nothing wrong with that."

"You still don't get it, do you?" she retorted, widening her eyes.

"Oh, I get it, but I don't think you do."

"You haven't lost your ability to be a real jerk."

A pained expression darkened Denton's features. "I can't undo the past. If I could—"

"I have work to do." Her tone was pointed.

His mouth worked, and she knew he wanted to argue. But he didn't. Instead he pivoted on his heels and walked out of the kitchen. Within seconds she heard the front door open and close.

Good. He was gone. Permanently, she hoped, though she knew better. She wasn't about to get out of this mess so easily, not when the lust was still riding so close to the surface for both of them.

Somehow she managed to force herself to put one foot in front of the other, go to her quarters where she immediately shed her clothes and stepped into the shower, trying her best to wash Denton off her body and out of her thoughts.

Feeling tears sting her eyes, Grace leaned her head against the tile and let the warm water flow over her, along with uninvited memories.

After they had made love for the first time that wonderful spring afternoon, she'd been so sure Denton loved her and would forever, that they would end up marrying and living happily ever after.

Then the bottom had dropped out of her heart and her world. Two days later, he had told her his dad's transfer had gone through and his family was moving out of state. But even then she hadn't been all that disturbed, confident that no matter where he was he wouldn't forsake her, that as soon as he helped get his parents settled and himself back to school, he'd send for her.

After all, they had made love. She was his.

Still, she'd cried when he'd told her. He'd consoled her with hot, wet kisses.

"Don't, Grace," he'd begged, his lips all over her face. "I'll see you again soon."

"Do you promise?" she'd whispered, staring at him through worshipful eyes.

He'd grabbed her hand and placed it on his chest. "I promise."

That had never happened. After the move, his dad had had the stroke, and though they'd corresponded through letters and occasional phone calls, she'd never seen him again. Until he'd walked up on the porch of the B&B.

And she never knew why. And still didn't.

In light of that, how could she have dropped her guard and kissed him back with such wanton need, such careless abandonment? She felt so ashamed. But she had no one to blame but herself. She could've stopped him, and she hadn't.

He had to leave soon. He just had to.

Clinging to that thread of hope, Grace stepped out of the shower, dressed, then went back downstairs. Her part-time helper Connie Foley was in the foyer dusting.

She was thin and petite with a sweet spirit and sweet ways. Although she varied her days, she was a hard worker, and Grace couldn't run the B&B without her help, especially when it came to the cleaning.

"I noticed we have another guest," Connie said in her soft, shy tone. "That's wonderful. Now we're full again."

Unwittingly Grace frowned, then followed it with a forced smile. "He may be leaving anyday."

"Oh," Connie said, appearing confused.

Grace saw no reason to unconfuse her. At least for the remainder of the day, Denton was off-limits. She prayed he'd feel the same way about her and stay gone.

"I noticed all the work you did in the gardens."

"It took most of the morning, so I'm running behind."

"Where are Mr. and Mrs. Brenner?" Connie asked.

Grace was in the middle of explaining about Ed's attack when the front door opened and the Brenners walked in.

"Boy, am I glad to see you two," Grace cried, hugging them both.

Zelma winked at Connie. "Now all her chicks are back in place."

"That's right," Grace declared. "My guests are my family."

"I know, honey." Zelma smiled and hugged Grace again. "Believe me, we're glad to be back."

"Hospital food sucks," Ed muttered in a tone as dry as parchment.

The women laughed, then Grace accompanied Ed and Zelma to their room where she left Zelma fussing over her husband.

Thank goodness neither had asked about Denton, Grace thought as she made her way into the kitchen to prepare for snack time, praying again that she wouldn't have to deal with him.

Then it hit her about Flora. He couldn't leave until he made good on his promise to help her. Darn!

She had just finished filling the tray with cheese cubes, cucumber sandwiches and homemade sugar cookies when the phone rang.

"Why, hello, Roger," she said after the unfamiliar voice had identified itself.

Roger Gooseby was the local grocer and mayor, whom she didn't see all that often because Connie did most of the grocery shopping. He was a large, robust man whose heart was as big as his body. Everyone in Ruby thought highly of him and his wife.

"How are you?" Grace asked. "And Cynthia?"

"The wife's fine. Actually, we were all fine and dandy until yesterday."

"What happened?"

"Something terrible, or at least it has the potential."

Grace curbed her fear. "Oh, dear, what's wrong?"

"Ruby's being considered for a nuclear power plant."

Shock forced Grace to sit down. "No way!"

"That's how I feel and everyone else I've spoken to."

"So what do we do?" Grace asked in a crisp tone.

"Get organized and fight the bastards."

"I'll do my part. Just keep me posted."

"Will do."

Grace remained seated long after the conversation ended. A nuclear plant in Ruby? The far-reaching repercussions were too vast to comprehend, especially for her as the owner of a B&B. Her head fell into her hands, despair wreaking havoc inside her.

First Denton. Now this. What on earth was going to happen next to upend her life?

"Would you be opposed to an old lady kissing you?"

"Why, shucks, no," Denton drawled, his tone dripping with humor. "In fact, I can't think of anything else I'd like better." Except being with Grace, watching her at work in the house and garden, that sweet, contented smile lighting her face.

But since that wasn't going to happen, he'd settle for a peck on the cheek from Flora and be damn glad to get it.

When he'd stormed out of the house, he'd started driving, having no idea where he was going. It was only after he'd found himself in Austin that an idea hit him, thrusting him into action. He'd find a contractor himself who could hopefully begin work on the nursery repairs immediately. Within an hour he'd done just that.

He had just told Flora the good news. She giggled, sounding like a schoolgirl, though her voice cracked slightly from age.

"You're a good man, Denton Hardesty," she said, touching her dry lips to his cheek.

"Thank you, ma'am."

"So the worker comes tomorrow," Flora said in a tone filled with wonder.

"Workmen," Denton stressed. "There'll be a crew here, getting this place overhauled and quickly, too."

Flora blinked back tears. "I still can't believe it."

"We can't have those newcomers messing with you old-timers."

Flora swiped at a tear that got loose. "Where's Grace? You should've brought her with you."

He wished. "She's too busy to run the roads with me."

"If I were her age and unattached, I wouldn't be." Flora winked. "That's for sure. I'd be bound and determined to hogtie you, boy."

Denton laughed, and it felt good. "And right about now, I'd let you."

Following his bout with Grace, a dose of this crusty old lady was what his battered senses had needed. Along with a cold shower, he added cuttingly. Grace's rejection of him had smarted. Hell, who did she think she was kidding? She'd been as hot for him as he'd been for her. He hadn't forced her to kiss him; he hadn't forced her to do anything. She'd been hot and pliant, giving as good as she got and of her own free will.

It had been her free will that had called a halt. He should be glad. Making love to Grace no matter how badly he wanted would not have been wise. Too many complications. Too many strings.

No, she had done them both a favor. Now all he had to do was convince his body.

"Maybe one of these days if I live long enough, I'll be able to repay you," Flora said into the growing silence.

Denton snorted. "Forget that. Even if you made a million, I wouldn't take a penny of it. I'm doing this because I want to."

"Again, you're a good man, and you deserve a good woman."

"How 'bout you and me gettin' hitched?"

Flora slapped him on the shoulder. "Go on, get out of here. This old lady has work to do."

After he left the nursery, he drove around town, taking in all the changes that had come about since he'd left. Man, how this little place had grown, and all for the better, too. Too bad there was nothing here for him.

Grace.

He gripped the steering wheel until his knuckles whitened. She was there all right, only not for him. He'd had his chance and squandered it. That road was now closed, which was best for both of them. Were it not for the aching hole left inside him from unquenched desire, he might have reconciled that within himself. But for now he couldn't.

If he had any sense, he'd do himself and Grace a favor. He would keep on driving until he reached Dallas, his home, where he belonged. For the most part this town, these people, were foreign to him. He no longer had anything in common with any of them nor did he want to.

His life, his needs were in the city.

Suddenly he found himself at the highway intersection. He didn't so much as hesitate. He turned and headed back to the B&B, back to Grace.

Ten

Grace moved like a robot on automatic pilot during the remainder of the afternoon, the mayor's disturbing call returning to mind. In fact, she worked herself into such a state she took time and made several calls to other B&B owners. Some had heard the news and others hadn't. But all were equally concerned and ready to band together to fight. The organizational part she was still leaving to Roger Gooseby, though she would do her part.

She feared for her business if Ruby was chosen. The other owners felt the same way. If she lost her livelihood, she would have no recourse but to return… No! She shut her mind to that thought, feeling panic well inside her. Ruby wouldn't be chosen. It simply wouldn't.

Now, at the moment, she was once again obsessing on Denton. He hadn't made an appearance during snack time or since, which was fine by her. Yet she found herself unconsciously flinching, then peering over her shoulder, every time a door opened and closed.

She figured she had so much to do—from replacing the wallpaper in her bath upstairs, to catching up on her book work, to planning the rest of the week's breakfast and snack menus, that she wouldn't have time to think about him.

Wrong.

Both her thoughts and heart continued to dwell on him, especially that lethal kiss. Even though she'd already beaten up on herself for her part in it, she truly hadn't wanted it to end. All the emotion, all the love she had felt for him was back, and her heart felt shattered all over again.

Surely she wasn't still in love with him. Unwilling to probe such a provocative thought, Grace tore out of the kitchen and made her way outside. Once there, she took several deep, gulping breaths, then felt the world suddenly right itself. The thought of being closed up was too much for her. She needed air and space.

Maybe she'd gotten her wish after all, she told herself, continuing to fight off the building sense of desperation. Maybe he'd already left.

Maybe the kiss had scared the living daylights out of him and he was halfway back to Dallas. For a second her world brightened. Then her sound judgment kicked in and warned her not to hold her breath. Anyway, she couldn't run from the emotions he stirred in her. She'd already tried to once and it hadn't worked. She had to face them, then defeat them, or she'd be lost.

But dammit, that wasn't fair. He'd broken her soul into little pieces and gotten away with it. No one should have to endure a second round of abuse. The answer was strength and resolve. She could and would pull herself back together one more time.

As soon as he left.

Holding her shoulders back, Grace made her way into the metal building where she stored her garden supplies. Shortly she was in the front yard, on her knees yanking out weeds. Maintaining her precious flower beds could be an everyday, all-consuming chore if she let it. Today, though, it was the panacea for her battered senses, and she welcomed the challenge.

"Hey, want some help?"

Grace looked up and Zelma was on the front porch, glass of iced tea in hand.

"No, thanks. You take care of Ed."

She made a face, then grinned. "That old coot. He's one for the books. He's in there holding court, ordering me around like you wouldn't believe."

"And you love every minute of it."

This time Zelma's grin was sheepish. "You're right, I do. I'm just glad he's going to be all right."

"Isn't that the truth," Grace said, wiping perspiration off her brow.

Zelma frowned. "Why don't you let Connie do that?"

"Because she has too much to do inside."

"I could help out on both counts."

"Not on your life. You're a guest, for heaven's sake. I'm supposed to take care of you."

"That's baloney. I'm used to working like a field hand."

"Well, not anymore. Ed's seeing to that. Now, you just relax and enjoy."

"All right. I'll take the old coot for a walk out back, then we'll rest in the swing for a while."

Grace grinned, wiping her face again. "Sounds like a good plan. I'll see you later." She paused. "I have something I want to discuss with you and Ed."

"What's wrong with now?"

"I'd prefer later." They were such a sound, responsible couple she wanted to get their take on what might happen concerning the nuclear plant threat, but not until she had her scattered emotions under wraps. Right now, she didn't.

If things had been different, she would have loved to get Denton's opinion on the matter. With his connections, he might even be able to help derail things. But that would be a dangerous move. She didn't want to involve him in town politics or anything else that was personal.

Forget him.

"Later it is," Zelma quipped, turning and going back inside.

Grace sat back on the grass for a minute, thinking she ought to go inside and get herself something to drink. Zelma would've brought her some tea had she asked. Ah, forget it, she told herself. It was getting late, and she should finish this flower bed, wind up this project for the day. She dreaded the evening, dreaded it stretching in front of her, long and lonely.

It was his fault.

If he hadn't come back to Ruby and turned her life upside down, her insides wouldn't be so mangled. It was in that moment that she heard the vehicle. Her heart faltered. He had come back. Both excitement and dread held her motionless until she felt his presence behind her.

"Something tells me we've been bitten by the same bug."

That low, husky voice that she'd come to associate exclusively with him further assaulted her already-raw nerves.

She scrambled to her feet. No way was she going to carry on a conversation with him sitting down. Although she wasn't nearly his height, standing up seemed somehow to even the odds, at least in her mind.

"And what bug would that be?" she said, trying to keep the tremor out of her voice. But it was hard, as he had a certain look in his eyes, a vulnerable look, as though he didn't know quite what to do next. If she was right about that, then that was probably a first with him. He usually oozed self-confidence.

"Work," he murmured, his eyes raking over her, seeming to concentrate on the vee of her shirt where she had a gathering of perspiration. "That's all you seem happy doing."

Color crept into her face. She couldn't even be around him without being aware of strong, sexual vibes. She didn't know how much longer she could play this cat and mouse game and endure.

"I guess you should know," she said lamely, trying not to stare at him.

"Do I still have my room?"

Their eyes met for another quick moment, then both turned away as if they'd been zapped.

Grace tried to find enough breath to speak again, but it was difficult. Now was her chance to tell him no, tell him he was no longer welcome, tell him whatever it would take to get rid of him.

"That's…up to you," she said. So much for the mental lecture.

"I'd like to stay."

"Denton—"

"How 'bout going on the porch?" He peered down, then back up. "If you're not through here, I can finish up later."

While she had no intention of letting him finish weeding the front beds, she didn't say that. Actually, the thought of just talking to him as if everything was normal as apple pie and ice cream left a bad taste in her mouth. Yet she couldn't let him know how she felt, how attracted she was to him, how *frightened* she was of that attraction.

Perhaps it was a thread of desperation she heard in his tone that made her turn and head toward the swing, then perch on one end of it. Thankfully, he chose the wicker chair next to her.

"I wouldn't blame you if you kicked me out."

Color rushed into her cheeks, knowing he was referring to the kiss. "That subject's off-limits."

"Would an apology help?"

"No."

"Didn't think so." He trapped her gaze. "I wasn't going to apologize, anyway, because I'm not sorry."

The intensity of his eyes seemed to literally burn her skin, deepening her color. "It's no big deal," she lied. "Just don't do it again."

He didn't respond for what seemed the longest time, then he said, "I've been at the nursery."

"Flora's?" she asked inanely.

"Yep, but not before driving to Austin."

She frowned. "I'm not following you."

He smiled briefly then explained.

"You mean it was that simple?" Her tone sounded dazed even to her own ears.

"Only if it all comes together. We'll see."

"I'm impressed and elated."

"I was hoping you would be."

Grace didn't dare probe that declaration for fear of sinking a little deeper into the surrounding quagmire. "I hope it isn't all for naught."

"What does that mean?" he demanded, narrowing his eyes and rubbing his slightly bristled chin.

She told him about her conversation with the mayor.

Denton let go of an expletive. "That's gotta be nixed."

"We all feel that way, but you know the kind of ammo it takes to fight that kind of thing."

"Do you mind if I do some poking, see what I can do?"

"Why would you do that?" she asked, voicing her skepticism.

"I think you know why," he said huskily, his eyes once again deep and searching. "For you."

Grace lunged to her feet, both her body and her voice quivering, "Stop it, damn you."

Before he could mount a suitable defense, she darted inside and slammed the door behind her.

She hated crying.

More than that, she hated feeling that awful sense of impending doom hovering over her like a dark cloud. She had tried to sleep, but couldn't. So instead of continuing to fight the bed, especially the pillow, she got up and made her way downstairs in the wee hours of the morning, hoping a glass of hot milk would stave off an attack.

She had just taken her cup out of the microwave when her hand began to shake, slopping the liquid all over the floor. But the mess was the least of her worries as her heart began to race off the charts, her breathing became labored, and her head spun.

She was having a full-blown anxiety attack, something she hadn't had in a long time. Giving in to the tears that ran down her face, she groped for the cabinet where she kept spare medication. Once she'd swallowed a tiny pill, she clung to the counter and waited for the room to settle.

"Grace, what the hell?"

Oh, dear Lord, not him, not the reason for her attack in flesh and blood.

"Go away, Denton," she whispered, between sobs. "You seem to have a talent for showing up at the wrong place."

"And at the wrong time," he added in a defeated voice.

"That's...right," she whispered, beginning to shake again.

"Grace, let me help," he pleaded. "You're ill. Even I can see that."

"No!" she cried. "I'm having an anxiety attack." Rarely did she share that secret with anyone. In fact, she kept it closely guarded, hating that weakness in herself. That was why she couldn't believe she'd just blurted it out, to him of all people, especially since she blamed him for bringing it on.

Denton suddenly closed the distance between them, and before she could get out of harm's way, he placed his hands on her forearms and drew her gently against him.

"Please, let me hold you," he said in a thick, tortured voice.

Heaven on earth was the thought that went through her mind. For the first time since the attack had rendered her useless, she felt safe, cocooned in a secure warmth that only his arms could provide.

Fool! she lambasted herself.

"Grace, Grace," he whispered, "I'm so sorry." He then ran a soothing hand up and down her back.

She couldn't speak; all she could do was cling to him.

Eleven

He knew he should push her away, that it was the sensible, logical thing for both of them. But how could he let her go when she was holding on to him for dear life? He didn't kid himself, though. Right now she was frightened, for some unknown reason, and he was her comforter. No way would he take advantage of her pain. Lord knows, he'd been down that same road with the plane crash.

Still, just having her in his arms and holding her was ripping his guts to pieces. He wanted more, so much more. He wanted to kiss her lips, suckle her breasts, lick her flesh all the way down to her toes.

Those erotic thoughts hardened him instantly, and he knew she felt him pressing against her. But that was the way it was between them, the way it had always been. When they touched, it was like a lethal combustion. Time or distance had not changed that.

All he could do now was hope he had the restraint to conquer his growing desire and not do anything else he would be sorry for.

"Shh," he whispered into her sweet-smelling hair. "It's going to be all right. You're going to be all right."

"No, I'm not." Her cry was muffled against his chest where he felt her tears soak his shirt.

"Yes, you are. Trust me on that."

She pulled back then and peered into his eyes. "I hate it when this happens."

"I'm sure," he said in a soothing voice, pulling her next to him again, only this time he couldn't stop himself from dropping featherlight kisses on her temple, then her cheeks, tasting her tears, *tasting her.*

A tiny sigh escaped her as he lifted her wide, tear-lined eyes to his, her lower lips trembling slightly. That was his undoing. With a groan he lowered his lips to hers, gently at first, then, when she didn't object, he deepened the pressure, becoming hard and hungry.

She moaned against him but still offered no objection, not even when his hand found its way to a burgeoning breast. He pulled on the nipple, feeling it bud under his fingers like a flower bursting to bloom.

"Grace," he whispered against her soft, moist lips. "I want you so much."

"Then…make love to me."

Denton pulled back and stared at her, unable to believe those broken words had come from her. But when she reached up and traced a finger over his lips, lingering on the moist inside of his bottom one, he knew she was serious.

Though his legs had all the consistency of water,

he forced them to move, with her adhered to his side. No words were exchanged, not even after they reached his room, where clothes were instantly discarded and they lay naked on the huge bed.

"Tell me what you want," he rasped, his gaze soaking up the beauty of her creamy-skinned body that still had all the curves in the right places.

"You. All of you."

He needed no second invitation, leaning over and taking her mouth once again in deep, hot kisses, tongues toying, then sparring. Fearing that he couldn't hold off much longer, but wanting to savor all of her, he pulled away and moved to her nipples where he pulled and tugged with his mouth until they were swollen and pulsating.

"Oh, Denton," she whispered, running her hands wildly through his hair before slowly making her way down his stomach to the crisp curls between his thighs. Velvet-like fingers surrounded his manhood, then moved up and down.

He moaned against the raw heat that shot through his body even as his tongue dipped in and out of her navel, further sparking the fire inside him to a feverish pitch. Still, he wanted to prolong the sweet misery, make this moment last forever.

It was then that his hand nudged her thighs apart and his tongue speared into her quivering moistness. Her hips bucked, and moans of pleasure erupted from her lips before he raised himself over her.

"Please, don't torture me anymore," she pleaded, reaching for him.

He thrust into her ever so slowly, his eyes glued to hers, watching the play of emotions across her face as he continued to move in, then out, extending the exquisite pain.

"Denton, please!" she cried.

This time he remained inside her, thrusting hard and high until they both cried out in unison and he collapsed on top of her.

"My sweet, sweet Grace," he murmured against her breasts.

Denton watched her for the longest time, determined to memorize every detail of her face and body, store it in his heart so that when he no longer had access to her he could draw on his vivid memory.

He stifled a groan, aching to touch a breast that was exposed to his greedy gaze. The streetlamp shone through the gauzy drapes and bathed her in a misty glow, allowing him that pleasure.

How could he walk away and leave her again? It would be even harder this time. But what choice did he have? None. His life was miles away from here. This time the groan escaped, and her eyes opened.

At first she seemed confused, then shocked at seeing him bending over her, watching her. Then she smiled, the most beautiful smile he'd ever seen.

"Thank you," she whispered.

He could barely talk around the lump in his throat. "For what?"

"For saving my life."

"I hardly think I did that." His voice was far from back to normal. He sounded as if he'd swallowed a rusty nail.

"Yes, you did. When I have one of my…attacks, I always feel like I'm dying."

"Oh, Grace, how long have you had those things?"

"Too long."

"Is that why you've been content and secure to stay here in quiet and peaceful Ruby?"

"That's part of the reason, but I also love it here. It's home."

Home. Did he have a home? Somehow he didn't think so. Suddenly that thought was unsettling. Even when he'd been married, he'd never really come home.

Denton crooked his elbow and stared directly into her eyes. "What triggers those awful attacks?" he asked, wanting to know everything about her, yet knowing he had no right. "Was it—" He broke off unable to find the right words to ask the deadly question that festered in his mind.

"You leaving me," she said, finishing the sentence for him.

He nodded on a deep sigh.

"No. They started much later." She turned away.

"Grace?"

She faced him again, but her eyes were shuttered. He had run into a brick wall. He knew there was more, but she had said all she intended to say on the subject. He had no choice but to respect that. He'd given up the right to pry long ago.

"For the most part, I'm okay," she said. "I have medication that usually kills them on target."

Her word choice made him smile. "That's good."

She stretched suddenly, and when she did her leg brushed against him. He got an instant response.

Her eyes widened. "Oh, dear."

He chuckled, then sobered. "See what you do to me, woman."

"That works both ways." Grace's tone faltered.

"So are you telling me you're wet?" he whispered, his eyes darkening.

"Yes," she said sweetly and simply.

The room was quiet for a long time.

Once they were sated again, Grace eased out of the bed and went into the bathroom. There she leaned over the counter and clung to it, deciding that she had indeed lost her sanity.

Lifting her head, she stared at herself in the mirror, wondering if she looked any different after having made love following such a long abstinence? No. In fact, there was a glow about her that said she'd been made love to countless times.

Regrets?

Did she have any? No. At least not now. As for the "later" of all this, she wouldn't deal with that now. She intended to block out the coming of dawn and with it the reality of the new day. At present she was enjoying a moment of heaven on earth, and she had every intention of wallowing in it.

"What took you so long?" he asked, a lazy smile on his lips.

She chuckled. "None of your business."

"I missed you."

"I'm...glad."

"Grace—"

Her name sounded like a cry, and the look on his face was tormented. She knew what was coming— *his regrets.* And she didn't want to hear then, not now, not ever.

"It's your turn," she said quickly, climbing back onto the bed.

"For what?"

"To share your secrets."

"What makes you think I have any?"

"Intuition."

"Mmm."

She poked him in the ribs. "Come on, confess."

"What makes you think there's anything?"

"Woman's intuition."

He snorted.

"Come on, confess. Something makes you pop antacids. And I'll bet it's not all your job."

Denton sighed deeply. "You're right, it's not. It's been almost a year now, but I was involved in a plane crash."

"Oh, my God, Denton, I had no idea."

"There's no reason you would. It was in the Dallas paper, but that's all, as far as I know."

When she didn't respond, he went on, "I walked away with barely a scratch, but I was the only one."

"That's unbelievable," she said, an obvious hitch in her voice.

"I know. There were three of us in a private jet, out for fun on a spring day."

She picked up on the pain in his voice and was glad he didn't try to mask it. Maybe talking about it would help purge some of the pain that had apparently been festering for so long.

"My best friend had just bought the small jet. He hired a pilot and away we went. We'd been in the air quite a while when something went terribly wrong." He paused, his lips thinning.

She clasped his hand in hers and squeezed it. "Go on."

"I don't remember a lot of the details. Maybe I've just blotted them out. Who the hell knows? The shrinks don't, that's for sure. Anyway, the plane lost power and down we went. My friend, who was sitting next to the pilot, died on impact. I was in the back. That may be why I survived. Again, who the hell knows?''

''It's hard to ever get over that trauma no matter how long you live,'' Grace said gently, nestling closer to him.

''I'm finding that out. Guilt eats at my gut constantly, and it's been hard to get my life back on track. Actually, I haven't,'' he added bluntly.

''It takes more time for some than others.''

''It's just since I've been in Ruby that I realized how exhausted and burned-out I am.''

It was on the tip of her tongue to tell him he was welcome to stay in town, that he was welcome in her bed, in her life. And while he was definitely confused for the moment, it wouldn't last. Asking him to stay here with her would be the same as trapping, then caging, a wild creature.

''I haven't popped an antacid in hours now,'' he commented, interrupting her thoughts.

''You really ought to throw those things away for good.''

''Maybe I can. Now.''

His gaze made another disturbing sweep of her naked flesh.

''We'll work on that,'' she said, her pulse rate zooming again.

''It wasn't burnout alone that kept me here.''

Grace didn't know where he was going with that heavily loaded statement, and she wasn't sure she wanted to know. She had sworn he would never have the chance to hurt her again. By allowing him carte blanche over her body, she had done just that. However, she was going to stick to her resolve and not dwell on or repent of that sin now. Dawn would come soon enough.

"I never forgot you, you know," he admitted into the silence.

"I find that hard to believe," she countered uneasily.

"That's understandable. I acted like an ass."

"I won't argue that point," she said in a dull tone.

"But I was scared, especially after I found out you were a virgin."

"That was no excuse."

"I know, but—"

"I wasn't going to force you to marry me," she responded in a bleak tone. "You should've known that."

"I did know, but I just lost it. I was too immature to handle a serious relationship. Ugly as it is, that's the truth."

She wished now she hadn't opened this can of worms. Rehashing the past was much more painful than she'd anticipated. But maybe it was something that needed to be done so that she could lay it to rest once and for all. She likened it to Denton talking about the crash.

"And I'll admit my parents didn't help," he went on. "When Dad told me he was being transferred and that I was expected to move with them, I felt almost relieved. Then he had the stroke…"

"They manipulated you, Denton, especially after they found out about us."

"You're right. They did. I could see that later. At the time I couldn't." He paused and drew a shuddering breath. "Then I did another stupid thing. I married a woman I didn't love and thought it would work."

"What do you want me to say, Denton, that I forgive you?"

"Do you?" he asked huskily.

Yes, she said silently, because I never stopped loving you. But she couldn't tell him that. Loving him was her problem, not his.

"Is my forgiveness important to you?"

"God, yes."

"Then you have it," she said in a small voice.

He stared at her through unreadable eyes, then he grabbed her and pulled her on top of him.

"Make love to me again," he whispered in a frantic tone.

Twelve

"**I** believe that was the best ever, honey."

Ed was referring to the breakfast they had all scarfed down, leaving nothing to put in the disposal.

Although Grace flushed with pleasure, she made an embarrassed gesture with a hand. "You say that every time, Ed."

"Well, I happen to agree with him," Ralph added in his low, easy voice.

Grace's eyes widened, and Zelma actually chuckled out loud.

"See," Ed said in a know-it-all tone.

"It was just bacon and eggs, for heaven's sake."

"Oh, for heaven's sake," Zelma mimicked, "it was much more than that. The grits casserole and fried green tomatoes were out of this world."

"Don't forget the homemade croissants," Ralph chimed in.

"Well, thanks, guys," Grace said, her face redder than ever.

Zelma cocked her head to one side. "To what do we owe this occasion?"

For a second Grace was tempted to ignore Zelma's direct question for fear of giving herself away, of blurting out the truth about her happy frame of mind, how she'd been hoping to impress Denton with her culinary skills.

Only he hadn't even shown up for the feast.

"I just felt like going all out," Grace said in as nonchalant and light a tone as she could muster. In reality her heart felt frozen inside her chest. Where was he?

"And the fact that we ate on the back veranda made the feast even nicer," Ed said, breaking into her thoughts before crossing to the sink, where Grace stood, and giving her a peck on the cheek. "Don't let my wife give you a hard time, honey. I don't have to have a reason. I just love being pampered, and I definitely feel that." He winked at Grace, making her laugh.

"Hey, you old coot, you stop flirting now, you hear?" Zelma demanded, a hint of laughter in her voice. "She'll have you so spoiled when we get home, I won't know what to do with you."

"Then don't go," Grace said off the top of her head.

Zelma appeared taken aback for a second, then said, "While that sounds tempting, my kids and his have other ideas."

"I know," Grace said. "It's just you can't blame me for trying. I'm going to miss you two something awful when you leave."

Ralph chose that moment to shove back his chair and stand. "Er...thanks again. I've got to get back to the salt mines."

"I'm going to miss you, too, Ralph," Grace said softly, giving him a sweet smile.

Seemingly embarrassed, he shuffled his feet before giving her a faint smile and walking out.

"What a strange man," Zelma said, shaking her head.

"Now, Z," Ed said in a loving but chastising voice, "he just does his own thing. Nothing wrong with that."

"Believe it or not, he writes some of the funniest and most adoring children's stories you'd ever want to read," Grace added. "He's given me several to read."

Zelma shook her head in wonder. "I choose not to believe it, but if you say so..." Her voice trailed off.

"You reckon he'll autograph a couple for our grandkids?" Ed asked, scratching his head.

"Ask him," Grace said.

Zelma rolled he eyes. "Not me."

Grace chuckled. "Then I will."

"By the way, where's the hunk?" Zelma asked unexpectedly. "I can't believe he missed this treat."

"I haven't the foggiest," Grace said in what she hoped was an even tone, though she turned away from their inquiring eyes just in case she hadn't pulled it off.

"Come to think about it," Zelma said, "I saw him leave as I was heading for the kitchen."

In spite of herself, Grace felt her heart falter. "Leave?"

"He had his keys in hand," Zelma responded with

a shrug. "I'll have to make it a point to tell him what he missed."

"I doubt he cares," Grace said before she thought.

Zelma's eyebrows lifted. "I detect a note of sarcasm hidden in those words."

"Now, Z, leave the child alone." Ed grinned at Grace. "She's famous for her matchmaking skills."

Grace forced a smile. "Well, she's wasting her time with me, Ed. Anyway, Denton's just passing through."

"Sounds to me like he's not passing anywhere, that he's pretty stationary."

"Zelma, honey, you're wasting your time," Grace said, forcing another smile. "Now you two get out of here, and let me get this mess cleaned up."

"All right, my friend," Zelma said, "we'll see you at snack time, if we're back, that is. We're going into Austin to shop."

Grace frowned. "Are you up to that, Ed?"

"You betcha. I'm feeling no pain."

"Trust me, the old coot is as full of piss and vinegar as he ever was."

This time Grace's smile was genuine. "You two are a piece of work."

A few minutes later she was alone with nothing but her torrid thoughts. Although she felt none of the regrets that she'd felt certain would hit her this morning, she did feel a keen sense of disappointment that she hadn't seen him. Was *he* sorry? Perhaps. Or just reluctant to face her for whatever reason—for many reasons? Suddenly battling a feeling of nausea, Grace placed a hand over her lower stomach and took several deep breaths. Momentarily she felt a little better.

Maybe he was upset with her because she hadn't

awakened him before she'd left, just as dawn was breaking. But he'd been sleeping so soundly, like a satisfied baby who had his tummy full. Well, Denton had been satisfied, all right, but not with food. Their marathon sex had done the trick. Too, she hadn't known what to say. Asking him to stay was out of the question. Asking when he planned to leave was also out of the question.

Both required nerve, a special kind of nerve that she hadn't developed. Oh, her skin had definitely thickened, but not to that extent. Who was she kidding? When it came to Denton nothing had changed; he had the same kind of power over her that he'd had years ago.

What did that say about her?

She still loved him and wanted to be with him the rest of her life. Not going to happen, she told herself. Or was it possible, after all? She sensed he cared deeply for her. Or was she wrong and their relationship was based on sex like it had been years ago? Although at the time she'd thought it had been much more.

Picking up a dish towel, Grace began wiping the cabinet until there wasn't a spot on it. Yet she kept on rubbing, wondering if he'd taken the easy way out again, or rather the chicken way, and left.

If so, fine.

Her lips tightened into a white line. If he wanted to pretend last night hadn't happened, then she could oblige him without a problem. Over the years she had become quite adept at hiding her emotions, especially after she'd been diagnosed with anxiety attacks. She could be just as blasé about their lovemaking as he could.

She could do no such thing, she told herself savagely, not when her heart was breaking all over again. Last night had rekindled so many heated memories she'd thought she had laid to rest in the secret part of her soul, that she was a basket case this morning.

Only because he'd left without reassuring her that last night had meant as much to him as it had to her. But she knew in the light of day that great sex was all they would ever have going for them, that a future was impossible.

She had no intention of leaving Ruby, and he had no intention of staying here. Give it a rest, Grace told herself, slapping the towel down on the cabinet. She could wrestle this demon the rest of her life and never conquer it.

All she had to do now was simply get through the time he remained, then begin to glue the broken parts of her heart and soul back together one more time.

Deciding to cut some fresh flowers for Connie to place in each of the rooms, Grace grabbed the scissors out of the drawer and headed toward the French doors that led onto the veranda.

She had just placed her hand on the knob when the phone rang. ''Darn,'' she muttered, not wanting to be trapped inside for a moment longer. Fresh air was what she most needed to help soothe her troubled mind.

Still, the phone was linked to her livelihood and she couldn't just not answer it. Crossing the room, she reached for the receiver.

It was Ward Pearson, a local rancher, the only man she'd gone out with since returning to Ruby. Although she cared deeply about Ward, she wasn't attracted to him and never had been. He was a widower

with grown children, and while he hadn't been pushy
in his efforts to woo her, Grace knew that if she gave
the slightest indication that she would marry him,
he'd take her up on it in a blink.

Not going to happen, especially now, not after Denton had breezed back into her life and proved anew
that marrying Ward would definitely be settling for
second best.

"Hello, Ward," she finally said, following his
friendly greeting. "Long time no hear from."

"I've been out of town. One of the girls had sur-
gery."

"Is everything okay?"

"Jim Dandy," he responded. "So what's going on
with you?"

"You haven't heard," Grace said flatly.

He seemed to have picked up on that certain vibe
in her tone because he responded accordingly.
"What's wrong?"

"Well, Roger's much more in the know than me,
but I can at least clue you in." She went on to explain
about the nuclear plant site and how everyone felt.

"That's not going to happen as long as I'm
breathing," he said in a low, terse tone. "No one's
going to put a blight on this town when there are
worlds of other sites that will work."

"You need to call Roger."

"I have a ton of messages, but I haven't listened
to any of them yet. I'm sure he's one of them."

"I'd say he's probably more than one."

Ward chuckled in his low, gruff voice. "When can
I see you?"

"Oh, Ward, I don't know."

"That seems to be your pat answer."

Grace felt a flush come over her face and was glad he couldn't see it. Guilt. That was what she was feeling right now and didn't know why. It was okay if she didn't want to go out with him, *sleep* with him. She was an adult and accountable to no one.

Except Denton, and only in her heart.

"It's not a good time. I have a full house, and you know how hectic that can be."

His deep sigh filtered through the line. "What if I won't take no for an answer?"

Although he spoke lightly, she knew he wasn't teasing. "I guess I'd be flattered."

"I just want to take you to dinner. Just think about it. Don't say no. Okay?"

"All right, Ward, I'll give your dinner invitation serious thought, although it might not be until next week."

"I can live with that. So I'll talk to you later, and don't worry about that plant. It's not going to happen."

"You have no idea how much better that makes me feel."

"Take care."

"Thanks, Ward."

She had just replaced the phone when she heard a sound behind her. Whirling around, she saw Denton standing in the doorway of the kitchen, his face devoid of color. She placed a hand over her chest, fear clutching at her. Had something happened? Other than his lack of color, nothing else seemed amiss. As usual, he looked as sexy as hell, even more so when visions of their erotic night flashed before her eyes.

He had on a pair of shorts and a T-shirt, as if he was about to hit the jogging trail. Maybe that was where he'd gone, only to correct that thought instantly as there wasn't one drop of sweat on him.

"Who was that on the phone?" he asked.

His blunt question took her so aback that for a moment she couldn't respond. Then when she did, she answered with a question, "Why do you ask?"

"I heard you mention the name Ward, then something about going out with him."

She was more than taken aback now; she was flabbergasted. "Were you eavesdropping on my conversation?"

"No, but I couldn't help but overhear."

Was he jealous? Was that what this was all about? For a moment her pulse leaped. "Actually, I was speaking to Ward Pearson, who's a friend."

"Are you two having an affair?"

She gasped, and her eyes widened. "Why...why would you ask such a thing?"

Silence fell over the room like a wet blanket.

"Because he's the client I'm here to see."

Thirteen

Money.

So that was what this was all about. Damn him! Grace warded off the sudden threat of tears and jutted out her chin. Jealous. Hysterical laughter almost erupted before she caught her lower lip between her teeth and bit down on it.

"I know what you're thinking—" Denton broke off as if searching for the words that would get him out of hot water.

"No, I don't think you do," she retorted, "or you wouldn't have said that."

It was obvious from the contrite look on his face that he wished he could recall his words and start over, but it was too late. As far as she was concerned, the damage had been done.

Last night had meant nothing to him. His career was heads above everything else.

"Tell me something, Denton, is the almighty dollar that important to you?"

This time his features darkened. "Dammit, Grace, if you'd just let me explain."

She stood her ground. "I asked you a simple question."

"No, it isn't," he responded through clenched teeth.

"Sure."

Her blatant sarcasm brought a flush to his face. "I knew you wouldn't believe me. That's why I wanted to explain."

"There are not enough words in the English language that would allow you to do that."

He muttered a curse just as Zelma rounded the corner. "Oh, I'm sorry," she said, halting midstride. "Sorry, I didn't mean to interrupt."

"I thought you two were going to Austin," Grace said.

"Me, too," Zelma replied, slightly down in the mouth. "But things didn't work out that way."

If the situation hadn't been so volatile, and her heart hadn't been hanging in shreds, she wouldn't have laughed at the picture Zelma made. For some reason her hair was all askew on her head. And her eyes were wide and smudged with makeup. She looked like someone out of a circus. And totally frayed.

"Sure I'm not interrupting?" Zelma's tone was as doubtful as her features.

"I'm sure," Grace said, dragging a deep breath through her lungs.

Zelma glanced from one to the other, then added

bluntly, ''Well, you two look as if you're about ready to blow a gasket.''

Leave it to Zelma to cut straight to the heart of the matter, Grace thought, hiding a smile.

Denton did chuckle, which definitely helped defuse the tension.

''I think that's a pretty apt term,'' he said, though the humor didn't seem to reach his eyes.

''Oh, dear,'' Zelma murmured meekly, resting her gaze on Grace.

''Don't pay any attention to him,'' Grace snapped. ''What did you need?''

Zelma waved a hand. ''Forget it. It's nothing that can't wait.''

''Our discussion is what can wait,'' Grace said, hoping that Denton would take the hint and disappear. Despite the fact that she still loved him, she couldn't bear the sight of him, not right now, anyway.

Zelma frowned. ''Oh, I don't—''

''Zelma!''

''Okay, okay. It's Ed.''

''What about him?'' Denton asked quickly.

Grace battled down her fear. ''Is it his heart?''

''No, no, nothing like that,'' Zelma said, the frown still in place, which made her appear even more bizarre. ''He has some kind of rash all over his back— big, nasty-looking welts.''

''Oh, my,'' Grace said, frowning also.

''I was hoping you had something I could put on them, some kind of antiseptic.''

''I'm sure I do,'' Grace said, glad for a reason to get away from Denton.

''Maybe you should call the doctor,'' Denton added, before she could so much as move a muscle.

Though he was talking to Zelma, Grace felt his smoldering gaze centered on her. She balled her fists, quelling the urge to throttle him. How dare he toy with her emotions as if she was his puppet on a string?

Cool it, she cautioned herself. Maybe she was making a mountain out of a molehill and she had misunderstood his motive. Maybe she should give him the benefit of the doubt and lighten up. Nah. She hadn't misunderstood. He'd been livid at the thought she'd messed up his chance to make a buck.

"Do you think it could be serious?" Zelma asked, a worried note in her voice.

Denton shrugged. "It might be caused by his medication."

"Well, he is on some new drugs since he had his attack."

"Let me go ahead and get you some ointment," Grace said, "then maybe you should call the doctor."

Zelma hesitated, then said to Grace, "Would you mind taking a look at it? I hate to ask, but under the circumstances—"

Grace patted her on the arm. "Say no more. I'll be glad to. I can't have anything happening to my favorite guests."

"You're going to have to stop spoiling that old coot."

Grace forced a smile. "Never."

"I'll let you look, too," Zelma said, facing Denton and bestowing a charming smile on him.

His lips twitched. "I'll pass. Two women making a fuss over poor old Ed is enough."

Zelma chuckled.

"Grace."

Because of Zelma, she didn't ignore him, though she refused to meet his eyes.

"We need to talk later, okay?"

"Maybe," she muttered before taking Zelma by the arm and pointing her down the hall toward her room.

Denton's expletive colored the air, but Grace kept right on moving.

"I think he's pissed," Zelma said, craning her neck and peering back over her shoulder.

Grace gritted her teeth. "He'll get over it."

Ass.

That word described him to a T, he thought, standing in his room and staring out the window after she'd turned her back on him and disappeared with Zelma, leaving him eating the dust of her vague comment.

She might not ever speak to him again, and he didn't blame her. Oh, she'd speak to him again, he assured himself, reality coming to his rescue. Under the circumstances, she didn't have much choice, but it wouldn't be the same.

He'd blown it.

And for no reason. The night they had shared had been incredible, a night he'd dreamed about often but never thought would happen. It had, then he'd rained on his own parade.

Before he had opened his eyes, he'd reached for her, only she hadn't been there. His eyes had popped open, thinking she might be in the bathroom. After checking, he realized she'd left.

Noticing the time, he figured she hadn't wanted to get caught sneaking out of his room after daylight for fear one of the guests might see her. But his disappointment had been acute at being deprived of the exquisite pleasure of rolling over and burying himself back inside her warmth.

God, but she'd been so wet, so needy. Just like him. Over and over. He'd lost count of the times they'd made love, several of those times she'd been on top, riding him until they had both cried out with release. Sex had never been that satisfying.

Just thinking about Grace made him hard, made him ache to dash down the hall, grab her and haul her back to his room.

Sure, Hardesty, when pigs fly.

He'd had every intention of going to breakfast just so he could be around her again, smell her, *touch her*. Accidentally on purpose. But he'd gotten cold feet, thinking that because she'd left his room without awakening him she'd had regrets, that she was sorry she'd given in to him.

With his mind playing those brutal tricks, he'd decided to go for a drive and think things through. If anything, his thoughts had become more muddled which was why, when he came to the nursery, he'd stopped, especially since the carpenters were there hammering away. Flora was outside, watching every move they made.

He'd stopped and spoken to the men and to her.

"Oh, Denton, I can't believe this is really happening, that you've given this old woman a new lease on life."

"My pleasure, Ms. Flora."

"Why did you do it?" She nudged him on the shoulder. "Was it to impress Grace?"

He looked appalled. "Whatever gave you that idea?"

"Huh! You can't fool an old broad like me who's been around the mountain a time or two. I haven't always been old and withered, sonny boy." She nudged him again and winked. "My old man and me played nasty many a time ourselves."

"Why, Flora Mantooth!"

"My point is I recognize that look when I see it."

He grinned, though his heart was beating much more rapidly than normal. "And what look would that be?"

"Like you could eat her with a spoon."

"I think your glasses need changing, Flora."

"You could do worse. That Grace is a favorite of just about everyone in Ruby."

"Shows Ruby has good taste."

"So make sure your intentions are honorable, sonny boy."

"I give you my word."

When he'd finally made it back to his vehicle, he'd felt as if he'd been gutted. He'd found it hard to believe that his feelings for Grace had shown to that extent. God, what had he gotten himself into?

That question had haunted him all the way back to the B&B and back to Grace. Suddenly he had ached to see her, to reassure himself that she wasn't sorry about what had happened between them.

It was shortly thereafter that he'd walked in and overheard her conversation with Ward. From that moment on, things had gone to hell in a handbasket.

Jealous. He was jealous of the client he hadn't even bothered to get back in touch with. Jealousy had been the driving force behind his knee jerk reaction to that call. He hadn't given a rip about the money, though he sure as hell wouldn't ever convince Grace of that, especially now. He'd just been so stunned that, first, it was the man he'd come to see whom she was talking to and, second, that he was asking her out.

The thought of anyone else touching her the way he'd touched her made him crazy. Jealousy aside, he had to face reality, too. If she and Ward were having an affair—that thought made his stomach revolt—then she just might feel the need to confess that she'd slept with him, Denton. In that case his deal would be nixed for sure. Somehow that didn't fit Grace's modus operandi, but then he really didn't know what made her tick.

So what if the deal went sour?

There were other deals with the same potential, even though this one might have been the one that bumped him up to partner. Partner, hell! If he didn't get his rear back to Dallas, he might not even have a job, much less a partnership.

But he wasn't ready to leave, not now for sure, not until he straightened this misunderstanding out with Grace. Then what? He broke out in sweat. Hell, he wouldn't think about that now. First things first.

Stewing wasn't getting the job done. He was going to have his say.

He found her on the front porch, a water bucket in hand, tending the plants. For a second he treated himself by just watching her. He took delight in everything about her from the lime-colored sleeveless dress that molded her slender figure to perfection, to her long, tapered legs that had plenty of room to move under the short hem and side slits, to her tousled hair that looked as if she'd just taken a tumble in the hay.

Which she had, earlier, with him.

Again he felt himself harden, wanting her, *needing* her.

Muttering a curse, Denton got out of his car and made his way up the steps. She finally turned and faced him, though she didn't say anything, her lovely features devoid of any expression. She wasn't going to make this easy for him, no sir.

Smothering a sigh, he crossed to the swing and sat down. "I'm sorry," he said simply.

"You should be."

"Does that mean you accept my apology?"

"No."

He swallowed another expletive. "I didn't mean it like it sounded. I don't care about the money."

"Yes, you do."

"Dammit, Grace!"

They both heard a door slam, their heads turning toward the sound simultaneously.

"Oh, dear," Grace whispered, clutching at her chest, her face going from red to stark white.

"Who's that?"

"The man you came to see, Ward Pearson."

Denton felt his own face drain of color. "Did you know he was coming?"

"No," she said in a barely audible tone.

"Hey, it's okay."

He watched as she took a deep, shuddering breath and plastered a smile on her face just as Ward's booted foot reached the first step.

"Howdy, folks," he said, tipping the edge of his Stetson, then glancing from one to the other as if he sensed the bad vibes in the air. "Am I intruding?" he asked in a low, gruff voice that sounded like cigarettes were his best friend.

Denton suspected that bourbon was the culprit instead.

"Hello, Ward," Grace responded, extending her hand, that plastic smile remaining in place.

He was long, tall drink of water, Denton thought, the consummate rancher, sporting a big truck and big bucks. He suspected that underneath his hat was a mop of gray hair or none at all. His face was severely tanned as if he lived in the sun. He wasn't a young man by any stretch. Still, he was nice-looking and was probably thought to be a great catch.

Pea-green jealousy almost kept Denton from rising and acknowledging Ward's presence with his own hand extended. "Denton Hardesty."

A shocked look narrowed Ward's eyes. "As in the investment broker?"

"One and the same," Denton said easily enough.

"How long have you been here?"

Denton picked up on the suspicion that now colored Ward's tone. Proceed with caution, Hardesty, not for your sake, but for Grace's. He would be the perfect man for her. When he was gone, Ward could step back in his rightful place. Again, that thought was so distasteful to Denton that he wanted to smash the other man's face.

Beautiful.

"Several days," Denton finally answered.

"I've left three messages for you, and they've gone unanswered." Ward's hostile gaze swung from Denton back to Grace.

Denton didn't have a comeback to that, so he said nothing.

"Now I can understand why," Ward declared flatly. "You've been otherwise occupied."

"Ward, please," Grace said, stepping forward.

Denton forced a curse back down his throat, then also moved forward. "Hey, it's not what you think."

Ignoring him, Ward whipped around and headed to his pickup.

Denton stood helplessly while Grace stared at Ward's back, a mortified look on her face.

Fourteen

"Grace—"

She held up her hand, cutting off his words. "Don't say anything, please."

"I know you're upset."

She glared at him. "That's an understatement."

"Look, I'm sorry if I screwed things up between you and Ward."

"Are you?"

He paused and stared at her for several long heartbeats. "No, dammit, I'm not."

"You're something else, Denton."

His mouth curled. "I deserved that, but while I know this seems to have gotten out of hand, it can all be straightened out."

"Don't worry about me." Her eyes flashed. "I can take care of myself. After all, I've been doing it for years."

"That's not the point."

Ignoring that, she said, "Why aren't you talking to Ward and trying to patch things up? Isn't that what this is all about?"

"No," he said, his jaw clenched so that his words sounded biting. "It's about you and me."

Grace shook her head in amazement. "You and me, huh? There is no you and me, Denton, and you know it." She paused. "Look, I'm going inside. I have things to do."

"Grace, don't do this. Let's talk about this."

She wanted to stay, to wallow in that pleading look, those huskily spoken words, but she knew he would just suck her under deeper, and she couldn't afford that. As it was she was barely hanging on to her sanity and her pride. One more push and she could topple over that edge.

"I need some space, Denton. Maybe we'll talk later." She paused again, her gaze raking over his. "Meanwhile, I suggest you call Ward and straighten things out. After all, that's why you're still here."

Before he could reply, she turned and went inside, not releasing her pent-up breath until she reached her room and closed the door.

She had just gotten out of the tub, where she had soaked in bubbles up to her neck, and dressed in a pair of shorts and loose blouse when the phone rang. For a second she was tempted to ignore it, but again, running a business that depended heavily on the phone, she couldn't afford that luxury.

"Hello," she said, trying to force some brightness into her tone.

"Grace, it's Ward."

Great.

Sinking onto the chaise lounge, she clutched the receiver tightly. "I'm glad you called."

"You are?" His tone held genuine surprise.

"Of course. We're friends."

"Look, I acted like a horse's behind, and I want to apologize for that."

"Hey, you don't owe me an apology. If anything, I owe you one."

"The hell you do. I acted like a jealous you-know-what, and I had no right."

True, she wanted to say, but she didn't. Ward was such a nice guy, but he wasn't the one for her, Denton or no Denton. She had to make him understand that without hurting or humiliating him further.

"But when I saw you and Hardesty," he added, regaining her attention. "I lost my cool."

"Denton's an old friend," Grace said lamely.

"Judging from the way he was looking at you, he'd like to be more."

How she wished that were so, but she knew better. Denton wanted to make love to her, not make a future. On the other hand, Ward wanted both. Too bad she loved the wrong man. Tears suddenly gathered in her eyes though she fought them back.

She wasn't about to cry over Denton. She'd wasted enough tears on him already to last a lifetime.

"He's just passing through, Ward. He'll be leaving as soon as the two of you meet."

"I don't know so much about that."

She felt herself panic. No way was she going to be responsible for Denton not getting his deal or at least having a shot at it. While he stressed he didn't care, she did. "Oh, please, I'd feel awful if you two didn't get together because of me."

"Hardesty might see that differently."

"Please, Ward, leave me out of this, okay?"

"Okay, honey, whatever you say." He paused. "Are you ever going to change your mind about me, Grace?"

She heard the pain in his voice and hated that she was the cause of it. But she couldn't lie to him. She couldn't make herself love him no matter how hard she wanted to. Her heart belonged elsewhere and always had.

"No, Ward," she said as sweetly as possible. "You're a great guy and I value our friendship—"

"I get it. You don't have to draw me a picture."

She flushed. "I'm sorry."

"You don't have to be that, either. I just figured it was time I knew exactly where I stood."

"There's someone out there for you," Grace said. "I just know there is."

"Yeah, Ruby's full of single women."

Through the pain she heard the humor, which she returned by chuckling herself. "Just like it's full of single men."

"Well, if friendship is all there is, then I'll take it."

"Thanks, Ward," she responded, a catch in her voice.

"Now, moving on, we need to meet about this nuclear plant crap. I've had my ear to the ground, and the rumbling's growing louder that Ruby's pretty high on the list."

"I'm ready to meet and load our guns. Just let me know the time and place."

"I'll talk to you later, then."

She was already drained, but now she felt really

zapped of energy. What a day. First her encounter with Denton, then Ward, then Denton and Ward together. No one deserved that. Suddenly she felt the urge to scream. When had her peaceful life disappeared?

When Denton drove into town.

Sighing, Grace got up and walked to the French doors that led onto the balcony outside her room. She opened them, stepped out into the refreshing spring air and clung to the railing. The evening was lovely, she told herself, made for lovers.

Stop it. She couldn't afford to let that thought run rampant or she'd be in a world of hurt. But it was hard when all she could think about was how it felt to have Denton inside her again, how she longed to experience that hard heat every day for the rest of her life.

Not going to happen.

Breathing deeply, the scent of the flowers heightened her senses, making her edgier than ever. Maybe a cup of hot tea on the front porch would soothe her soul. She would love to visit with Zelma and Ed; they never failed to buoy up her spirits. But they had finally gotten off to Austin and wouldn't be back until late.

As for Denton, she figured he was in his room, walking the floor with his ear glued to the phone, tending to business.

What she wanted to know was when he was leaving.

Surely he couldn't afford to remain in Ruby much longer. His boss was bound to start hollering for real and demand that he return to the office. There was just so much one could accomplish by phone.

Hopefully, now that Ward had returned and they had met, Denton would make the deal of all deals, she told herself with sarcasm, then fire up his BMW and head back to Dallas, back to civilization, as he called it.

Taking another whiff of the flowers, Grace made her way back inside, but she didn't linger. She headed downstairs to the kitchen where she made some flavored tea, then went onto the front porch only to pull up short.

Denton occupied the swing.

If she hadn't had a firm grip on the cup, she would've dropped it.

"Oh," she murmured, suddenly conscious of the fact that she didn't have on a bit of makeup and her hair was mussed. More important, she didn't have on a bra. Under any other circumstances it wouldn't have bothered her, except her nipples had gone instantly erect at the sight of him.

Feeling her mouth go dry, she swallowed hard. Even after he was gone, every time she walked out the front door, she would still see him in that swing looking like the big, sexy hunk he was.

Damn him and his intrusion in her life.

"You're not happy to see me." His words were a flat statement of fact.

"No, I'm not," she said with equal bluntness.

His features suddenly looked tired and strained. "I couldn't stay cooped up in my room a second longer."

"That's how I felt," she admitted reluctantly, not wanting to dwell on his long, bare legs splayed out in front of him.

"You can sit down, you know."

"I know." She didn't move an inch.

"Even on the swing with me."

Was that humor lurking in his tone, or had she imagined it? It didn't matter; either way she was not in the mood to indulge him.

"I know that, too," she muttered, fighting the urge to dash back in the house like a frightened doe. Instead, she stiffened her spine and forced her demeanor to remain unruffled. He was not about to get the upper hand here. This was her porch. If anyone was the invader, it was him.

Besides, she couldn't run from him and the emotions he evoked in her, not when she'd let him make love to her. To play the outraged virgin at this point was a bit ludicrous.

"Are you in love with him?"

At first his words didn't register. Then it hit her what he'd said, and she stared at him wide-eyed. "What?" she asked simply because she was so stunned.

He released a harsh sigh. "Don't make me repeat it. Next time, I might choke on the words."

"Are you referring to Ward?"

"Of course." He leaned his head to one side while his eyes stabbed her. "Who else?"

Loaded question, one that she would dodge at all costs.

"You know I'm not in love with him," she retorted, red-faced.

"How the hell would I know that?"

"If I had been, I wouldn't have made love to you."

"God, Grace," he said, standing, his voice tormented, "I never meant to invade your space like this."

"Is that your way of telling me you're sorry we made love?" The words came out a raspy whisper.

"No," he said in a strangled tone. "I—"

"I know what you're thinking, that I'm a love-starved old maid who's grateful for the crumbs you threw me."

He closed the distance between them in one long stride and clutched her arm. "That's hogwash!"

She peered down at his hand on her flesh then back up at him. Green eyes lingered on her brown ones, both dark and filled with secrets. "Is it?" Her voice was broken.

"Yes," he whispered.

Fifteen

His lips were everywhere.

And she didn't want the sweet torment to end, even though she craved to feel the hard strength of him inside her.

She had no idea how they had gotten from the porch to his room, to his big bed. Yes, she did, she told herself, only she hated to admit the weakness that had made her give in to the burning need he created inside her.

When he'd grasped her arm, stared down at her and seduced her with those hot, green eyes, she had turned to putty. She remembered parting her lips then hearing him groan before his lips ground into hers—hard and deep.

The next thing she knew they were on the bed, naked, laving each other with mouths and tongues.

"Oh, Grace, I want you so much," he rasped, closing her mind to everything except him and what he was doing to her body.

"Oh, yes," she whispered, squirming under the feel of his tongue between each toe before moving up the inside of her leg to the apex of her thighs.

He had already made her crazy, having kneaded and suckled her breasts until they were full and wet with the juices from his lips.

Now she gasped and grabbed a handful of dark hair as his tongue made contact with her wet center. "Ohh," she gasped again when blessed relief instantly flooded through her.

"I love pleasing you this way." The rasp of his voice sounded as if he'd just swallowed sandpaper as he shifted his position so that his full-blown manhood replaced his tongue.

"Denton, Denton," she muttered incoherently.

"I can't wait any longer." His hungry eyes were on her.

"Neither can I," she cried, touching the tip of him, guiding him inside her.

Holding her with strength and intensity, flesh met flesh and hips rocked against hips until both their cries of satisfaction rent the air.

What a perfect spring day to be at the nursery, perusing the plants, Grace thought, that is, if one liked tiptoeing among carpenters. She almost smiled.

She'd had to escape the house. The walls felt as if they were closing in on her. She didn't want to think about Denton. Yet he was all she did think about. Consequently, her nerves had been driving her, rather than the other way around. That was when she'd found Zelma sitting on the front porch, swinging

while Ed slept. Off the top of her head, she'd asked
Zelma if she'd like to go to the nursery with her.

Zelma hadn't hesitated. Now they had just arrived,
and Grace was still reeling from shock. The old di-
lapidated premises had received a face-lift, though the
transformation was not totally complete. Denton had
certainly lived up to his promise to Flora, which both
relieved and pleased Grace.

She'd been afraid...

"Honey child, you ought to snag that man."

"That's what I've been trying to tell her," Zelma
said, inclining her head and giving Grace a knowing
look. "For more reasons than one." She paused and
swept her hands in a circle. "Why, just look at what
all he's doing for Flora here."

"Don't that beat all," Flora added, a dazed sound
to her voice. "If I was just a tad younger, he could
sure eat crackers in my bed."

Zelma grinned, then winked at Grace.

Grace quelled a sigh, staving off the urge to throttle
her friend, actually both of them, she corrected. They
were ganging up on her, and it wasn't fair.

"So?" Flora's tone was as pointed as her eyes.

"So, nothing," Grace replied, with as much indif-
ference as she could muster while at the same time
masking her irritation. The last thing she wanted was
to hurt the old women's feelings. Still, Denton was
an off-limits subject, considering the volatile nature
of their relationship.

If they only knew she'd spent the night with Denton hot and hard inside her....

"Are you all right, dear?" Zelma demanded into
the sudden silence, her gaze concentrated on Grace.

"You look sort of peaked, like Ed does sometimes when he can't catch his breath."

"I'm...fine," Grace said lamely. "Just felt dizzy for a sec."

"It's all that talk about gettin' herself a man," Flora said without pulling any punches. "Why, that rancher's been trying to rope her for months now, and she won't have nothin' to do with him. And he's got more money than God."

"Flora!" Grace shot her a look. "Give it a rest."

"Well, I don't know anything about this rancher," Zelma chimed in, "but I think you've lost your mind not to go after Denton."

"And just what, pray tell, would I do with him?" Grace asked before she thought.

"Marry him," Flora said bluntly.

Grace made a strangled sound. "Yeah, right."

"Well, that's not so far-fetched, my dear," Zelma put in. "The looks he often gives you are hot enough to scorch the earth. So don't play the innocent with me."

Flora bobbed her head up and down like a cork. "Or me. I've seen the same thing."

"Hey, you two." Grace held up her hands. "Cut me some slack, okay? Denton is simply passing through."

"We'll see," Zelma said loftily.

Again Grace wanted to throttle both women as they turned and winked at each other as if she didn't see them, as if she didn't know what was going on. But it really didn't matter. So what if she indulged them in their little game of romance? They were playing cupid and having a ball doing it. Why spoil their fun time? She knew the truth, and that was all that counted.

Despite the fact that Denton might look at her with undeniable heat, that hot streak would burn itself out just as soon as he climbed in his BMW and headed for Dallas. Suddenly a tight squeeze on her heart robbed her of her next breath.

But she recovered, not wanting to call more attention to herself by having an anxiety attack.

Grace peered at her watch, then back up to Zelma. "I'd best get what I came after and go back to the house. I have work to do."

"Speaking of working," Flora said, "I hope it won't take these fellows much longer to wrap things up around here."

Grace smiled. "I'm sure it won't, at least not the way they're working."

"I still can't believe this is happening," Flora said, her cataract-clouded eyes wide with wonder. "It makes me kind of scared at the thought of operating such a fancy place now."

Grace hugged her. "You'll be just fine. However, you will have to hire someone to help you, I would imagine. Your business is going to double or better."

"Oh, Lordy," Flora wheezed, grabbing her chest. "I hope I'm up to the challenge."

Zelma gave her a pointed but reassuring look. "Sure you are."

"Come on, dear," Grace said, a lilt in her voice, "strut your stuff. Pick me out some new plants for my porch."

A short time later Grace was back at the B&B, digging in one of the pots on the side porch. Zelma and Ed had decided to go back into Austin, and Ralph was in his usual spot in front of his computer. The only one out of place was Denton.

She had no idea where he was, except that maybe he'd gone to try to smooth things over with Ward, still hoping to get his business. When she'd driven up from the nursery and his car had been gone, her heart had dropped to her knees, thinking that perhaps he'd already cut out to Dallas without so much as a good-bye.

In her heart of hearts she had known that wasn't true. There would be real closure this time, but it still wouldn't lessen the emptiness, the pain of losing him again. But when she had involved herself with him, she had known the end result. Nothing had changed, despite another night of passion in his arms.

As before, she had left his bed and crept into hers. However, this time she hadn't escaped without him knowing. He had grabbed her arm, which had frozen her to the side of the bed. Without peering back at him, she'd whispered, "What?"

"We have to talk," he'd responded.

"Not now," she said, a break in her voice.

"When?"

"I'm...not sure."

"Later today?" His tone was low but forceful.

She licked her bottom lip. "We'll see."

"Grace—" This time there was exasperation in his tone.

"I don't see that we have anything to talk about."

He withdrew his hand and muffled an expletive.

That was when she walked out. Now, as she dug in the dirt, she longed for the feeling of well-being that always stole over her. It didn't come. She remained uptight, wired and close to tears.

Battling back the threat of tears, Grace jabbed her trowel deeper in the dirt.

"My, but that must be some difficult soil."

Startled by the unexpected sound of a voice, Grace jerked her head up and stared into the face of a man she'd never seen before. He had more than his share of unkempt hair, which she suspected was prematurely gray as he seemed rather young. He was of medium height, but nothing else was medium about him, certainly not his girth. It was distended far too much to be comfortable.

Though she sensed his impatience, his grin was friendly enough.

"Are you here to inquire about lodging?" she asked, straightening to full height.

"No wonder he's not back," the man mumbled.

Grace pushed a loose stand of hair back and blinked. "Excuse me?"

"I'm Todd Joseph," he said suddenly, extending his hand. "Denton's boss. Is he around?"

Grace felt her stomach hollow as she removed her gloves and forced a smile.

"Mr. Pearson's out on the range, working cattle."

Denton smothered a sigh. "I guess it'll be late when he gets back."

"If he does at all." The housekeeper shrugged. "Sometimes he spends the night out there."

"Well, tell him Denton Hardesty came by and that I'll catch him later."

The lady nodded, then closed the door.

When he returned to his vehicle, Denton didn't crank it. He merely sat there, feeling limp and deflated, something that made him want to kick butt—his in particular.

He rubbed his head, feeling it pop, as though he had a zinger of a hangover. He had to get his act together. He couldn't continue to indulge himself to this degree or he might as well chuck his job.

For what? He sneered. Dance attendance to Grace? *Yes, dammit.*

Why not? Since he'd been in Ruby with nothing but great weather, great food, great company, he'd become a new person. He'd become humanized. Seeing that smile on Flora's face and feeling her wet kiss on his cheek had done something good for his soul, something that hadn't happened to him in a long time, far too long to even remember the feeling.

Damn sad.

So what did this mellow feeling mean? Was he trying to convince himself that he wanted a steady diet of Ruby and its laid-back lifestyle? No. He didn't think so. What he did want, however, was a steady diet of Grace.

He'd rather be with her than anyplace on earth. What he felt for Grace was more than the constant gnawing of sex. He was smitten with her every move, her infectious laughter, her flashing eyes, her sharp tongue.

All wrapped up together, she presented an enchanting package. And he didn't want to leave Ruby without it. *Without her.*

Only after he felt the throbbing in his head ease some, did he start the powerful engine. But instead of heading toward the B&B, he went by the nursery. He had no intention of stopping. Once Flora got her claws into him, all avenues of escape were usually blocked. He grinned without restraint. Most times he didn't even mind that, even enjoyed jawing with the sharp-witted old woman.

Not today. He merely wanted to keep an eye on the workers, to make sure they were there and work-ing. Since he'd struck out with Pearson, something he hadn't been looking forward to, anyway, he couldn't wait to get back to Grace, test her temperature fol-lowing last night's lovemaking session—more incred-ible than the last time.

How could he leave her?

Sweat, followed by cold chills, broke through his skin. He had no choice. No matter how much he liked it here, he couldn't stay. Not indefinitely, that is. Not even much longer, either, he reminded himself. Al-ready he was pushing the envelope with Todd, who blew smoke out of his ears every time they talked, which was becoming several times a day.

In reality he knew he couldn't continue to operate his million-dollar-plus business from afar. Yet he hated like hell to leave without Grace.

Suddenly he braked and pulled off the road. Why the hell hadn't he thought of that before? Of course. That was the answer. That would work. All he needed was the quality time to pull it off.

He turned onto Live Oak Lane only to groan, then let go of another expletive. None other than his boss's green Cadillac was parked in the drive. Todd himself was parked on the front porch, seemingly deep in con-versation with Grace.

"Damn!"

A face-to-face confrontation with his boss had been something he'd hoped to avoid. Didn't appear things were going to work that way. Todd waited for him to get out and make his way onto the porch. Denton figured his boss was angry. The line around his mouth and his stiff stance said as much.

"I was hoping it wouldn't come to this," Todd said without preamble, glaring at him.

Ignoring him, Denton faced Grace and smiled. "Would you excuse us?"

Without returning his look, she said, "No problem."

Once they were alone, both men were silent. Todd was the first to speak, his tone sardonic, "I'm assuming that piece of work is why you're still here."

Denton stood his ground, not so much as flinching. "You got that right."

Sixteen

"**W**ell, I'll have to hand it you, she's a looker."

For some reason that observation irritated Denton no end. But then, having his boss show up here in Ruby was irritant enough without bringing Grace into the equation.

"However, I don't think she's worth throwing your career down the toilet." Without being asked, Todd then lowered his heavy frame into the swing, propping a foot over his knee. "I haven't seen any woman worth that." His tone was filled with acid.

"And you think that's the case here?" Denton asked, holding on to his temper by a mere thread.

Todd sneered. "I think you know the answer to that."

"What the hell are you doing here?" Denton demanded, noticing that Todd appeared far too comfortable in that swing. Hopefully, Grace wouldn't pull one of her hospitality stunts and bring out a tray loaded with her special goodies and her flavored iced tea. Todd wouldn't budge another inch for sure.

On second thought, he'd be surprised if Grace reappeared. She had sensed the climate when she'd walked off and wouldn't want to get involved in a discussion between him and his boss.

"I'm here to help you come to your senses," Todd said flatly.

"I wasn't aware that I'd lost them."

Todd snorted, and this time his belly shook. "Only a woman would come between you and money."

Denton felt his stomach burn. "You don't know what you're talking about."

"Are you in love with her?"

"Dammit, Todd, mind your own business."

"Hey, that's exactly what I'm doing, good buddy. In case you haven't noticed, we're pretty closely joined at the hip, which means your business is my business."

"So the partnership's still in the offing?" After he asked that, Denton held his breath for fear of what the answer would be. He wouldn't blame Todd if he did can him. He definitely hadn't been his usual, driven, professional self since returning to Ruby. But he didn't need Todd to tell him that.

"Only if you get your rear back to Dallas and on your accounts."

Denton felt a flush steal into his cheeks, more from anger than embarrassment. He could hold his own against this man regardless of who he was or what he represented. When he'd gone to work for Todd, he'd been looking for a job. He could do so again. Still...

"So are you in love?" Todd pressed.

"No."

"Well, you gotta be in lust then. Nothing else would keep you in this godforsaken place."

"This is where I grew up." Denton's tone was on the defensive, and he didn't know why. He'd knocked Ruby more times than he cared to admit. But then that was before he'd returned and Grace— Nipping that thought in the bud, he let go of a pent-up sigh.

Todd's voice hardened. "I wouldn't be bragging about that."

"Okay, you've made your point," Denton muttered. "You've driven here and slapped my wrist."

"I came here because I want to know what the hell's going on," Todd stressed. "You know how much I depend on you, and it's been awful without you in the office. Any moment now several deals are threatening to go to hell in a handbasket."

"I still haven't made personal contact with Ward Pearson," Denton said, hoping to take some of the heat off himself and calm Todd down.

"And why not?"

"He had to leave town and has just returned." That wasn't all a lie, Denton reminded himself, though he couldn't quite look his friend straight in the eye. "In fact, I just tried to visit with him, and he's riding his range."

"Gawd."

"You're in the hill country, remember?"

"I feel like I'm on another bloody planet."

Denton almost smiled.

"So see Pearson tomorrow, wrap up that deal and head for North Texas."

Todd's words weren't phrased as a question but rather a statement of fact. And even though there was no overt threat, Denton heard one in the undertones. With Todd, push had definitely come to shove.

"If he's back, I'll see what I can do." Denton's tone was calm but firm. While he agreed with Todd about his absence, he wasn't about to let him think he could browbeat him into submission. That old dog wouldn't hunt. Anyway, before he left Ruby, he had something to take care of, but Todd didn't have to know that.

"If you snag the deal, our company will be flying high."

"And I'll be full partner," Denton added to the sentence.

"That was the deal." Todd fell silent, then peered up at him. "You still haven't told me what's going on between you and that honey inside."

"And I'm not going to, either."

"Ah, so you do have the hots for her." Todd grinned, then stood. "Can't say I blame you."

"Get out of here."

"Aren't you going to offer me some refreshments?" Todd asked in a taunting voice.

He nodded his head across the street. "The station sells drinks."

"Man, you do have it bad."

"Don't push your luck, my friend," Denton said in a gruff tone.

"No problem. I'm going. Give your little lady my best regards." Todd slapped Denton on the shoulder. "Just remember what you went through with your ex."

"Stuff it, Todd," Denton muttered harshly.

"Oh, speaking of exes. Yours called."

"Marsha?"

"Yep."

"What the hell did she want?"

"More money, she said."

Denton laughed with biting humor. "She's crazy!"

"I agree. She took you to the cleaners when you divorced."

"Wrong. I chose to give her the cleaners," Denton declared. "There's a difference."

Todd shrugged his massive shoulders. "Whatever."

"What did you tell her?"

"That you'd call her."

Denton scowled. "One day I'll do you a favor."

Todd threw back his head and laughed, then ambled down the steps. "I'll see you in Big D."

Grace would have loved to be a fly on the wall out on the porch, she thought, as she mixed the dough for rolls. On second thought, maybe not. She could imagine the barbs zinging between the two men. Her delicate ears probably couldn't have survived. She smiled at such an absurd thought. Still, she figured the climate was as cold as the Arctic. She had sensed that immediately.

Even though Todd What's-His-Name seemed like an amicable enough guy, he was as hard-nosed and driven as Denton, or he wouldn't have shot off in search of his prodigal employee.

Grace's smile suddenly fled as did the warmth around her heart that had remained with her following their intense but sweet night of lovemaking. She knew he didn't love her. Yet she'd never felt so loved or cherished in her life.

And he would be leaving. Today, most likely. Maybe with Todd.

This time her heart almost stopped completely, and for an instant the room spun, but, taking several deep breaths, Grace regrouped and everything righted, except her heart.

She tackled the dough like it was her enemy, kneading it until it was in stringy pieces. Then realizing what she was doing, she stopped, washed her hands then patted her face with cold wet fingers. She had returned to the kitchen with every intention of preparing a tray and taking it to the porch, only to change her mind. She hadn't wanted to overstep her bounds. Too, Denton certainly hadn't been in the entertaining mode.

Once the dough was back intact and the rolls in the oven, Grace stood still for the longest time. And listened. Finally she heard an engine crank. Swaying, she held on to the countertop and waited.

When Denton drove off, part of her would leave with him. But he couldn't stay, the rational part of her mind cried back. That wouldn't work, either. He would soon be miserable and make her miserable, as well.

So Todd's arrival was a godsend. Denton had to go before he set up permanent residence in her soul.

"My, something sure smells good in here."

Grace forced a smile on Ed and Zelma. "You say that every morning."

Ed chuckled. "That's 'cause it's true every morning." He paused and turned to Zelma. "We're sure going to miss this, dear."

Zelma poked him in the ribs. "You just don't know when to keep your mouth shut, you old coot."

Grace sobered, her eyes shifting from one to the other. "You're leaving." Her words came out sounding like a death knell.

"Oh, honey," Zelma said in a conciliatory tone, rushing over and giving Grace a hug. "You knew this time had to come. We're coming back, though."

"When?"

"Moving, in fact."

Grace's eyes lighted. "Oh, Zelma, that's wonderful."

Zelma winked at Ed, who was heading for the bowl of fruit on the counter and helping himself. "We told the kids last night."

"And?" Grace held her breath.

Grace hesitated, then grinned. "They said go for it."

"All right!"

Grace knew Denton had walked into the room, though he hadn't said a word. His animal magnetism never failed to precede him. "What's so exciting in here?"

Zelma turned and, after hugging him, told him the news.

His gaze rested briefly but deeply on Grace, who somehow kept herself from flushing. "I know you're thrilled."

"Beyond words," she said softly.

Their eyes lingered a second longer before she turned away, troubled by the shadows that lurked in his. She wondered when he would tell her he was leaving, as well.

Zelma actually voiced the question. "So, when are you heading back to the city?"

"Soon."

"Didn't you just have a visitor?" Zelma asked, apparently not ready to let him off the hook so easily.

If her insides hadn't been in such turmoil and there hadn't been so much at stake, Grace would've smiled at seeing Denton on the hot seat.

"Zelma," Ed said, "that's none of your business."

"Oh, poppycock. Nothing's a secret around here."

"Guess not," Denton said drolly.

"So, why didn't you invite your friend to breakfast?"

"Zelma!"

She flapped her hand at him. "Oh, Ed, give it a rest."

Grace's eyes met Denton's again. This time there was a smile in them, and he winked, melting her heart on the spot.

"Despite my better half," Zelma said to Denton, "I'm not letting you off the hook."

"That was my boss from Dallas, who's after my hide to leave here."

"Hey, everyone," Grace said suddenly, unable to bear the turn in conversation, for fear she'd fall apart in front of everyone. "Let's eat. I've set us up on the porch."

For the next hour, conversation was impersonal and lively. Even Ralph joined them and added a couple of author anecdotes that were humorous. Just as everyone was finishing, Connie arrived.

Denton, along with everyone else, excused himself and went to his quarters. A short time later Grace heard him on the phone. She forced herself to concentrate on her business, but it was hard, especially when she knew her world was about to come crashing down on her again.

She was losing all her guests at one time, which happened often. Zelma and Ed were packing and loading up. And while she was saddened by their departure, the fact that they were coming back to live in Ruby eased the pain. Ralph was also leaving, having completed his novel right on deadline.

As far as Denton was concerned, she expected him to fly out of his room at any time, briefcase in hand and climb into his BMW.

"We'll see you soon," Zelma said one last time and after one final hug, before getting into the car. "Meanwhile, we'll keep in touch by phone." She pulled Grace's head closer and whispered, "Don't you dare let that hunk just waltz out of your life. I know there's something going on between you two, and I don't mean just between the sheets, either."

With her face scalding-red, Grace stepped back. "One of these days…"

Zelma merely chuckled as Ed backed out of the drive.

The remainder of the day passed like molasses running uphill, despite the fact she was so busy with bookwork and housework. Yet she kept listening for Denton to make his move. He didn't. If he left his room, she was unaware of it, though she did leave and run some errands.

Now, as she was about to make her way upstairs to take her bath, Denton's door opened. She paused mid-stride, their gazes meeting and holding. He looked exhausted and rumpled. She'd never seen him quite so disheveled.

"I know, don't say it." He shoved his hand through his hair, further mussing it. "I look like the bloody wrath."

"Okay, you do, but I won't say it."

A smile flirted on his lips. "Are you alone?"

"Yes." The fact that she was now alone in the house with Denton was something she refused to think about.

"Would you like to go out to dinner?"

Her eyes widened. "I thought—" She clamped her lips together.

"Are you ready for me to leave?" His eyes were broodingly intense.

She swallowed. "No. Of course not."

"So what about dinner?"

"Why don't I fix something here instead?"

His eyes raked slowly over her. "You wouldn't mind?"

"Uh, no, not in the least." Her voice sounded breathless, but she couldn't help it. "I'd rather."

"I'll clean up, then, and join you."

Their gazes lingered on each other for another moment, then he turned and went back into his room. She wilted against the doorjamb, her mind splintering in a million different directions.

What was that all about?

Seventeen

Despite the hovering tension, the meal went off without a hitch. As he had at breakfast, he made her laugh with several stories about clients. She in turn related some of the weirdos she'd had at the B&B. All in all, the intimate dinner went much better than she'd expected, though by the time she poured their coffee, she thought her insides would explode.

He'd been so close, so within touching distance, yet she couldn't touch him. Once she did, she wouldn't stop. She sensed he felt the same, as he seemed to make it a point not to make direct contact with her skin, only her eyes, devouring her through them.

They had just settled down in the living room with coffee when the doorbell chimed.

Denton frowned. "Who the hell...?"

"I have no earthly idea," Grace said, getting up.

"Don't answer it," Denton muttered to her back.

Ignoring him, she opened the door. Roger Gooseby, the mayor and grocer, stood on the porch, hat in hand.

"May I come in?" he asked without preamble.

"Of course," Grace told him, fighting off a sinking feeling in the pit of her stomach. She didn't want anyone or anything to encroach on her last few hours with Denton. Time with him was at a premium.

Once Roger's tall, lean frame had cleared the entrance, she gestured for him to be seated, but not before introducing him to Denton.

"Would you like me to leave?" Denton asked.

"No," Grace said quickly. "It's about the nuclear plant, isn't it, Roger?"

"That it is," he said, barely able to mask his fury.

"What's happened?"

"The powers-that-be are apparently looking at us real close, like second from the top."

"Oh, dear," Grace said, glancing at Denton then back to Roger.

"When I get back to Dallas, I may be able to help," Denton put in.

"You think you can help?" Roger's tone was brusque.

Denton stretched his legs in front of him. "Maybe. I have a connection that might make a difference."

Roger's leathered face brightened. "We'd sure appreciate anything you could do. Meanwhile, Grace, I've talked to several others, and we'd like you to be our spokesperson, travel to Washington, if need be."

"That's a smart move, Mr. Gooseby," Denton said.

"Roger," the grocer corrected. "Formalities don't play around here."

"No."

At first Grace knew neither man had heard her answer. They were too busy becoming chummy, which was a waste of time. Once he left Ruby, Denton wouldn't ever see Roger again.

"What did you say?" the mayor asked, cutting his head around.

"No." There. She said it again.

"But...but why not?" Roger spluttered.

Denton's gaze pinned her. "Yeah, why not? You'd be the perfect one, considering your personality and your devotion to this town."

Grace shook her head vigorously. "I'll do anything else, but I won't be in charge."

"We sure need you, Grace," Roger said, his tone gruff. "If this thing doesn't get nipped in the bud, Ruby's going to be in a world of hurt."

"I know, Roger." Grace paused a second and rubbed her temple. "I'm in business, too. But I'm not the right person."

"I disagree," he countered bluntly. "I think you're the perfect person."

"I'm sorry, but I won't do it."

He scratched his head, then released a harsh sigh. "Well, I guess that's that. If you change your mind, holler. Meanwhile, we'll try and come up with an alternate person and plan."

He stood then, and Grace followed suit, extending her hand and giving him a forced smile. "It will work out. It just has to for all our sakes."

"Let's pray." Roger nodded in Denton's direction, then added, "I'll see myself out."

Once the mayor was gone, the room fell silent. Grace couldn't bring herself to look at Denton, knowing he was disappointed in her. His disappointment seemed to roll off him in waves. The fact that she cared what he thought made her furious.

"If you aren't willing to fight for Ruby, then why don't you leave?"

"And go where?" she bit back sarcastically.

"To Dallas?"

She gasped. "To Dallas?"

"It's not another planet, you know," he pointed out on a dry note.

"As far as I'm concerned it is." She paused, then added, "And just why would I even consider such a thing?"

"Because I ask you to."

Grace went weak all over. "And what would I do?"

He didn't hesitate. "Live with me."

For a moment she had thought— "As your mistress?" Voicing those words made her sick to her stomach. Why couldn't he say he loved her? Because he doesn't. He never has and never will. How much longer was she going to let this man have charge over her body and soul?

"That's not the term I'd prefer to use."

Grace laughed a hollow laugh. "Oh, really. In any case, I don't think so."

He flushed. "Dammit, Grace—"

"I'm not leaving Ruby. Ever."

"Why the hell not?" he exploded. "You're wasting your time and your life in this godforsaken place."

"How would you know?" she lashed back. "You still don't know anything about me."

"I know enough to know you don't belong here."

"Instead I belong there as your little bimbette."

He cursed. "It wouldn't be that way, and you know it."

"I don't intend to ever be your mistress or any man's. Is there anything about *that* you don't understand?"

"Dammit!"

He might as well not have spoken. She was on a roll and didn't intend to stop until she'd had her say. "Man, oh, man, it sure didn't take you long to start bad-mouthing the peace and quiet."

"We're not talking about me," Denton countered, his lips white around the outer edge.

He was not happy, Grace knew, but neither was she. "Well, again, I love what I do and where I'm doing it."

He scoffed. "You'd love it in the city."

Livid, she retorted, "This may come as a shock to you, but I haven't always lived here in this godforsaken town as you call it." She paused and watched his nostrils flare, knowing she'd pushed the right button. "I was an assistant district attorney in Houston until I couldn't stand the rat race any longer and walked away."

Her words fell into the room with the punch of a huge anchor falling overboard on a ship. Denton merely stared at her in disbelief, his jaw slack. "You're putting me on."

"You know better than that," she snapped.

He rubbed his slightly grizzled chin in an agitated move. "You're an attorney?"

Again there was shock, which he didn't bother to conceal, adding to her fury. "Is that so hard to believe?"

"Yes," he said bluntly, "considering your lifestyle now."

"Well, it's a fact."

"What made you give all that up?"

"When I started having anxiety attacks," she said with simple honesty.

He blew out a breath. "That's certainly a kicker. But couldn't you have just cut back—"

"I made my choice, Denton," she responded softly, "and I've never regretted it."

"You mount a mean defense, Grace Simmons."

This time a smile flirted with her lips. "After all, that's what attorneys do."

He stared at her long and hard with an unreadable expression in his eyes. "I still say you're wasted here."

"And I still say that's *not* going to change."

They glared at each other suddenly, their breathing elevated.

"You know you want me."

His thickly spoken words almost buckled her knees. "I never denied that," she whispered, toying with her lower lip.

He groaned, his eyes darkening. "All I can think of right now is how nice it would be to have you in my bed every night and every morning."

"Why are you doing this?" Her tone was agonized.

"Because I can't stand the thought of being without you, of leaving you." He closed the distance between them, reached for her hand and placed it on his crotch. Though she sucked in her breath, she didn't move her hand. She reveled in the feeling of ecstasy his pulsating hardness was bringing her.

"Then don't," she finally managed to get out, lifting her eyes and meeting his, all the while keeping her hand on him.

"Don't what?" He sounded as if the words were dug out of him.

"Don't leave."

"I have to."

"No, you don't." Her hand squeezed him.

He groaned again and closed his eyes for a brief second. When he opened them again, they were dark with passion. "My job's in Dallas."

"Mine is here."

"You're making me crazy."

"Not any crazier than you're making me."

"I'll be good to you, I promise," he pressed urgently. "You won't ever want for a thing."

Except your love.

As though she'd been burned, she dropped her hand and stepped back. His eyes narrowed as he sucked in his breath and held it. "I don't want for a thing now, Denton. And I'm my own person, not a kept woman."

He let an expletive fly. "Don't you think that's a bit outdated?"

"Maybe."

"Hell, people move in together every day. It's no big deal."

"It is to me," she countered quietly.

"Grace—"

She held up her hand and cut him off. "Enough. I'm going to bed."

A heavy silence followed her words.

"I'm not giving up."

"You're wasting your time. But I'll see you in the morning—if you're still here, that is."

Another stinging expletive followed her out the door.

"You won't regret this, Ward."

"I'd better not."

Denton withdrew his hand. "I'll fax you all the necessary papers when they're done."

"Whatever. Just as long as I don't have to go to that hellhole for anything."

Denton shook his head, wondering if everyone in Ruby felt that way about cities. "I'm sure it's all doable by machines."

Ward shoved his hat back on his head and squinted his eyes. They had just left the rancher's big, airy kitchen where they'd cussed and discussed the deal until Denton had finally gotten his name on the dotted line. Now they were outside, standing beside Denton's BMW.

"One more thing," Ward said, his crusty voice sounding even crustier.

"Anything."

"You'd better handle her with gentle, loving care."

Denton blinked. "Excuse me?"

"You know who and what I'm talking about."

Denton felt heat sting his face and not from the sun, either. "Grace is a grown woman with a mind of her own," he responded tersely.

"In this case, I hope she uses it wisely."

With those choice words, the rancher turned and made his way back up the steps.

Denton merely shook his head and climbed in his vehicle. Yet he didn't start it. He was still somewhat dazed by the rancher's veiled warning. Talk about putting him in his place... He didn't think this kind of person existed anymore or that anyone cared that much about his fellow neighbor and friend.

He didn't remember this closeness growing up here, or maybe he just didn't recognize it for what it was—friends looking out for friends. Not bad, if you liked someone meddling in your business, which he didn't.

So what now?

He stared at the azure-blue sky and thought he'd never seen a more perfect day. How come the sky never looked like this in Dallas? And how come he never felt this relaxed, like he had finally stitched the seams of his frayed life back together for the first time since the crash? He'd begun to think that tragic event had messed with his mind permanently. But since he'd been here, his gut had uncoiled, and he'd actually laughed and smelled flowers, literally.

Ah, to hell with that kind of thinking. That would only get him in more trouble, mess with his mind in a different way. These country people were getting to him. He couldn't allow that. His goal was to get Grace out of here.

Himself as well.

So what was he waiting for? He'd gotten the deal that would elevate him to partner. But for some reason it no longer seemed that big a deal. Maybe it was because he had no legitimate reason for remaining in Ruby another minute.

Except Grace.

And he had no intention of leaving without her. After they had parted last evening, he'd gone to his room, taken a much-needed cold shower, then called

Ward's house and found that he had returned from the range and would see him first thing this morning.

Now he had to make a decision. He could forget her, forget how hot and pliant, how willing she was to please him in bed, how much he ached to be with her, *in* her. He could forget her smile that could and would explode into laughter at unexpected times, her lovely curves, her warm generosity…

Or he could plead with her again to go with him. He'd just have to use more patience, devote more time to her than he'd thought, plead his case more eloquently. That latter thought made him smile.

An attorney.

Amazing. Yet he couldn't figure out why he'd been so shocked. After all, Grace had all the right stuff to do anything she wanted. He just couldn't believe she'd chosen the field of law.

His smile spread. He would bet she'd been one tough litigator, waltzing into that courtroom looking like a delicate rose, only then to jab with hidden thorns anyone who crossed her.

Ouch!

Suddenly disgusted with those crazy thoughts and his blatant waste of time, Denton sped off toward the B&B. He was nearly there when he saw it. *Smoke.* It curled out of the kitchen window. The old home was on fire.

Grace! Oh, God! His heart almost stopped as he rammed down on the accelerator.

Eighteen

By the time he finally made it into the drive, Denton's legs were so heavy he didn't know if he could move them. But move them he did, fear for Grace's safety giving him the strength he needed to hurl himself out of the car and into the house.

"Grace!" he shouted at the top of his lungs. "Where are you?"

No answer.

His panic burgeoned as he dashed to the kitchen where the billows of smoke were pouring through the door. In the distance he heard the sound of fire engines. Without them, this old structure wouldn't have a chance to survive. If they didn't hurry, it wouldn't, anyway, he thought in desperation, taking the stairs three at a time.

"Grace!" he called again. Where the hell was she?

He dashed in and out of every room while all sorts

of terrible images colored his mind. The thought of her lying unconscious on the floor somewhere made him crazy. By the time he covered the entire house, his lungs had been stretched to the breaking point with both anxiety and smoke.

Coughing into his handkerchief, he finally dashed outside and sucked fresh air deep into his lungs. That was when he noticed her sitting on a stone bench under a huge oak, looking as lost and forlorn as a young child who had just buried her favorite pet.

Without saying a word, he closed the distance between them, reached for her and pulled her trembling body against his chest. She didn't protest.

"Are you all right?"

"I'm…fine."

"Are you sure?"

"I'm sure." She raised her head, her tear-stained eyes glistening.

"You scared the hell out me," he muttered, reaching out and trapping a tear with a finger.

"Again, I'm okay," she said, her voice shaky.

Still, he didn't stop running his hands over her. For his own peace of mind, he had to keep reassuring himself that she had indeed escaped injury.

"But my house isn't," she wailed suddenly, slumping against him and burying her head in his chest.

"Don't," he'd said brokenly, feeling so helpless, so damn useless.

He loved her.

That truth hit him with all the force of a sledgehammer upside his head. For a moment he reeled, the mental punch setting him back on his heels. In reality, he'd probably never stopped loving her. When push had come to shove, he'd been just too young and too pigheaded to know that.

"My…house…"

"Shh, it's okay. If the house goes, it can be rebuilt."

"That's easy for you to say," she'd sobbed.

"Hey, it will be easy. As long as you or anyone else didn't come to any harm, nothing else really matters."

"Thank God all the guests had gone and Connie wasn't working."

"What about you?"

"I had just come from the grocery store. I saw the smoke when I turned the corner and called the fire department from my cell phone."

"Your quick actions probably saved the house."

She didn't respond, just remained quiet in his arms until the fireman came after them, having assessed the damages and the cause, the fire having started from a faulty electrical switch in the kitchen. Once that had been taken care of, they made their way to the front porch. She couldn't seem to remain inside even though the smoke damage was not all that bad.

"I should be asking you if you're all right," she said out of the blue, facing him.

"Why?"

"You're so uptight."

"Dammit, Grace, I told you, you scared the hell out of me. Of course I'm uptight."

"I'm…sorry."

"I'm not leaving without you."

"I'm not going to Dallas," she said softly, meeting his intense gaze head-on.

"Then I'll stay here."

Her jaw dropped. "Why, you won't, either."

His cell phone chose that moment to ring. Cursing, he reached for it. "Dammit, Todd, I know it's important. Look, I'll call you back." With that he slammed his phone shut, and for a moment another silence fell between them.

"Your boss has spoken." He heard the bitterness in her tone and the resignation.

"I'm not going back, Grace."

She cut him an incredulous look. "And just why would you stay here?

"Because I love you, and you won't leave."

Her eyes widened and her lips parted. "You…love me?"

"Yes," he rasped, "and I want to marry you."

"Oh, Denton," she cried, flinging herself back in his arms, tears gushing down her cheeks. "I love you, too, you big oaf."

"So will you marry me?"

Laughter bled through her tears. "Just try and stop me."

She didn't think she would ever feel him inside her again. She was happy she'd been wrong. Yet she still couldn't believe that Denton loved her and wanted to marry her.

If he hadn't proved his love over and over with his hands, his lips, his tongue, his manhood, she still might not be convinced. But every place he touched, *every touch,* spoke of love and commitment. He seemed to worship her body as he made love to her over and over.

Even now, with the sunlight filtering though the sheers, he was continuing to love her.

His mouth was suckling a breast while a hand was cupping the warmth at the apex of her thighs, a finger sliding in and out of her wetness at will. She moaned under the sweet assault, snaking her hand down to him and surrounding his hardness.

He moaned, opening his eyes and staring into hers.

"Turnabout's fair play," she whispered, her eyes and voice soft and warm as honey.

"It's your time to be on top," he ground out, shifting her until their positions were reversed and he was hard and high inside her, her breasts full and throbbing under the tutelage of his hands.

"Oh, yes, darling," she cried, feeling him expand inside her.

He stared up at her through dazed eyes. "Tell me when."

"Now!"

It was then that she felt him explode, and she cried out in exquisite relief as she rode him harder and harder. His moans were the last thing she heard before lowering her cheek to his sweaty chest and feeling his arms close around her.

A short time later she peered up into his fervent gaze, then stretched.

He tapped at her lips, an indulgent smile on his face. "You look as satisfied as a cat."

"I am," she responded, grinning. "Hey, don't you think we should get up and get moving."

"Nope."

"In case you don't remember, buster, I had a fire here yesterday. I have things to do."

"And I guess you think I don't."

Suddenly Grace frowned, feeling her heart lurch. "As a matter of fact, what are you going to do?"

After he'd confessed his love and his intention to remain in Ruby, they hadn't talked about anything. Instead they had made love, which had been fine with her. But now, reality was staring them in the face, and they had to deal with it, though she was reluctant.

It still hadn't soaked in that Denton loved her and wanted to marry her. Even more mind-boggling was his intention to live in Ruby. That was why this conversation was so important.

"First things first, my darling," Denton said.

"I'm listening."

"When will you marry me?"

"As soon as you want."

"How about a large wedding?"

"No, absolutely not." Her tone was as emphatic as her words.

"Are you sure? I don't mind, though I'd rather not go through that long process."

"Not to worry, I don't, either. I just want our wedding to be small and cozy."

He kissed her. "Our wedding. I do love that thought."

"What about your parents?" She hated asking that loaded question, but she didn't have any choice. When she'd dated him years ago, Earl and Shirley Hardesty hadn't thought she was good enough for their son. She suspected they would feel the same way now. And while she wasn't marrying his parents, she knew it was important for Denton to have their approval. Hers, too, for that matter.

"What about them?"

"Don't do that. You know how they feel about me."

"Hell, that was years ago. You've changed.

They've changed. Mom's been riding my butt to marry again and give them some grandchildren.''

''Really?''

''Really.''

For some reason she went short of breath. ''And how do you feel about that?''

His eyes blazed into hers. ''I hope we've already made a baby. Nothing would please me more than to watch your tummy swell with our child.''

''Oh, Denton,'' she cried, pulling his head down and kissing him with ardent passion.

''If you have any more questions, then you'd better behave,'' he said in a strained voice. ''I'm on a tight leash here, and you're running out of time.''

She smiled, having felt his hardness once again poking in her lower stomach. ''I still want an answer to my question. What makes you think you'll be happy here? I really can't ask you to give up your dream for mine, Denton. If so, you'll come to resent me.''

''Hey, who said I'm giving up my dream?''

''You. This partnership in the company is what you want.''

''It's what I thought I wanted. There's a difference.''

''But—''

''No buts, my darling. What I really want is you and a plant nursery.''

''Huh?''

''You heard me. I'm going to buy Flora out, if she'll let me.''

Grace looked at him aghast. ''Are you serious?''

''As serious as your fire.''

''Oh, Denton, I don't know what to say.''

"Say that you'll get up and fix me some break-fast."

"I can't," she wailed. "I don't have a kitchen."

"Then I guess I'll go get us something. Already having to wait on my wife."

She grinned, then winked. "Ain't it sweet?"

Nineteen

They were on the front porch a short time later, having just finished bagels, cream cheese and fruit. Now they were in the swing drinking the rest of the coffee.

"Not nearly as good as your chow-down grub, but it'll do in a crunch."

"Again it's a good thing all the guests are gone, though I have no idea how long I'll be out of commission."

"Not long. I'm going to find a contractor today."

Grace frowned. "That's not your responsibility."

"Hey, woman, let me take care of you, okay?"

She shrugged, a warm feeling replacing her concern. "Okay."

He grinned. "Man, you're easy."

She giggled, happier than she'd ever been in her life, though she knew there would be a lot of rough spots to get over. But if they truly loved each other, then they could make it.

"Denton—"

His cell phone rang. "Dammit," he muttered, grabbing it.

She turned her head and tried not to listen, but she couldn't stop herself. It was Todd, of course, and from the gist of the conversation he was livid. Her heart plummeted to her toes.

Even after he flipped his phone shut, the silence lingered.

"Don't go," she whispered.

"I have to. All hell's broken loose, and it's something I'm responsible for."

She lunged out of the swing and walked over to a post.

"Grace, it's okay," he said, coming up behind her but not touching her. "Actually, it's better than okay. While I'm there, I'll go ahead and wrap up things in the office, then I won't have to go back."

She swung around. "I don't want you to go at all."

"You know better than that, honey. I have an office, a home, lots to take care of."

"Do it later."

A deep frown doubled the wrinkles in his forehead. "I would, if it weren't for the crisis in the office."

"I still wish you'd wait," she said, feeling panic growing inside her, remembering the other time he left town and never came back.

"Hey, what's this really all about?" he asked, running the back of his hand down one side of her cheek.

"I'm afraid you'll get there and decide not to ever come back."

He released a sigh. "Like I did before?"

"Yes."

"I was a stupid boy then, Grace, who didn't have sense enough to get in out of a good, hard rain."

"Still—"

He gave her a hard, wet kiss. "That's not going to happen this time. I know where I want to be and with whom. Returning to Dallas is not going to change that."

"How can I be sure?"

"You can start by trusting me."

"Yeah, right."

His face turned red and his lips thinned. "Don't make this any harder than it is. Hell, I don't want to leave you, either." He paused, then snapped his fingers. "Why don't you come with me? That's the solution to this problem."

She really pushed the panic button then. "No way. I'm not leaving Ruby."

"God, Grace, you're hardheaded. Actually, that's the perfect solution, what with the house being out of commission and the repair work about to start."

"No," she said adamantly, her anxiety expanding.

"Dammit, what do you want me to do?"

"I told you. Don't go."

"I have to, and that's that."

She stiffened and stared at him for long moment. "If you walk down those steps and drive off, you need not bother to return."

He flinched visibly as though she'd slapped him in the face. Then his face darkened with suppressed anger. "You can't mean that?" he said harshly.

"Every word."

"But that's crazy! You're being both stubborn and irrational."

"I've told you how I feel."

"Well, I'm sorry, but I have no choice, and that's how I feel."

"Then I guess that's that."

He appeared ready to explode, but when he spoke, his voice was under control though it shook, "Again, if you don't trust me, then our love is doomed, anyway, so what the hell."

Refusing to let his tone and the devastated look on his face crack another hole in her heart, she turned her back.

He gave a strangled oath, then she heard him stalk down the stairs. Seconds later his vehicle was roaring down the drive. Somehow she managed to remain upright until she made it inside the house. Then she sank to the floor and sobbed.

"How much longer do you intend to go on like this?"

"Like how?" Grace asked innocently of Zelma, who was sitting at the bar sipping a cup of hot apple cider.

"Don't play the innocent with me, dear. It won't work."

"Oh, Zelma, I can't talk about it." Grace clamped down on her lower lip to keep it steady. "It hurts too much."

She knew she looked like hell, had ever since Denton left Ruby, which had been three weeks ago now. Although she cried herself to sleep every night, the days were tolerable, maybe because she'd been so busy. Despite their split, Denton had followed through with the promise of contacting a contractor, who had started working two days later. The man and his crew had been a lifesaver, getting the B&B back in operation on record time.

She had two of the guest rooms filled and the other one soon to be that way. Meanwhile Ed and Zelma had returned to Ruby and rented a house until they could build.

Grace couldn't imagine what she would've done without Zelma. She'd been both an emotional and physical rock, even though sometimes, like now, she made Grace crazy with her logic.

She didn't want to see herself as the heavy here— only Denton.

"So life goes on as is, huh?" Zelma was saying.

"And it's a good life, too,"Grace said, still on the defensive.

"Sure." Zelma slid off the stool and peered around the kitchen. "I have to say this place actually looks better. I love the cream-colored paint you chose."

"Thanks. I'm pleased, too."

"I'm worried about you, Gracie. The spark's gone. It's a good thing the nuclear plant issue's been settled in our favor. You're definitely not up to that kind of fight."

"You're right, I'm not."

"Do you think Denton had anything to do with them choosing another site?"

"Maybe. He said he was going to use what influence he had. And the fact that he went through with contacting a contractor for the house leads me to believe he followed through with that, as well." She doubted he went through with purchasing the nursery from Flora, however. She hadn't had the courage to go there, much less pose such a question.

"What a man."

"Don't, Zelma."

"Okay, as long as you start working on getting yourself back together. I hate seeing you like this."

"I'm working on it," Grace said in as light a tone as she could.

Zelma was quiet for a while as if in deep thought, then she leaned over and hugged Grace. "He's right, you know. Love without trust isn't true love."

"Zelma!"

"I know I said I'd back off, but you're too damn stubborn for your own good. But then you know that."

"Maybe, but I have to do what I think is best."

"And you think being miserable and alone is best?"

Grace flushed. "You don't know all the details."

"I know what you've told me, and that's enough to know that you're wrong."

"Please, let's drop the subject, okay?"

"Whatever," Zelma said with a shrug, then stood. "I've got to run. I'll call you tomorrow."

Later that evening Grace climbed out of the shower and dressed in a casual pair of slacks and top. Once her makeup was done, she stared at herself in the mirror. All dressed up with no place to go.

Tears filled her eyes and she cursed silently. She missed Denton. The hole in her heart grew bigger every day. What did she expect? She played that awful evening over in her mind every time she closed her eyes, always with the same conclusion. Denton was right: if she couldn't trust him, she didn't love him.

But she did love him. More than life itself.

So what was her problem? Suddenly it hit her that

she didn't have a problem other than her pride, which seemed to lose its importance now. Her breathing quickened. Was it too late to repair the damages? But to do so, she'd have to leave Ruby and go to Dallas.

She grabbed her chest and visibly staggered backward. Could she do that? Could she leave her safety net and take a chance and go for the gold?

Without the net?

Sweat dotted her skin, and her breathing turned more rapid. No, she wouldn't have a panic attack. She would ignore her elevated breathing and her rapid pulse and take action by doing what she should've done days, weeks, ago.

By damn, she was going to the city. To Denton.

"Hell, Hardesty, I'm so sick of you moping around here like a lovesick puppy, I could puke."

"Thanks, Todd, and you can go to hell."

"I have a better suggestion. Why don't you go get laid. Maybe that'll take the edge off."

"Not interested."

Todd rubbed the back of his neck, then stared back at Denton out of bleak eyes. They were in Todd's office discussing a client who had given them trouble and whom they were considering dropping. It was a touchy matter that required Denton's full concentration, an asset that was hard to come by.

He moaned inwardly. He couldn't think about her, talk about her, dream about her without coming apart at the seams. Todd, more than anyone else, knew this. But he was getting tired of it, too, and Denton couldn't blame him. He had to either come to terms with his loss or change the terms.

"I wish the hell you were interested in something," Todd muttered under his breath.

"I am. Grace."

"Then why aren't you there with her, for God's sake? I want you to do what will make you happy, and Lord knows, you're one miserable sonofabitch."

Suddenly Denton stood. "You're right. I am going to do something about that. I love her too much to let her off the hook that easily.

"It's about time you started thinking with your brain instead of below the waist."

For the first time in a long while, Denton grinned. "Good advice."

Several hours later he mounted the steps of the B&B with his heart in his throat. He nearly choked on it when Grace chose that moment to open the door, her purse and keys in hand.

"Oh," she whimpered, pulling up short and staring up at him, shocked.

He swallowed forcefully. "Uh, hi."

"Hi."

Silence.

He swallowed again. "Were you going somewhere?" he asked inanely, drinking in her beauty, her smell, aching to touch her, taste her.

"To Dallas," she whispered, "to see you, to ask you to forgive me."

It took what seemed like eons for her words to soak in, but when they did, he cried with joy and at the same time he grabbed her and buried his face in her hair.

"Oh, Grace, I love you, and I'm sorry, too."

She pulled back, love shining from her eyes. "You

have nothing to be sorry for. You just loved me, and I couldn't see that.''

"Let's get married.''

"Now?''

"Now.''

She laughed. "Let's do it!''

With a loud shout he swung her up in his arms and carried her down the steps. "Oh, by the way, I bought the nursery.''

"Fantastic!''

He paused and stared down into her adoring, up-turned face. "Know that you're loved from the depths of my being,'' he whispered before lowering his head.

She clung to him as her greedy lips collided with his.

* * * * *

THE BARONS OF TEXAS: KIT

by
Fayrene Preston

FAYRENE PRESTON

published her first book in 1981 and has been publishing steadily ever since. This is her third book for Silhouette Books, and she is delighted to be on board. Fayrene lives in north Texas and is the mother of two grown sons. She claims her greatest achievement in life is turning out two wonderful human beings. She is also proud to announce the arrival of her first grandchild: a beautiful baby girl. Now she has even more to be thankful for.

Prologue

Des.

The name of her stepcousin broke the peace of the cold winter morning and eased its way into Kit Baron's consciousness.

She didn't even flinch. As much as she hated the fact, Des Baron was never far from her thoughts, especially when he was in residence at the ranch, as he was now.

Like an apparition that haunted, Des—his dark eyes, his enigmatic smile, his long, lean body—seemed to hover, waiting for an opportunity to infringe upon her thoughts. It was crazy, and she had no answer for it. She simply had learned to endure until he once again left the ranch and she was able to breathe more freely.

As she continued toward the saddle barn, the gravel crunched beneath her feet and she forced her thoughts elsewhere. The dawn was just beginning to break over the horizon. All over the ranch, activity had been going on for hours. There had been a freeze during the night, but the day would warm up with the sun, and in the meantime, she didn't mind the cold. It cleared her head.

She loved winter mornings on the Double B, but then, she couldn't think of a day or a season she didn't adore. She had been born on it, and despite the harsh way her father, Edward Baron, had raised her and her sisters there, she had fallen in love with the land at an early age. Tess and Jill had gone in other directions, eager to be gone from the place and make their fortunes elsewhere. But now that their father was dead and Kit had had time to put her own personal stamp on the ranch, it was more than her home, it was her life.

Its wildness and unpredictability suited her down deep in her bones. She identified with the land that remained untamed, despite man's best efforts. It was her own personal kingdom.

As she drew closer to the barn, her steps quickened.

The saddle barn was a constant in her life. As a child, it had served as a place to hide from her domineering father, a place to dream of a happier life.

But even there, Des had managed to imprint himself on her memories. One summer evening, when she had been seventeen, she had fled to the barn after her father had verbally torn her to shreds over something so inconsequential she couldn't even remember what it had been. But she did remember Des Baron.

Coming into the barn, he had heard her crying. Following the sound, he had found her up in the loft in the farmost corner. Without a word, he had gathered her into his arms. But soon the comforting strokes had turned more urgent, and murmurs had turned into kisses. Soon heat was coursing between them. If he hadn't finally torn away from her...

But he had. And that night she had learned that Des was a danger to her like no other. With incredible ease he could make her want him to the point that nothing else would be important, make her fall beneath his spell until he was her entire world.

She couldn't allow it to happen.

Living under the heavy thumb of her father had made her vow she would never again allow herself to be dominated by a man. Once in a lifetime was more than enough.

And so, in public and on the surface, she had competed in an idiotic contest with her sisters to win Des's agreement to marriage. She and her sisters had each wanted to marry him because of business reasons that had to do with their father's will and, ultimately, control of Baron International, the family business. Privately, though, she had remained extremely wary of Des.

Damn the man.

Why wouldn't he stay out of her mind?

Just inside, she flipped on the light and started down the wide hall between the stalls. Immediately the scent of the sweet hay and straw, and the commonplace smell of saddle soap, leather and horses, enveloped her. Since childhood, she had equated the smells with comfort, with home, with safety.

She could hear Dia already moving restlessly in his stall, kicking out and whinnying nervously. Something had upset him.

With a frown, she made a fast stop by the tack-and-feed room, snatched an apple from the refrigerator, grabbed his halter off a peg and hurried to him. His head came up, his neck stretched out of the stall, and he nickered a greeting.

"Mornin', Dia," she said softly, giving him the apple and reaching up to stroke his neck. "What's wrong, boy? Did one of the barn cats get in your stall and spook you? Or are you just overly anxious for our run this morning?"

She knew she was. Whenever Des was home, she remained constantly on edge. And he had come in last night.

She rubbed Dia behind the ears, trying to soothe him with her presence and their well-known routine.

A sorrel quarter horse stallion with a blond mane and tail, Dia had been named Diablo by his former owner, who had cautioned her against buying the "crazy devil." Early in his life, Dia had been put into bad hands that had left him traumatized, with a hatred of all men. His former owner had been about to put the horse down. When she had found him, she bought him immediately.

She had spent two-thirds of her life under the

thumb of her father, who had been a devil of a man. In comparison, Dia was a lamb, though no one else on the Double B thought so. But then, no one else understood him as she did. Some men had the ability to crush a person's soul. Dia's soul had been crushed. She had restored it.

She opened the stall door and walked in. Dia practically pranced in place with eagerness. "I know, my beauty," she murmured as she slipped the halter over his head.

He loved their early morning ride as much as she did. It was their one guaranteed hour together, when no one bothered them and they could be alone with each other, the wind and the land. But it was more than eagerness for their ride that had him going this morning. Something else was up.

She cast a critical eye around the stall, then went outside again for a shovel. Turning the straw over, she failed to see anything obviously wrong.

She walked Dia out into the hall and crosstied him in the aisle. He pawed the sand beneath his hooves, and the other horses, sensitive to his mood, moved and nickered restlessly.

"I've been waiting for you."

The gruff voice sent a chill down her spine. She whirled around as Cody Inman stepped out of an empty stall three doors down. Suddenly Dia's nervousness made sense. "What are you doing here?" If there was a choice, no one ever entered the barn before she took Dia out.

"Like I said, I've been waiting for you. We need to talk."

Cody was a compact, muscular guy with dark curly hair, somewhere in his late twenties. He had been working on the ranch for about eight months. A couple of times he had been in the group she had gone dancing with. But last night it had inadvertently worked out so that it had been just the two of them.

With Cody at her side, she had flown one of the ranch helicopters into the nearest town, where she had heard there would be a good band playing, and for a short while she had enjoyed herself. But he had ended up drinking too much and had come on to her. As a result, she had been forced to cut the evening short.

Now she studied him, irritated that he had intruded on her private time. From the rumpled look of him, he hadn't been to bed, and from his slurred words, he had been drinking ever since they had returned.

As head of the Double B and everything on it, she was in charge of what was basically a man's world. She sometimes walked a fine line between boss and woman, but she was in no position ever to forget who she was. And she never did.

She had two rules. She played only with those who knew she was playing, and she never allowed the situation to get serious. She had thought Cody understood her rules. She had thought she could use their night of dancing as a shield to protect her from dwelling on Des and speculating on the reason he was home. She had been wrong.

Yesterday morning she had received an unexpected

message from Des, saying he was flying in and wanted to see her. She had panicked and set about to make sure she was busy.

Trying to avoid Des was a knee-jerk reaction with her, one she should have outgrown years ago. Still, going out dancing was something she had done a hundred times before with a hundred different ranch hands.

But no more.

No more.

If nothing else, this situation with Cody had taught her it was not a wise thing to do.

"Back away, Cody. You're making Dia nervous."

"Everything makes that devil nervous."

"I don't know where you're supposed to be working this morning, but it's not here." Though there were always exceptions, generally speaking only the ranch's longtime, most trusted hands were allowed to work around the main homestead, which was comprised of the main two homes and their support buildings. "Go sober up, then get to work."

She strode to the tack room and returned with a bucket of grooming tools.

He caught her elbow. "No way, sweetheart. I'm taking the day off. Besides, I'm with the boss. No one is going to get too bent out of shape over it."

His grip hurt. "Cody, you're drunk. Go do as I say."

"Don't tell me what to do! I'm not some common ranch hand. You and I clicked last night, and I'm not going anywhere until we've settled a few things."

She jerked away and went to Dia. At her touch, he calmed, but his skin twitched and the white rims of his eyes showed. "There's *nothing* to settle. Last night was fun, until you began to drink too much, but it's not going to happen again."

"Last night was special, you know that. But then you gave me the brush off, and that's not right. There can be something really sweet between us if you'll just let it happen."

She gave a sound of exasperation. "Tell me something. Am I speaking a language other than English? *Pay attention. Nothing* is going to happen between us."

"Come on, baby. You're a wild one, but I've made up my mind—*I'm* going to be the one who tames you."

"Tame me? Are you for real?" She used both brushes on Dia's back in an effort to hurry his grooming.

"Look, Kit, all I want is to go out with you again. What's so bad about that? We can have some more good times, get to know each other better."

"Do yourself a favor, Cody. Get out of my sight— *now.*

Even though she had done her best to keep her tone level, Dia must have heard something in her voice. He reared, kicked his hind legs out, then returned to pawing. "It's okay, boy."

She was able to get Dia's blanket and pad on without incident, but when she returned from the tack room with the saddle, Cody intercepted her.

"Come on, honey," he said coaxingly, blocking her path and grasping her shoulders. "We were hot last night. *You* were hot."

At his touch, true anger flashed through her. "Get your hands off me or you're going to be very sorry."

She pushed against him, using the weight of the saddle to throw him off balance. He staggered backward but quickly recovered. She turned away, but then heard him give a yell of anger. Before she had time to respond, his weight hit her back and she fell forward onto the saddle, hitting the ground and knocking the air out of her.

Dia gave a scream of fury and reared, but there was nothing she could do about him now. She rolled off the saddle just as Cody came down on top of her.

"Get *off* me, you bastard."

"No way, Sugar. You're mine now."

His lips crushed down on hers with bruising force, and she tasted blood.

She forced herself to relax for a moment, until she felt him loosen his grip and shift his legs. Then she jerked her knee up into his groin. He gave a loud groan and fell off her.

She scrambled to her feet and wiped the blood from her lip. "Collect your pay and be off the ranch by noon. You're *fired.*"

Cody groaned again.

She quickly saddled Dia and led him out of the barn. By the time her weight settled into the saddle, Dia was moving forward. She reined him in, attempting to hold him to a walk. "Easy, boy. Let's warm up first."

She flipped her hair free of her jacket collar, and as they passed the next barn, she saw Tio, one of the ranch's longtime cowboys, and lifted her hand to him.

"Kit?" he called out. "What's wrong? You're lookin' like thunder this mornin'."

"Just a guy who can't take no for an answer."

"Well, now, that ain't right, no sir. You want me to handle him for you?"

"Don't bother. I took care of him."

Free of the outbuildings, she eased Dia into a lope, then gradually into an easy gallop. When she thought he had warmed up enough, she let him run flat out.

The whole unpleasant scene with Cody could be traced back to her reaction to the news that Des wanted to see her. How incredibly stupid of her.

Des.

Where was he?

What was he doing?

Why did he want to see her?

One

Careful of her split lip, Kit took a sip of the hot coffee, leaned back in her rocking chair, propped her booted feet atop the porch railing and scanned the lake. The breeze rippled across its surface as the sun lit the water silver.

She hadn't meant to ride as far as the lake this morning. Normally she let Dia run for only a quarter of a mile, then slowed him to a lope for perhaps another quarter of a mile, after which they would head back to the barn.

But this morning neither one of them had seemed to want to return home just yet. So she had given in to the need to lengthen her time away from the waiting ranch business and turned Dia in the direction of her small cabin, which sat atop a bluff, overlooking the Double B's largest lake. She was glad she had.

Truthfully, Dia *never* wanted their morning ride to end. As for her, she was still upset about Cody. She cast her mind back on the few times she had been with him. For the life of her, she couldn't think of a thing she had done to lead him on.

But… Cody was a relatively new hire and didn't know her well. And they had been alone….

She sighed. In retrospect, it had been a mistake to invite him to go with her, but it was over now. Hindsight was a wonderful thing and, in this case, totally useless.

She took another sip and refocused on her surroundings. The lake cabin was one of her favorite places. As soon as her father had died, she'd had it built, along with a corral and a small barn. It had been one of her dreams. Here there were no phones. Here no one ever bothered her. Often she and Dia would ride out on a summer evening. She would swim and spend the night, then, the next morning, after another swim, she would head back to the house.

She scanned the lake. Unfortunately, it would be much too cold to swim this morning, and it was time she returned to her work.

A faint roar disturbed her musings. Curious, she got up and walked to the corner of the long porch so that she could peer around the side of the cabin. The roar was coming from the south, which meant it was coming from the direction of the homestead.

She shielded her eyes and picked out a vehicle,

speeding toward her at what she estimated to be well over fifty miles an hour, raising a cloud of dust behind it.

She stiffened. Surely it wasn't Cody. Surely their encounter in the barn had been enough to discourage him. But no…

It was a truck, she realized, as it drew closer. And it looked like the one her Uncle William had given his stepson, Desmond Baron, when he had graduated from law school.

Her pulse quickened, and her brow crinkled.

If it was Des, why would he seek her out here? His message had said he had wanted to talk to her. Was it so important he had felt the need to come after her?

It had to be him. No man on the Double B would dare abuse a ranch vehicle by driving it that fast over what was little more than a track. But with her Uncle William's death four months ago, Desmond Baron now owned fifty percent of the entire Baron empire. He could do anything he wanted to.

With a sigh, she sat her coffee cup on the railing and went down the steps to meet him.

If Des had been raised in a city instead of on a working ranch, his appearance might have stopped at classically good-looking. But he had been raised on a vast ranch and had conquered most of its jobs by the time he was fourteen. With time, the rough, outdoor life had branded him with a ruggedness and sexuality that seared as hot as the West Texas sun. His thick, dark brown hair was styled away from his brow and in short sideburns in front of his ears. His brown eyes were as sharp and all-seeing as a hawk's.

With the force of his intelligence and personality, he had the ability to dominate any situation, whether it was in the courtroom, where he had earned a reputation as one of the toughest, smartest defense lawyers in the country, or on the ranch, where every hand viewed him with respect. He was as hard as the plains on which they had both been reared, so what did he want with her?

As he climbed out of his car, her heart somersaulted. She hadn't seen Des since the reading of the will, which had occurred right after Uncle William's funeral. Now his jeans wrapped his lean hips and long legs like a Christmas present. His boots were well worn, and beneath a sheepskin vest was a beautiful pine-green sweater. It looked hand-knitted, and she couldn't help but wonder if a woman had made it for him. The home where he'd been raised sat less than a mile from hers, and she'd had countless opportunities to watch him from afar, starting when she first became aware of him as a little girl. There had always been women in his life. Gorgeous women who seemed willing to do anything for him. She'd never liked any of them, not that it mattered.

His scent of leather and spice came to her on the breeze as he stopped in front of her. Funny. From the first time she had been this close to him, though she had tried her best, she had never forgotten the way he smelled. Or anything else about him, for that matter. "Good morning, Kit."

"Good morning." His sharp brown eyes seemed to cut to her very heart, and his deep voice resonated inside her. No wonder he won the majority of his cases. Just last week she had read that his latest trial had ended with a victory for his client. Most of the trials he conducted ended the same way. Opposing lawyers rarely had a prayer against him. "What are you doing out here?"

He paused, his gaze touching on her red hair.

"You really should have a phone installed out here."

It didn't escape her that he hadn't answered her question. "Usually I'm not here that long."

"Still, in case of an emergency, you should carry a cell phone."

His tone was mild, not dictatorial or judgmental. Nevertheless, she instinctively defended herself. "It's not like I'm out here all the time." She swung an arm to indicate her surroundings, causing her jacket to shift partially open and reveal her sweater. His gaze dropped to her breasts, and she silently cursed as she felt her nipples harden. "Besides, the ranch isn't going to fall apart if I'm gone for a few hours now and then."

"Actually, I wasn't thinking of the ranch. I was thinking about you. What would happen if you had an accident and needed help?"

She slipped her hands into the fleece-lined pockets of her jacket. "My managers know where the cabin is, along with my routine. If I was missing for more than a few hours, they'd come straight here."

"What happened to your lip?" he asked, causing her to take a quick mental left turn.

Her hand flew to her mouth and the split lip that remained slightly swollen. "I must have bitten it."

"Must have?" His gaze roamed her face, searching. "Don't you know for sure?"

"I bit it." She didn't want to tell him the truth. Despite her reassurances to herself, she still couldn't help feeling that she could have handled Cody better.

"It must have been a hard bite." He reached out and gently touched the spot. "And it looks like a fresh wound."

Heat flashed through her. She recognized the feeling from that long ago summer night when he had taken her in his arms. Why couldn't she forget? She moved her head slightly, dislodging his touch. "It's fine."

In a casual move, he shifted the lapel of her jacket aside, baring the portion of her sweater he had seen when she had gestured. "Is this your blood?"

She glanced down at her sweater. She hadn't realized her lip had bled so badly. That damn Cody. "What's brought you all the way out here? If you had just waited, I would have been back soon."

With a quickness that nearly took her breath away, he stepped forward and slid one hand along the side of her jaw, tilting her face up. "Kit, would you tell me if you were in trouble?"

His move and question took her by surprise. His touch warmed her skin. "I'm not sure what you're talking about."

"*Are* you in trouble? Because if you are, I'll help."

With his hand on her, she could barely think. Could he have heard about her argument with Cody? But no, that didn't make sense. For better or worse, she had taken care of the matter. "Why are you here, Des?"

He let his hand drop away. "You're needed back at the homestead."

"Why? I don't have any appointments scheduled until this afternoon." She didn't have a clue what he was thinking, and instinct honed over time kept her from trying to find out. With Des, it was better if she kept her distance. "Oh, never mind. I was about to head back anyway. I'll just close up."

"Wait."

His grim tone halted her as she was about to turn. She eyed him cautiously. Because of her father's cruelty in keeping her and her sisters under his thumb, and later, because of her wariness of Des, she'd never been close to him. But even she knew he wasn't acting normally. "What is it?"

"Someone's been killed, Kit."

"Oh no! Who?"

Death on the ranch wasn't a complete shock. Working with large animals, as well as heavy machinery and equipment, offered too many chances for accidents. But she always hated to hear about it.

"Cody Inman."

She stiffened. How could that be? After she had left, he hadn't even been supposed to go to work, only draw his check from the paymaster and leave. "Cody

Inman?'' she repeated to make sure she'd heard correctly. ''But I saw him right before I rode out this morning.''

''That's what Tio said. A little while after you left, Tio went into the barn to start his work and found the body in one of the empty stalls. Since you weren't around, he came to me. I called the sheriff, then drove out here to get you.''

She nodded. ''Of course.'' How had Cody managed to get into an accident on what should have been his last few hours on the Double B?

''How awful.'' However Cody had acted toward her, she felt a deep pang of sadness for him. Just last night he had been so alive, dancing and laughing with her. But then he'd begun to drink and come on to her, and then this morning…

Questions raced through her mind as she tried to grapple with the fact that a man she had argued with mere hours before was now dead.

''How did he die?''

''You don't know?''

Confused, she stared up at him. ''How would I know?'' He didn't answer. ''Des? How did he die?''

''It looks like a blow to the head with a blunt object. Perhaps a shovel.''

The air went out of her. ''Are you saying Cody was *murdered?*''

''That's right.''

''But I don't understand. How could such a thing have happened?''

"That's what the sheriff wants to question you about."

"Okay, I'll close up here and be there as soon as possible."

"No. Just leave Dia here and come with me. We'll have someone bring a horse trailer out for him."

"Is that really necessary?"

"The sheriff will be waiting to talk to you." He paused. "So, *now* do you want to tell me how you got that split lip?"

She hadn't told him. And for the most part, Des didn't say much on the drive back to the homestead, which was fine with her. She'd given him the general outline of what had happened, but no details. Her morning encounter with Cody was still not something of which she was proud. It had been a situation she had let get out of her control.

Thoughts of Cody and the way he had died kept her busy. She kept trying to come up with scenarios for what could possibly have happened, but for the life of her, she couldn't come up with one that made sense.

But then, Des also occupied a large part of her mind. She attempted to ignore him by fixing her gaze on the passing landscape, but time and again his nearness drew her thoughts and senses back to him. Despite her attempts to ignore him, it had always been like that. With resignation, she wondered if it always would.

When he finally pulled up to the saddle barn, she breathed a soft sigh of relief.

She didn't recognize several of the cars and trucks parked there, but she did recognize the sheriff from a picture she had seen in the paper, put there when he had first come to their area nine months earlier. A tall, lanky man in his late thirties, he stood beside one of the trucks, speaking on a cell phone, but as soon as he saw them, he hung up and waited expectantly.

"Have you had any dealings with this sheriff?" Des asked quietly as he cut off the engine.

"No. Any problems we have with the men we try to handle ourselves." Her hand went to the door handle.

"Wait a minute." Des leaned over and clasped her wrist, and his arm pressed against the softness of her breasts.

Heat filled her lungs and, uncontrolled, her nipples hardened. No matter what, she couldn't seem to stop herself from responding to him.

"Listen to me, Kit. The sheriff's name is Moreno, and his reputation is that he's ambitious. So I want you to say as little as possible, and when in doubt, let me answer for you."

"What are you talking about?" She pushed against his arm.

He straightened away, but the severity of his tone didn't lessen. "Don't volunteer anything he doesn't ask. And if I tell you not to answer a certain question, don't."

She glanced through the windshield at the sheriff,

whose gaze was now trained on her. "He just wants me to tell him what happened."

"Actually, he wants you to make his job easy by confessing. Right now, you're the only suspect for Cody Inman's murder."

Her mouth dropped. "Suspect? Confess? But that's ridiculous."

"It's also the truth. So just be careful what you say."

"This is absurd." Suddenly she felt as if she were suffocating. Cody was dead, and Des was focusing his entire attention on her. It was too much. Her legs were shaking as she climbed out of the truck.

"Ms. Baron." The sheriff touched the brim of his hat in greeting.

"Sheriff Moreno." Her nerves were strung tight, but there was no point in taking her mood out on him. It wasn't his fault. "Sorry to have kept you waiting, but I didn't realize anything was wrong until Mr. Baron came to get me."

Des stepped up beside her, and the sheriff's gaze shifted to him, then back to her again. She wouldn't have been surprised to see a hint of intimidation enter his expression. After all, Des had an international reputation as a lawyer, and she ran one third of Baron International, specifically the massive ranching division. But the man's demeanor remained businesslike and aggressive.

"I'll get right to the point. I understand you were the last person to see Cody Inman alive."

"No. The person who murdered him was the last person to see him alive."

"Of course."

Des was standing so close to her that the warmth from his body filtered through her clothes to her skin. She supposed it was his way of supporting her, but she didn't need his support, and she certainly didn't want it—at least, not this kind.

The sheriff once again glanced at Des, then back at her. "Let me put it this way. It looks as if you were the last person to see Cody Inman before he was murdered. In fact, one of your hands—"

"That would be Tio."

He checked his notes and nodded. "Tio Rodriguez. He indicated that you and Mr. Inman had had a problem this morning."

She nodded. "In fact, I fired Cody right before I left for my morning ride." Beside her, she felt Des stiffen.

The sheriff's brows shot up so high they almost disappeared beneath his hat. "You fired him? Was that because of something work related?"

Slowly, as if it were a perfectly natural gesture, Des reached out, circled her wrist with his long fingers and lightly squeezed. She felt something lurch near her heart. The questioning didn't bother her. Des, however, did. "No," she said, impatient to get away from both men. "It was personal."

"How so?"

"You don't need to answer that, Kit."

Des's sharp tone tightened her nerves, making her

response even quicker. "We went out last night and—"

"You and Mr. Inman? Just the two of you?"

"That's right."

"And what happened?"

"To put it as simply as possible, Sheriff, Cody wanted our relationship to go farther than I did."

"Kit—"

"And did you and Mr. Inman fight over this?"

"Kit! *Stop answering.*"

She glanced at him again. His jaw had tensed, and his eyes had darkened. "I've got nothing to hide. Cody and I definitely fought. But did I kill him? No, I did not."

"I see."

The sheriff didn't believe her, she realized with a small shock. On the Double B her word was law, and she wasn't accustomed to being doubted. Slightly shaken, she scanned the faces of the men who had gathered around him. Several of them looked confused, even skeptical. Great. Just great.

The sheriff nodded toward her lip. "Did you get that injury in the fight?"

"He kissed me."

"And the kiss split the lip?"

"That's right. He wasn't exactly gentle."

"Uh-huh. Made you mad, did he?"

"He made me very mad."

"That's enough." The authority in Des's voice cut between the sheriff and her. "If you need any further information, Sheriff, make an appointment with Ms.

Baron *through me*. Kit, I'll see you back to your house." His strong hand on her back quickly turned her and headed her back to the car.

"Wait a minute!" the Sheriff yelled. "Ms. Baron, I'll need to ask you to come down to the office. We'll need your fingerprints, and I'll want to question you further."

"She'll come in later," Des said, raising his voice, but not stopping until he had her in the truck and they were driving away.

Two

Kit slammed the front door shut in Des's face.

Damn the woman. A muscle clenched in Des's jaw as he opened the door and went in after her. He found her in the living room, lighting a fire.

"What were you thinking about, talking to the sheriff like that?"

She wheeled on him. Her green eyes flashed, vivid with anger, and her long red hair curled like flames against her shoulders. "Don't *ever* do that again to me."

"Do what? Save you from incriminating yourself?"

"Don't ever again tell me what to say or not to say. And don't *ever* give me an order in front of my men. You may own fifty percent of this ranch, but *I* run it.''

''Listen to me, Kit. You can't tell the sheriff everything you did without expecting to be arrested. Not in this case. Why didn't you do as I *said?*''

The logs began to burn behind her but she barely noticed. ''Do as you said?''

All of his career, he had faced hostile clients, lawyers, judges and juries. Part of his success was that he was always able to remain cool under fire. Staying calm and above the fray was one of his trademarks. No one ever got to him.

Kit got to him.

He wanted to shake her. Worse, he suddenly realized, he wanted to kiss her. Lord help him, where had that come from?

''Whether you realize it or not, Kit, you've gotten yourself into a serious situation. And just because it was *me* who gave you the advice, doesn't mean you had to go against it.''

''That's not what happened.'' She stripped off her coat and threw it across a chair.

''That's exactly what you did. Admit it. You hate for anyone to try to tell you what to do, but this case is different, and you need to realize it. In this case, you don't know what's best. *I* do. And believe me when I say, you told him entirely too much.''

She threw up her hands. ''For heaven's sake, get over yourself. The women you go out with must not have any brains, but I do.''

''You're not hearing what I'm saying. Dealing with

men like that sheriff is what I do for a living, and I know what I'm talking about. Let me do my damn job.''

''This isn't a job you need to concern yourself with. Whatever happened, happened in my realm. I'll take care of it.''

He shook his head. ''Trying to defend yourself is the worst thing you can do.''

''I'm not trying to *defend* myself.''

''Then tell me what you think you're doing.''

''Telling the truth about what actually happened.''

He gave a sound of disgust. ''Prisons are filled with people who told the truth. At this stage of the game, everything you say is important. Even *how* you say it. You have to be careful, and you weren't.''

''What are you talking about? The sheriff didn't indicate he suspected me.''

''If you believe that, you weren't listening.''

''Don't be ridiculous. Cody's body was just found. It's way too early for the sheriff to *suspect* anyone.''

''Granted, it's early, but have you ever heard of quick arrests?''

''Of course, but—''

''Ideally, authorities like to make an arrest within the first twenty-four hours of a crime. After that, witnesses can go foggy, crime scenes can be tampered with, or any number of other things can happen. Kit, face it. That's exactly what may happen here, because, unfortunately, it looks as if everything so far points to you.''

"That's not true. They haven't even found the murder weapon yet."

"Are you telling me that if the murder weapon turns out to be a shovel, or any one of the implements used in that barn, your fingerprints won't be on it?"

"No. They probably will be—" Abruptly she broke off and swiveled back to the fire. "I don't have my own silver-plated shovel, Des. At one time or another, I've probably used and touched everything in that barn."

She was electric, all fire and fury. But he also saw the fragility there. He had always been able to. He had often heard his adoptive father, William Baron, grumble about the stricter than strict way his brother Edward was raising his three daughters. He hadn't seen Kit on a daily basis or even a monthly one, but rather over time and at various stages of her life.

Living on the same ranch, he'd had a unique perspective from which to watch her grow up. As a little girl, she had tried in vain to battle against the tyranny of her father. As a teenager, she had become subdued and resigned to living beneath her father's thumb.

Her father's death when she was twenty had finally given her the freedom to come into her own, but that had also been when her rebellion kicked in. It had seemed to him that during those years she had been all flash and fury, yet she had also taken the reins of the ranch. Now she had everything she ever wanted, including power. The problem was, she now seemed to be rebelling against him. Worse, he felt the effects much more than he should.

He took a steadying breath, but it didn't have the desired effect. He couldn't seem to hold on to his objectivity. Deep down, he was frightened for her. Even more frightening to him, he was coming to realize he badly needed to keep her safe. Where had that come from? And when? "I'll put an investigator on this Cody Inman and find out about him."

"Don't be stupid. You won't find anything unusual about him. He was just an ordinary ranch hand."

"He was a man who hurt his boss, a woman. He tried to force himself on you, or have you forgotten?"

"Of course not."

"Odds are good that somewhere he's got a bad history, and I need to find out what it is. It could make a difference in the trial."

"Trial?" she practically sputtered. Her hair flew out around her as she spun around. "There's not going to be a trial—at least, not with me as a defendant."

"Calm down. I'm just thinking ahead. It's what I do."

Her brow furrowed with anger. "Who asked you?"

"Damn it, Kit—" He stopped himself and forced another deep breath through his lungs. He wasn't going to be able to help her unless he could regain his composure. Unfortunately, his temperature was rising by the minute.

She affected him way too deeply.

For most of his life he had deliberately stayed away from her and her sisters. Their father's will had stipulated that unless Kit and each of her sisters made his idea of a fortune within ten years of his death, they would lose their thirty-three and one-third percent portion of Baron International. Even though she was the youngest, Kit had already met the first condition of the will, earning that fortune plus more. Her sisters Tess and Jill had, too.

In addition, they had all known that his step-father, their father's brother, would leave his fifty percent of the corporation to him upon his death, which would essentially give him control of the company, unless the three of them voted together at all times, leading to a stalemate.

The sisters had quickly come up with the theory that if one of them could obtain control of his fifty percent of the Baron empire through marriage, she could thus control Baron International. So, like her sisters, Kit became caught up in the mad game of trying to get him to succumb to her charms. She and her sisters had actually competed to get him to the altar.

Most men would have reveled in the attentions of three beautiful women, but under the circumstances, he had decided reticence was the intelligent response. Fortunately for all concerned, the game had come to an abrupt halt when Tess and then Jill had married. In effect, they had given up everything for love and left the path to him wide open for Kit.

But then, suddenly, she had started to shun him. It didn't make any sense to him, and anything that didn't make sense bothered him.

She had always intrigued him, and now that he was

no longer preoccupied with his father's health or a trial, he had vowed that this was the trip home when he would find out why she was going out of her way to avoid him.

But now, just when he had decided to seek her out, fate had stepped in before him. A murder had put her in peril, and he wanted, needed, to help.

But she continued to confuse him.

She made his mind veer away from the subject at hand and on to the fact that she was the most desirable woman he had ever seen. At the moment she was practically vibrating with anger at him, yet all he could think about was how much he would love to kiss her.

The knowledge was a shock to his system.

He shrugged out of his vest and carefully placed it on the back of a sofa. "Let's go at this a different way. You told the sheriff that Cody had wanted to take your relationship farther than you did. What exactly was he to you?"

"Just a guy to go dancing with." She wrapped her arms around herself and began to pace. "I never meant it to be serious."

"Then why did you go out with him in the first place?"

She fixed him with a straight gaze. "Do you plan to take every woman you go out with to the altar. Or even to bed?"

"I've never dated a woman who ended up dead the next morning."

"Then obviously you've been lucky and I was unlucky. But believe it or not, I didn't know Cody was going to be murdered.''

He shook his head, frustrated beyond belief with her, with himself. And he knew what the problem was. He was letting himself get too involved, something he never allowed with clients. Yet even armed with that knowledge, he couldn't stop himself. ''Your flirtations have always been within inches of getting out of hand and you know it. It's called playing with fire, and sooner or later it was bound to get you into trouble.''

She made a sound of anger. ''You know *nothing* about how I handle my personal life.''

''I know enough. I've seen you on the dance floor with one guy after another, and, honey, let me tell you something. The way you dance is an invitation to every red-blooded male in the state.''

''That's *not* true.''

She looked as if he had struck her, but at least she was finally listening. ''It's true all right,'' he said, his tone grim. ''The last time I saw you at a party, you were wearing a little nothing of a white dress, and every man in the place was salivating.''

She stared at him, her green eyes wide and gorgeous. ''You remember what I was wearing?''

He frowned, as surprised at himself as she was. ''It doesn't matter. Let's get back to Cody. What happened when you were out with him last night that made him think he could have a future with you?''

Years ago, he'd had firsthand experience of how easily she could melt against a man. Even now, just looking at her made him want to grab her into his arms and make love to her. In fact, he couldn't get the idea out of his mind. So he didn't even want to think of her in another man's arms. The very idea infuriated him.

She made a vague gesture. "Nothing extraordinary happened."

Nothing extraordinary. She would probably classify the kiss they had shared in the barn all those years ago as nothing extraordinary, too. Hell, she probably didn't even remember it. But he did. He always would.

He crossed to her and gripped her arm. "That's where your faulty thinking comes in. *You* are extraordinary. You turn those green eyes on a man, you press that sweet body of yours against him, and I guarantee a man's going to feel something."

He couldn't help himself. He pulled her against him, and his throat went tight. He hadn't felt her body against his since she was seventeen. Then he had kissed her and hadn't wanted to stop. Now he felt the same way. It was completely inappropriate. It was totally astounding. "Exactly *how* hot and heavy did you get with him?"

She twisted, trying to free herself. Her breasts and thighs rubbed against him, making him hard. What little control he had left was about to disappear. Suddenly he was quite sure he was about to do something irrational, and abruptly he let her go. He needed to help her situation, he reminded himself, not harm it. He needed to remain clearheaded.

Looking shaken, she rubbed herself where he had gripped her and moved away. "Hot and heavy? Charming phrasing, Des. Really charming."

It was a clumsy phrase, but his vaunted word power had deserted him. He drove stiffened fingers through his hair. He knew better than anyone the need to keep personal feelings out of this, but the thought of her in danger made him crazy. "You know what I mean."

"*No.* In no way did I lead him on. *Furthermore,* nothing hot and heavy happened. At the bar, he forced a kiss on me and I brought the evening to a quick halt."

"And after that, what happened? Did he just accept your decision?"

She shrugged. "He got a bit sulky. After we got back to the ranch and I went to drop him at the bunkhouse, he tried to kiss me again, but he didn't get very far."

"How did you manage that?"

"I had one of the guys at the hangar secure the helicopter for me, I dropped Cody off, then I came home."

"And do you know what he did after you left?"

"I don't have a clue. Except…"

"Except what?"

"Well, it was obvious this morning that, whatever else he did, he went off and began drinking heavily. When we were together, he had two beers."

"How many did you have?"

Resentment flared in her eyes. "None of your business."

"Someone's going to ask, Kit. It might as well be me."

"I had one. Okay? I had one."

"Is that usual for you?"

"What are you getting at?"

"To your knowledge, has anyone where you were last night ever seen you drink a lot? Or even get drunk?"

"*No.*" Her eyes darkened with her anger. "Do you honestly believe I would have had more than one beer when I was *flying* home?"

He studied her for a moment, believing her and wondering how his planned quiet talk with her had turned into this angry confrontation. Then he silently answered himself. He had just realized that he cared too much. "Okay. You said you dropped Cody at the bunkhouse. Did anyone see you drive off in your car alone?"

"Probably. What difference does it make? I was dropping him off at the bunkhouse."

"When you're involved in a murder case, you have to backtrack and look at every single detail. For instance, the person who saw you two drive away from the hangar together could have thought that you were bringing him here. He could have assumed you two were lovers, and if the sheriff heard that, he could have decided you two had a lovers' quarrel and you killed him in a fit of rage. It happens a lot."

"But it *didn't* happen in this case."

"Had you slept with him, Kit?"

"*No.*"

The relief he felt was out of all proportion to what it should have been. "When you're involved in a murder case," he said quietly, "you have to look at everything."

"But *I'm* not involved." She started to pace again, her long legs eating up the ground behind the big sofa, her hair gleaming in the light.

"You're involved, Kit. You were the last person to see Inman alive, and you admitted having an argument with him. You admitted to a physical fight with him. Lord…" He wearily ran his hand through his hair. "You're a smart woman, Kit. You've run this entire ranching empire by yourself for nine years. So why can't you see that you're in trouble?"

"And why can't *you* leave me alone?"

She grimaced, as if she didn't like what she had just said. He didn't like it, either. As a matter of fact, he hated it, because he didn't have an answer. He tried to find one that made sense. "Because, Kit, you need advice of counsel. You don't realize how serious this is."

She halted and directed a level gaze at him. "Contrary to what you may think, I *do* see this as serious. Someone, while in *my* employ, has been killed on the Double B, which is *my* land. I take that very personally and will help however I can. But the sheriff needs to get his focus off me and look somewhere else."

"That's just it. He doesn't have to look somewhere else. Not if his mind is made up. And think about

something else. Wouldn't it be a coup if he were to
arrest the well-known Kit Baron and make it stick?
The local district attorney would be drooling. The
publicity would shoot them both into national prom-
inence. There would be the possibility of book deals
and interviews and maybe made-for-TV movies. It's
happened before.''

''But I *didn't* do it.''

He waved dismissively. ''I know you didn't.''

She blinked. ''You do?''

''Kit, you're incapable of intentional cruelty *or* a
cold-blooded killing.'' She was so beautiful, so stubborn. He felt an aching near his heart. He was in
serious trouble. How was he going to help her when
it was all he could do just to contend with the new
feelings for her he had just discovered?

''Worst-case scenario,'' he said absently, trying to
figure out answers to the questions he was asking
himself, ''we could plead self-defense.''

She picked up a vase and threw it at him as hard
as she could. He ducked as it whizzed by his head
and crashed against the wall behind him. ''Damn you,
Des Baron!''

A deafening silence descended between them, and
it grew in intensity and volume until Des wanted to
put his hands over his ears to drown it out. Instead,
he fought to regain his composure.

''You know,'' he said calmly, ''if anyone but me
had seen you throw that vase, they might just believe
you could lose your temper at a man who made you

angry, maybe even do him bodily injury. Maybe even kill him.''

He saw her shudder as if a cold chill had slid down her spine. At last one of his points had hit home.

''Get out,'' she said softly.

''I'll leave. For now.''

Three

Des.

Kit groaned softly. For the last ten minutes she had been rereading a paragraph in a romantic suspense book she had started earlier in the week, and she still didn't have a clue what it was about.

She thrust it aside. It was useless to try to concentrate on anything tonight. Des was the only thing on her mind, and she couldn't get him off.

All her instincts were shouting at her that earlier this morning, with very little effort, her encounter with Des could have turned from anger to passion. And if it had…

The potential for instant passion between them had always been the thing that, deep down, she had feared. Yet for some odd reason, the charged sexual tension between them had taken her totally by surprise.

It had seemed to take Des by surprise, too, though she couldn't really be sure. She couldn't begin to guess. His father had understood him, but since Uncle William's death, she doubted anyone did. He was a brilliant enigma.

She pushed herself up from the couch and walked to a window. Outside, sleet had begun to fall, but inside her home, it was warm and cozy, just as she liked. But tonight, even the surroundings she had worked so hard to achieve couldn't soothe her.

So much had happened today that was awful and bewildering. Someone had killed Cody, and the sheriff was looking closely at her as the person who had done it. If it wasn't such a bizarre tragedy, she might have laughed. Even funnier, stranger, was the fact that Des, whom she had avoided for years, had declared himself her lawyer, her defender.

She could cope with the sheriff, but Des was a different matter. She could well understand why for years women had made fools of themselves over him. At seventeen, she would have made a complete fool out of herself if he hadn't stopped their kiss. She groaned at her thoughts.

She had wrapped up business earlier this evening and treated herself to a long soak in a bath. Then she had slipped on a pair of big socks, a pair of silk pajamas and her cashmere robe. It would have been a perfect night to relax, perhaps even finish the novel she was reading, except she couldn't get her mind off the murder. And Des.

Des.

If he had kissed her this morning, she would have responded. She knew it in her bones. She wouldn't have been able to control herself. Worse, her response would have been so easy, so automatic, so natural. And what if it had gone even farther?

If nothing else, her musings on what, in reality, was nothing more than a kiss that hadn't happened told her she had been absolutely right to avoid Des for all these years.

The doorbell chimed, startling her and breaking into her thoughts. For a moment she simply gazed toward the sound. No matter who it was, she was in no mood to see anyone. She would love to simply ignore whoever was there, along with whatever problem they were bringing with them. Unfortunately, it wasn't in her to shirk any kind of responsibility.

Reluctantly, she went to answer it and found Des standing under the light on her porch. Her heart leapt, and her hand flew to the neck of her robe, pulling it tight in a protective gesture.

She had been thinking of Des and he had appeared. Slivers of ice coated his dark hair and the shoulders of his long fleece-lined coat.

Staring at him, a painful truth hit her. She had been waiting for him. Oh, Lord. Her heart shouldn't beat this fast every time he was near. Her pulse shouldn't race. She couldn't let it happen. She didn't know if he planned for them to spend a great amount of time together. But even if they spent only a small amount of time with each other, she was going to have to build a formidable defense against him.

"May I come in?"

She hesitated. "It's very late."

"Not that late."

She gave in much too easily and gestured him inside. Standing back, she watched as he shrugged out of his coat and hung it on a brass tree, then walked into the living room. She followed. The jeans he was wearing looked newer than the pair he'd had on this morning, but they still hugged every line of his hips and his long lower body. A soft-looking navy blue sweater stretched across his wide shoulders and chest and hugged his lean midriff. She could smell leather and spice and soap.

He looked wonderful. And disconcertingly desirable. "Has something happened?"

"Nothing new, if that's what you mean."

"Then why are you here?"

He glanced at her, then slowly turned his attention to the room, taking in everything about it. "This is nice," he said at last. "I didn't notice it earlier."

No, he hadn't. *Earlier* he had been concentrating very hard on her. "Thank you."

"I had heard you gutted the house and redid everything inside it."

"Yes."

He hadn't told her why he was there, which she considered a bad sign. If she knew what was coming, she could defend herself better. However, by focusing on her home, he was giving her a temporary reprieve from whatever was on his mind, and she took it.

She had decorated everything in the softest of colors, with pillows and books piled everywhere. It was her private refuge, a refuge he had invaded. And, damn it, just her luck, he looked right at home there.

His long fingers flicked at a gold tassel on a tall pillow, trailed over a soft leather chair; then his hand closed around a porcelain figurine of a woman in eighteenth-century dress and lifted it. It was so delicate he easily could have broken it, yet he held it carefully, examining its graceful lines with obvious appreciation.

Those same fingers had gripped her arms and pulled her against him.

Suddenly she had trouble swallowing. "Can I get you something? Bourbon? Scotch?" She didn't want him to stay long enough to have a drink, but, unfortunately, *she* wanted one.

"A brandy, please." He put the figurine down and strolled over to the fireplace. Holding his hands to the blaze, he remarked, "Dad told me you had redone the place, but I haven't been here in years."

She had never invited him into her home. She rarely invited anyone, though one or both of her sisters would occasionally stay a couple of days.

From the mantel, he picked up a delicate porcelain box with pink and yellow roses on its lid, gazed at it as if he didn't know how it had gotten into his hand, then put it down again. "The house is unrecognizable from your father's day. I remember a series of dark, boxy rooms—very plain, very small, very basic.''

"Yes.'' She'd knocked down walls and added windows and doors. She'd wanted the wind to be able to blow through the rooms and the light to be able to fill them. And she had succeeded. Now her home nourished her.

"I understand why you wanted to make it your own.''

Of course he did. Growing up as close as he had, he wouldn't have been able to miss the oppressive, rigid way her father had reared her and her sisters. But she wished with everything she had that he didn't understand. It made her feel too vulnerable. She poured her own drink, then sloshed a bare half-inch of brandy into a snifter and handed it to him.

"Actually, I wouldn't have been surprised if you had razed the house to the ground.''

"Doing it this way was just as effective.'' She sipped at her own brandy, then returned the glass to the bar. She had thought the brandy would help her nerves and relax her tight throat. It didn't. Since he had arrived, her nerves had tightened to the point that she was now afraid the drink might make her sick.

"I'd say it was better.''

She thought about that. "I suppose so. I took what my father had built and recreated something bright, clean and healthy in its place. There's absolutely nothing left of the man who built it.''

"Good for you,'' he murmured.

The softness of his voice grated along her skin and

warmed her stomach. She pulled her robe tighter around her.

His gaze dropped to his brandy snifter. "Were you able to make arrangements to get Dia back all right?"

They had talked about the house, and now they were talking about her horse. As long as they weren't talking about the sexual tension that was between them, she would be okay. "I took a trailer out and got him."

One corner of his mouth turned up. "Didn't trust him to anyone else, huh?"

"Not really. Then I had to put him in a different barn than the one he's used to." Her gaze lingered on his lips entirely too long. She crossed to the fire and nudged the burning logs with a poker. "He's not happy, but for the moment, there's no other option."

She was doing the same thing as he was, she realized. She was trying to soothe the tense, heated air with small talk. The problem was, she wasn't any good at it. Neither was he.

"I talked to the sheriff this afternoon," Des said. He's conducting a very thorough forensic investigation, but he should be through with the barn by tomorrow afternoon."

"I know. He called here and told me. He also insisted again that I come in for fingerprinting."

"I don't want you to have to do that."

"I told him I would be in sometime tomorrow."

His gaze cut to her, and he exhaled a long breath. "I don't want you to do that."

"It would only antagonize the sheriff further if I

didn't. Besides, by going ahead and getting it over with, it shows I'm willing to cooperate." She paused, then finally asked, "Des, what are you doing here?"

"I thought we should settle what we started this morning."

Her nerves jumped. "I don't think there's any need to say anything more."

He set his snifter on a nearby table. "I totally disagree with you. There's every need. To start with, I lost my professional objectivity with you, something that's nearly unforgivable, considering my profession."

Oddly, she felt insulted. The term *professional objectivity* made her feel like a client with no personal ties to him, and, strangely, she resented it. However, a large dose of objectivity about him was exactly what *she* needed. She just wished she could figure out how to achieve it. "I'm sure you've already gotten it back."

He gazed at her for a long moment, and she found herself holding her breath. He affected her way too much. He always had.

"The truth is, I was worried about you, Kit. I still am."

"Don't be. There's no reason. And there's also no need for any more lectures. I've thought it over, and I fully comprehend the gravity of what's going on and how it involves me."

He nodded. "Good. I've already begun an investigation."

"You don't have to. I'll be doing my own."

"Kit..." He paused, seeming to consider carefully what he was about to say. "Do you remember when you were a little girl?"

"I try very hard not to."

He gave a chuckle that sent a warm tingle down her spine.

"Well, *I* remember," he said softly. "When your father would start to thunder at you and it all got too much for you, you used to run away from the house. After a couple of hours, your father would send the hands out to look for you. But somehow I always knew where to find you. You'd be up in the loft of one of the barns, at the very back, curled up behind a hay bale."

She tried to remember the frightened child she had been instead of the sexual woman she had become, but failed when she suddenly realized he was in front of her—too close. She hadn't even seen him move.

"You'd be curled up in a tight ball," he murmured, "trying your best to be invisible. I'd hold out my hand to you, but you'd shake your head. I'd tell you that it would be much better if you'd let me take you back to your house. I figured it would go easier on you if you returned voluntarily. But you were so stubborn. You always had to do it the hard way—your way—and you'd never accept my help."

Gently he closed his hand in her hair. "Please, Kit. This time, don't do it the hard way. This time let me help you."

Dazed, confused, she stared up at him. With that

soft mesmerizing voice, and that gentle, fiery touch, he was an extremely dangerous man.

Damn it.

"I can do this by myself, Des."

"I know that, but with me here, there's no reason for you to have to. Come on, Kit, I'm one of the highest priced lawyers in the nation, and I'm offering you my services free. I'm experienced. I'm damn good. I can help. *Let me.*"

With a sigh, she looked up at him. "You're not really going to give me a choice, are you?"

"Not really."

She slowly nodded. "Okay, then. Just to show you that I've actually learned something since I was a little girl, you can help. But if at any time during our investigation I feel we're not getting along, I can tell you to leave. Understood?"

"Good," he said simply. "Good."

His eyes dropped to her lips, then slowly, hesitantly, he lowered his face toward hers.

She had time to pull away, actually plenty of time. But she surprised herself by not moving. Instead she waited for, anticipated, what would happen next. And by doing so, she was going against everything she believed.

Still she waited, and then her waiting was over. It was as if he didn't give a second's thought to what she had said. It certainly didn't seem to faze him. His warm, soft breath feathered over her skin. She lifted her face as if the warmth was a benediction. Then, exquisitely, his lips brushed back and forth over hers.

Automatically, it seemed, her mouth opened and his tongue pushed inside. A thrill jolted through her. She thrust her tongue against his, feeling his tongue's moist roughness, tasting its sweetness, savoring the sensuality.

His hands slid up and down her spine, moving the cashmere of her robe and the silk of her pajamas over her skin in an erotic caress. One kiss turned into two, and two into three, and the kisses went on and on.

Warmth crawled along her bloodstream until it enveloped her entire body. Soon, insidiously, it changed to blazing heat. It felt so good, so wonderful, that she vaguely wondered why she had tried so hard to deprive herself all these years. Oh, she knew she had a reason, a sure belief that she should stay away from him. But at this moment, it didn't seem to matter. Truthfully, she had never known kisses could be so all-encompassing, so totally absorbing.

She melted against him, just as she had when she was seventeen. Except… The fire was somehow hotter now, the blaze inside her stronger, his lips more firm and sure. Again his tongue plunged deeply into her mouth, and she slid her arms around his neck and threaded her hands up into his thick hair.

On some level she knew these kisses went far beyond what she should be allowing, but the compulsion to continue was much too strong to stop now.

She pressed her body closer to his, shamelessly undulating her hips until she could feel the hard ridge of his arousal. It was crazy. She had tried so hard for so long to stay away from him, and now she couldn't get close enough.

Gently, firmly, he pushed her away, making space between their bodies.

An involuntary cry of protest and denial escaped her lips. "Ah, don't make that sound," he murmured, his voice hoarse and broken. "It hurts me, too. But if we continue this much longer, I won't be able to stop."

The reality of what he was saying cleared her head. One part of her wanted to sink back into the heat where she didn't have to think and feel. The other part of her, which was now thinking straighter, knew that there were innumerable things wrong with them continuing.

Suddenly she felt as if she had been put through an emotional wringer, and weariness rapidly overwhelmed her. Without meeting his eyes, she stepped away. "Good night, Des."

He hesitated. "I didn't mean for—"

"Good night."

"You want me to go?" he asked stiffly.

"That's exactly what I want."

"Then good night, Kit."

Four

―――――

Des.

The next morning, Kit pulled back the drape of the living room window and gazed outside. It promised to be raw and gray all day.

Earlier, she had taken Dia out for their run, but, unlike yesterday, she hadn't been tempted to lengthen their time away from home. Today's run hadn't brought her problems into focus as it usually did, nor had it cleared her mind.

Des dominated her thoughts at a time when it was imperative she should be thinking of Cody's murder and how to help herself. It was no solace to her that she had been right all these years to avoid him. He could so easily fill her life to the exclusion of everything else. He could dominate her as her father had done, and she wouldn't even be tempted to run away.

She was angry at herself for having been so easy, and she knew that everything that had happened between them had been her fault. She had known the kiss was coming, and she should have said no.

Don't think about it, she ordered herself.

Easier said than done, she answered herself.

She was really losing it, she reflected ruefully.

She forced her thoughts back to Cody's murder. She didn't know anything about this sheriff. Des had said he was ambitious. To her way of thinking, it would be odd if he wasn't.

But if he *was* looking for a quick, expedient end to this case, circumstances had unwittingly made her the perfect solution. And because of that, any clues he would be looking for would be clues that linked her to the murder. He wouldn't be interested in anything or anyone else.

Des had been right. The innocent person didn't always go free. Oh, maybe in books and the movies, but not in real life.

But the last thing she wanted was for Des to help her.

She did not want to be beholden to him. Plus, last night had proven to her that she couldn't keep her head when she was around him. She had lost her temper. She had melted when he had touched her. She had made a fool of herself.

Briefly she closed her eyes. Somehow she was going to have to gain control over both herself and the situation with him. She was going to have to help herself.

If she hadn't killed Cody, someone else had. But who?

Last night, after Des had left, she had turned on her computer, opened a file and checked the reports of every one of her managers. Finally, she had found the one who had overseen Cody. A quick call on the man's pager resulted in a callback and the information that a man named Scott McKee frequently worked and hung out with Cody.

The doorbell rang, and she went to greet him. "Good morning, Scott."

He was a young man, still in his twenties, around five feet ten inches tall, with a stocky, muscular build. He swept off his hat to reveal the beginnings of a receding hairline. "Ms. Baron."

She had been in a group several times with him, and he had always called her Kit, but she didn't ask him to call her Kit now. This morning there was a definite formality to his demeanor and to the occasion.

"Let's go to my office."

She led the way down the hall to the big room that overlooked the back garden. She took her chair behind her desk and, with a wave of her hand, indicated that he should sit in one of the chairs in front of her. "Coffee?" She pointed toward a sideboard, a coffeepot and a stack of mugs she had previously set out. He shook his head, clearly uncomfortable in his surroundings.

"Then I'll get right to the point, Scott. I'd like to know about your friendship with Cody Inman. Were you close?"

He shifted awkwardly in the chair. "I wouldn't say we had what you'd call a real friendship. Depending on where we were each assigned, we'd sometimes work together. We bunked fairly close, too."

The first thing on her mind had been to get him settled so that she could begin questioning him, but now she studied his face. He looked uneasy and apprehensive.

"Did you ever hang out with him when you weren't working?"

"Once in a while. Damned shame he was killed."

"I'm not just sorry about his death, Scott. I'm angry. I value every person who works on this ranch, whether I know them well or not."

She paused, but he had started to studiously examine the near edge of the desk and didn't say anything.

"Someone committed murder here. Until we find out who, other people could be in danger."

"I hadn't thought about it like that."

"But it's true."

"Yes, ma'am."

"Did you have reason to be mad at Cody recently?"

He looked at her. "No. Did you?"

She returned his look as calmly as she could manage. News traveled fast on the ranch. By now he knew what had happened between her and Cody. By now everyone did.

Scott retreated into silence, and her heart sank. Scott was feeling awkward with her because he thought it possible she had killed Cody. Did others feel the same way?

Something in her screamed.

This ranch and her place on it were her pride and joy. This ranch was all that she had, all that she wanted. And the respect of each and every person who worked on the ranch was something she valued highly. Now she saw that with some she might have to work hard to regain that respect.

"Do you know of anyone who didn't get along with Cody? Anyone he fought with recently? Anyone who didn't like him?"

He shrugged, glanced at her, then returned his gaze to the edge of the desk. "Not really."

"Think hard."

"The thing is, he was pretty much a regular guy. Nothing too special about him. He worked hard. And when he played, he played hard." His voice dropped. "Just like we all do, I guess."

He was thinking of her, and it was one more reason to find out who really had killed Cody.

"Good morning," Des said, walking into the room, taking it over with his forceful, magnetic presence.

Scott immediately straightened. "Mr. Baron."

Des dropped down into one of the other chairs and looked at her. "Morning, Kit."

She nodded stiffly, losing her train of thought. "I didn't expect you."

"I just thought I'd drop by." He turned to Scott. "I don't think we've met. I'm Des Baron."

"Yes, sir. I know who you are. I'm Scott McKee."

"Scott sometimes hung out with Cody," she inserted by way of explanation.

"Good, then don't let me interrupt. Go on with what you were doing and I'll just listen."

Continuing with what she had been doing was easier said than done. With Des in the room, it was hard to remember there was anybody else there. Des had a personality that was difficult to ignore, and she didn't think she felt that way just because she was inexplicably drawn to him. A glance at Scott told her that Des was having the same effect on him. No matter how one regarded Des, he was a force. In some ways he could be like a Texas tornado, knocking down everything that stood in his way.

With one more look at Des, she returned her attention to Scott. "Did you see Cody night before last or yesterday morning?"

The younger man shifted in his chair, obviously miserable at being in the spotlight. "There was a late night pickup game of poker. I saw him then."

She inched forward in her chair. "You mean *after* he and I came back?"

His gaze shifted to his knee. "Cody did mention something about being out with you."

She just bet he had. He had probably been bragging. *Damn it.* She couldn't forgive herself for having such lousy judgment.

"Was he one of the players?" Des asked quietly.

"Yeah."

"Were you?"

"I dropped out when he came in."

"Did you stay, though?"

"For a while, then I left."

"Did anyone lose big after Cody came in?"

"Not that I can remember. The stakes weren't that high, not like right after payday."

She reached for her pen. "Give me the names of everyone who was there."

Scott hesitated momentarily, as if he was considering whether or not he was about to betray someone. Thankfully he apparently decided he wasn't and reeled off the names of five players.

"Well, there was Cody, of course. Then Mike Stillwell, Red Tinsdall, Scooter Garner, Burt Salatore and Johnny Don Galvez."

She wrote the names down. "Is there anything else you'd like to tell me?"

Scott shook his head.

"Then thanks. I appreciate it."

Scott surged to his feet. "That's all?"

She nodded. "That's it. You can get back to work now."

He couldn't get out the door fast enough. At any other time Kit would have laughed. Instead she turned to her computer and quickly input the names of the men he had given her. Then she sat back and waited while the files printed out.

"I meant to ask you last night," Des said. "Are your fingerprints on file anywhere?"

She looked over at him. "No."

He nodded. "Fingerprints aren't really what the sheriff is after, anyway. He knows that getting your fingerprints isn't going to do him a lot of good, so he's using them as an excuse."

"What for?"

"I've made a couple more phone calls about the man, and it seems he's big on intimidation. What he really wants is to get you into his office, where you'll be on his turf. Then he'll have you go over and over the story, hoping that if you tell it enough times, and he asks the same questions in different ways, you'll eventually trip yourself up and reveal that you killed Cody."

"Then he's in for a disappointment."

He smiled, and it was one of the most brilliant smiles she had ever seen him give. She felt as if she had just been struck by lightning. How on earth was she supposed to ignore a smile like that?

"So what's your plan? What are you going to do first?" he asked.

"I'm going to find these five men and talk to them."

"Then let's go."

"That's not—"

He raised his hand. "I really want to come with

you. As your counsel, I'll be helping you to make the case that you're innocent.''

So his reason for wanting to come with her wasn't personal. She should learn from him. She turned back to the computer and punched in more commands.

''What are you doing now?''

''I'm accessing my managers' reports that tell which employee works under them, when and where each employee worked on a given day, and what they accomplished.''

He chuckled. ''If there's one certainty on a ranch, it's that conditions can change at any given moment, sending the ranch hands off in an entirely different direction for an entirely different task.''

She nodded, taking in the deep, warm sound of his laugh. ''I get the reports at the end of each week. I haven't yet received this week's reports, but last week's will give us a place to start.''

Us. She had said *us*. She desperately needed to erect a formidable barrier against him, but unfortunately, one chuckle, one smile, one twinkle in his eyes, and she was wondering what it would be like to kiss him again. She quietly sighed. After this whole mess was over, and he left, she would definitely put him out of her mind.

They found Bill Ridley, one of her managers, fairly easily. He was at one of the big hay barns, supervising several men who were unloading a flatbed of hay.

Bill had worked on the ranch ever since she could remember. According to his file, he was fifty-three years old. His dark hair already held slivers of silver, and he had a belly that hung over his handtooled belt. To her relief, he seemed genuinely delighted to see her. Obviously he wasn't one of the ones who thought she could have killed Cody.

"Kit, Des, it's great to see you."

Des shook his hand. "Good to see you, too. It's been a while."

"Sure has." Bill's gaze flitted between them. "What are you two doing out this way?"

Kit spoke up. "I need some information on Cody Inman."

Bill's grin faded. "Damn shame about his murder. I almost couldn't believe it. Fistfights are a common enough occurrence. Sometimes a man can get beat half to death before the fight is broken up, but I don't think we've ever had a murder on the Double B."

She nodded. "I've sure never heard of a murder, though who knows what happened in the early days."

"You're right about that. It was pretty rough-and-tumble back then."

"I can well imagine." She handed him her hand-written list of names. "Listen, my records indicate these men have been working under you. I need to find out what shift they're working and where they are."

He glanced at the list. "Any reason I should know?"

"No. It's just that they were all at a poker game two nights ago with Cody, and I just thought it might be good to talk to them. Can you help me?"

"Sure thing. Got the assignments in my pickup over there." He quickly walked to his truck, pulled out a clipboard, then returned. "Okay, well, let's see. Burt and Red are up on NW Section 258, checking out the herd for me. They'll be there for a few days. As for Mike, he left at first light for Oklahoma and his sister's funeral." He flipped to another sheet; then, using his finger, he scanned it. "Oh, right. I sent Scooter and Johnny Don up to Oklahoma City to pick up a special order. I expect 'em back tomorrow." He looked at her. "Is that any help?"

"It's a great help. Thanks. I just want to touch base with these men as quickly as I can and see what they can remember. Now that I know where they are, I can arrange my schedule accordingly."

"Good idea. Be sure and let me know if you need anything else."

"I will."

His good humor returned. "Hey, Des, how long you home for this time?"

"Indefinitely."

"You're *kidding*."

"No."

"Hey, that's great news."

Kit started, sharing Bill's surprise and then some. Des was never home for long; he usually stayed only a few days. But now he was staying *indefinitely*?

If Des noticed her surprise, he didn't show it. "Yeah, I've decided not to take on any more cases, at least for a while. I'm going to do a little consulting from here. The computer age has provided us with instant communication, and I've decided to give it a try.''

''Well, it'll be good to have you home.''

Des smiled. ''I agree. I miss the Double B when I stay away too long.''

''Before we start out to find them, I need to stop by my office and pick up the men's files.'' Kit was a bit amazed at herself for forgetting something so basic. Agitated, nervous, she finger-combed her hair away from her face. ''I can't believe I went off without them in the first place.''

''You've had a lot on your mind,'' Des murmured, turning his truck toward her house.

''Yeah, I guess so.'' What an understatement, she reflected. ''So when were you going to tell me about your decision to start working from the ranch? Or did you plan to just let me figure it out gradually when you didn't leave?''

''I would have told you at the appropriate time. It's just that since Cody's death, we've had…other things to talk about.''

Another understatement. ''Yes, we certainly have.''

Something in her voice must have drawn his attention. He looked over at her. ''It's getting to you, isn't it?''

''Of course it is. I don't see how it could be otherwise. It's not every day I'm suspected of murder, you know.''

"Would it help if I promised you that you've got nothing to worry about?"

A promise was an intangible thing, but instinctively she knew that a man like Des wouldn't make one lightly. The fact that he had meant he felt he could back it up. The thought made her feel good, which wasn't good at all. She was putting her trust in someone other than herself, something that over the years she had schooled herself not to do.

She deliberately pushed the thought aside and returned to his astounding decision. "Sure," she said casually, then changed the subject. "So when did you make the decision to stay home?"

"It's something I've been thinking about for a while."

"But it's such a radical decision. Have you considered the very real possibility that you may miss the excitement of trial law?"

"Sure, but I've had that excitement. After a while, it gets old."

"So does everything."

"Not everything. For instance, you can't tell me that you ever find life on the Double B old."

A grin broke out on her face before she could censor it. "No chance. Every day is different."

He smiled. "Exactly. And I love the ranch, just like you do. I wasn't born here, but my roots are here. I don't feel truly at home any other place."

If she had ever given the matter a moment's thought, she might have realized that he would feel that way. Still…what was it going to mean to her to have him living on the ranch all the time?

For one thing, avoiding him was going to be much more difficult, maybe impossible. And there was something else bothering her. She had always considered the ranch *her* domain and hers alone. Thankfully her sisters' interests had always lain elsewhere. "You need to know that *I* run the Double B, and that I definitely don't need anyone else's help."

He chuckled. "That's such a *Kit* thing to say."

"Are you saying I'm predictable?"

He laughed. "*Never.* In fact, I'd be a complete fool to say that."

She shook her head. "You could never be a fool." She had never thought she could be one, either, but because of last night, she had changed her mind.

"Thank you. And just to ease your mind, let me state for the record that I have no plans to so much as stick a finger into the running of the ranch. I think I said it before. You're doing an excellent job."

"But since you now own fifty percent of Baron International, you are legally entitled."

"I know."

"And you just told me you loved the ranch."

"I do. But I wouldn't like to run it. All the details would keep me from enjoying it."

"The details are fun."

Humor glinted in his eyes. "Now you sound as if you're trying to talk me into helping you run it."

Lord help her, he was right, and it was just another

sign of how mixed up she was. "Okay, so then what *are* you going to do here?"

"Basically, give myself the luxury of time."

"I still don't understand."

"I'm going to enjoy being home, Kit." He pulled the truck to a stop in front of her house. "Looks like we've got company."

Her next question to him died in her throat. The sheriff's car was parked alongside a van with *The Courier* emblazoned on its side. It was the name of a local newspaper. "What's going on?"

"I'm not sure, but let's go find out. Just remember to be careful of what you say, and when in doubt, let me do the talking."

She almost smiled. "I think we've been over that ground before."

"Who won?"

She chuckled. "You did, but there'll be no argument over this. I'll handle it."

Five

"Hello, Sheriff Moreno," Kit said in greeting. "Are you here to conduct more forensics testing?"

The sheriff glanced at Des, then back at her. "I have someone handling that as we speak, and we're also still searching for the murder weapon."

"Good. I sincerely hope you'll be able to find something that will help you."

"Oh, I'm positive I will."

His tone registered as sarcastic, but she decided not to rise to the bait. She gestured to her house. "So why are you here and not down at the barn?"

"Ordinarily I would be, but in your case, I decided it would be best to drive out and escort you into town for your fingerprinting."

He had just insulted her. Beside her, she felt Des stiffen. "I already told you that I would come in sometime today."

He shrugged. "There was always the possibility that you might forget. I thought I'd better make sure you didn't."

"You're way out of line, Moreno." Des spoke quietly, but a vein beat prominently at his temple.

The sheriff cut his gaze to him. "I disagree."

"Then you're wrong."

"What I *am*, Mr. Baron, is *thorough*."

The smile that touched Des's mouth held no humor. "Actually, what you *are* is a whole other conversation best saved for another day. For now, I will just tell you that Ms. Baron is not going anywhere with you at this time unless you are prepared to arrest her."

"I seriously doubt if that's really what you want me to do." Something close to a smirk formed on the sheriff's face.

"You know damned well you can't arrest her. You don't have enough evidence."

"That's debatable."

"Then we'll debate it in court."

Sheriff Moreno's chin came up. "Later, perhaps. But for now, let's just say that I'm extending a *courtesy* to Ms. Baron."

"Call it what you will, but for now, leave this property. Ms. Baron will drive into town in a timely manner."

"Which could mean anything at all."

Up to that point, Kit had been fairly neutral on the sheriff's behavior, but now she realized she actively disliked him. What was more, Des was very close to losing his fabled composure. She put a staying hand on his arm. "Let me speak for myself."

"Excellent idea, and just why I'm here," a smooth female voice said.

Kit looked around at the woman who had been standing off to one side. She had almost forgotten there was somebody else there, but now she remembered the newspaper van.

"Hello, Ms. Baron. I'm Ada de la Garza." The petite woman had her dark hair swept up into a tight French twist and wore a camera-flattering red wool suit, though there were no cameras in site.

Kit eyed the business card the woman presented to her. "A reporter."

"That's right. And I plan to do a story on everything that has been going on out here."

"You mean the murder?"

Ms. de la Garza smiled broadly and, with a flourish, produced a notebook and pen. "Exactly. Hello, Mr. Baron. It's so nice to meet you." Her gaze was openly flirtatious. "I'm sorry, though, for the circumstances. Perhaps when this whole unfortunate mess is over we can meet again."

With hidden amusement Kit looked at Des expectantly. He had cut his teeth on women like Ada and knew just how to handle her.

He smiled charmingly. "I'm afraid my schedule is always packed, and that's just the way I like it."

He had left Ms. de la Garza with no place to go, yet he hadn't been cruel. Kit not only applauded his method, she realized she would have been upset if he had shown even a small amount of interest in the woman.

"I see." Ms. de la Garza appeared slightly dented yet nevertheless determined. She returned her attention to Kit. "Ms. Baron, our readers deserve to know every detail of the circumstances surrounding the murder of Cody Inman. For instance, I understand the two of you were seen dancing at a bar the night before the murder. Was the affair between you serious?"

"No—"

"And how long had that affair been going on?"

"We weren't having an affair. That was the first—"

"Oh, you were at the *start* of the affair." As the woman made notes, she fired another quick question at Kit. "Tell me, Ms. Baron, what was it about Cody Inman that got past that famous princess-of-all-you-survey attitude of yours and suddenly made all your other men fade into the background?"

Kit didn't know which outrageous remark to respond to first. "What *other* men?"

The red lipstick on Ada de la Garza's wide mouth gleamed as she smiled knowingly. "Oh, please. Now's not the time to play coy. Obviously the man had something that attracted your attention. For instance, he must have been good-looking, right? Perhaps with that cowboy sort of machismo that most of the men out here seem to have."

"I don't know what you're talking about," Kit said flatly.

"Oh, come on. You know exactly what I'm talking about. After all, you're a woman who's obviously *very* aware of men. You work day in and day out surrounded by them. What could be more glorious for a woman like you? The temptations must be enormous, and you're certainly no angel."

Kit was horrified at the woman's perception of her. Where on earth had it come from? She glanced at the sheriff, and something about his smug expression told her that he had tipped off the reporter. If de la Garza wrote the story using the prejudicial things she had said to her so far, it would play right into what the sheriff wanted.

She looked back at the woman. "Why are you saying those things? You and I have never even met."

"But I've seen you around. Everyone has. You have a way of making sure you're noticed."

"I beg your pardon?"

Des firmly clasped Kit's arm. "Ms. de la Garza, if you want an interview, then call for an appointment." He tugged Kit toward the house and fell into step beside her.

The reporter followed them. "How about an interview right now, Kit? I'm here. You're here. And there's no time like the present."

Kit didn't know which she hated more—the woman's familiar use of her name, or the idea of her personal life becoming public property to be talked about over the breakfast tables of people she had never even met. "I don't think so."

"Come on, Kit. You know I'm going to write the story with or without your help."

The woman was rude and abrasive. And she was also blatantly unsympathetic to her. One reason could be that she had the look of a woman who saw all other women as competition. But the better explanation would be that trashy stories with juicy details were always top sellers. Still, the woman had given her a glimpse of how other people must see her, and her confidence was shaken.

"Kit, did you hear what I said? Call me."

"Call for an appointment," Des repeated to the reporter, opening the front door.

"It won't be an accurate story unless Kit gives me her side."

"Then don't write it." Without another word, Des ushered Kit into the house.

With a barely muffled groan, she headed straight for the couch in the living room, sank down onto it and buried her face in her hands.

Des sat down beside her and hung a loose arm around her shoulder. "Don't let that woman get to you. She's simply not worth it."

"Something about her scares me, Des."

"That's understandable. She's a predator, and you're sensing it, that's all."

Kit scrubbed her face with her hands. "A predator disguised in a smart red suit with the ear of the public and using our constitution's First Amendment as a weapon. That makes her a *powerful* predator."

"Ignore her."

"I'd love to, but I'm not sure she's going to let me. And what am I going to say to her when she comes after me again? That I refuse to answer on the grounds that it might incriminate me? Good grief, just saying those words makes me sound guilty."

"As long as this case is open, you can't be faulted for trying to protect yourself. And saying that is well within your right."

She looked over at him. "You're talking like a lawyer."

He smiled softly. "We've agreed that I'm *your* lawyer, remember? And even if we hadn't, speaking like a lawyer is a hard habit to break, particularly when it involves someone I care about."

He had just said he cared about her. It was an extraordinary statement, but most likely made to reassure her that she would come out on the other end of this nightmare whole and well. She prayed he was right, but she wasn't reassured.

"You know," she said slowly, "I had no idea so many people thought so badly of me."

"You heard that from *one* person, Kit. *One.* Moreover, she's a person who's out to get something from you. She wants the fame she thinks she'll get if she exploits you." His tone turned disgusted. "She and the sheriff have that in common."

The fact that he was right didn't lessen the impact

the reporter's words had had on her. If anything, it meant the woman would do her worst.

He pulled her closer to him. "Kit, since you were old enough to be aware of your circumstances and the people around you, you've known that you had to be cautious of everyone in case it was just your name and fortune they were attracted to."

She gave a hollow laugh. "And most of the time it was exactly those two things they were attracted by."

"I'm sure there were many who fell into that category. I had more than my share of that type trying to hang around me, too. But along the way you've managed to make many true friends. I know that for a fact. Plus, you have your sisters and—"

She shook her head. "We're not close."

"That's not their fault. There's nothing they'd like better than to be close to you. And I know without a doubt that they'd be here for you on a moment's notice if they knew you were in trouble."

Her eyes widened in dread. "You won't tell them, will you?"

"I'd like to. I think you could use their support."

"Des, no!"

"Okay. If you don't want me to contact them, I won't."

"Please don't. And don't let it slip to their husbands, either. I know you talk to them." She couldn't think of anything worse than having her sisters hovering around her, feeling sorry for her.

"Fine. But have you considered that when de la

Garza's first article hits the paper, it will more than likely be picked up around the state, perhaps even the nation? Your sisters are bound to hear of it sooner or later.''

''I'll deal with that when and if it happens.'' Lately she seemed to be putting off facing quite a bit. She relaxed her body against his and pressed her face against his chest. She didn't fully realize what she had done until she inhaled her first breath of him—spice, leather, sensuality. All in all, he was a man she was getting much too close to.

Another time the idea would have alarmed her so much that she would have pulled away. But right at that moment she felt a bottomless need to be comforted, and his warmth and strength were doing just that.

So she stayed right where she was. He didn't say anything more, and she didn't, either. And while he held her, time and her worries were suspended.

Kit dialed her sister Tess's number, then sat back and waited. She didn't know when she had decided to call her sisters. She just knew that one minute she was telling Des not to contact them and the next *she* was doing it. At the moment Tess was in Austin, where her husband, Nick Trejo, was a professor of archaeology at the University of Texas.

''Tess, this is Kit.''

''Well, *hi*. This is a surprise.''

She didn't doubt it. She could count on the fingers

of one hand the times she had called either of her sisters lately.

"A *pleasant* one though," Tess hastened to add. "How are you?"

"I'm okay." She had tried to think of a way to ease into the news, but she hadn't been able to, so she simply told her. "Listen, there's something you should know. Something has happened here. I'm afraid one of the ranch hands has been murdered."

"Oh, Kit, how awful. Did I know him?"

"No. He had been with us less than a year."

"Who did it?"

"No one knows at this point, but for whatever reason, the sheriff thinks I did—or at least he's trying to prove I did."

"You've got to be kidding."

"Believe me, I wish I was."

"But why *you?*"

Kit proceeded to lay out everything for her sister, telling her exactly what had happened and, for good measure, including the part about Ada de la Garza. She left out only those things that had occurred between Des and her that might be construed as remotely personal. How could she give her those details? She hadn't yet come to terms with them herself.

"Thank goodness Des was home," Tess said. "I know he's being a big help."

Kit's mind wandered to the kiss they had shared. It had been helpful only in that it had taken her mind off the murder. But it had also left her terribly confused.

"Kit?"

"Oh, I'm sorry. Yes, he is."

"Okay, I've got one of the jets here at the airport. I'll be there by this evening."

"No, *don't*. There's honestly no need. Des and I have everything under control." She nearly stumbled over the words. "As a matter of fact, I'm waiting for him now. We're about to go out and interview a couple of the men who were playing poker with Cody the night before he was murdered."

"Are you sure? Because I'd really like to help. I mean, if nothing else, I could field calls, hold your hand…whatever is needed."

"No, I'm positive. I just wanted to let you know what was going on here. I wanted you to be prepared in case you were told about it before it's resolved."

"I'm glad you did. Have you told Jill yet?"

"I plan to call her as soon as I hang up with you."

"Kit, promise me you'll call if you need any backup or anything else. And for heaven's sakes, please keep me up-to-date on what's going on. I'll be worrying like crazy."

"Don't. Honestly, Tess, everything is going to be fine."

"You're sure you've got everything under control?"

She almost laughed in her sister's ear. "I'm positive. Bye for now."

Hanging up, she said a short prayer that she was ̄ht. Then she picked up the phone again and dialed

* * *

Later that afternoon, as Des guided his truck over the bumpy trail, Kit sat in the corner watching the snow whirl around them. They were heading for the Double B's NW Section 258 to interview Red Tinsdall and Burt Salatore, because according to manager Bill Ridley, that was the section where he had assigned them.

"I'm glad you called your sisters."

"I guess I am, too, although what I was afraid of happened. They both wanted to fly in. I had a horrible time trying to talk Jill out of it. Tess was a little easier to convince."

"Jill's pregnant. She could be feeling especially protective."

"Maybe." For a moment she allowed herself to wonder what it would be like to be pregnant with the baby of the man she loved. A yearning stirred near her heart.

"I still think we should have held off on this trip until morning," Des said, interrupting her musings. "That sky is getting lower by the minute."

"I know."

When he had come to pick her up, he had warned her that the weather looked as if it were going to turn bad and had suggested that they put off the trip until tomorrow. But the weather reports she had received that morning hadn't indicated a storm, and she hadn't been willing to wait.

"I also told the sheriff I'd come in to see him today. But I really want to talk to Red and Burt before

I do. I'm hoping they'll know something that will be helpful.'' She paused. "The sheriff will have to wait for his fingerprints a little longer.''

"Good.''

She glanced at him. "You didn't have to come.''

"Yes,'' he said quietly. "I did. And we can still turn back. Just say the word.''

"I want to keep going. The sooner we can find out who really killed Cody, the better off I'll be.'' *We.* Somehow she had become very familiar with using the plural when it came to the two of them. Amazing. She gazed out the window. "Besides, this truck can handle a little snow.''

"Yeah, it can. A *little*. But it's steadily getting worse.''

She bit back a sharp retort. He was only trying to help her, she reminded herself. "It'll be okay. We're almost there.''

In fact, it was some time later before they pulled up to the line cabin, and the sun was already beginning to set. And Des had been right in his weather prediction. The snow had gotten worse.

"I can't see any sign of life.''

She followed his gaze. There were no footprints in the snow anywhere, and there was no smoke coming out of the chimney. She climbed out of the truck. "The guys must still be out on the range, but I'm sure they'll be back soon.''

"Then why don't you go in?'' he said, already heading for the back of the cabin. "I'll bring in some wood.''

"You don't want any help?" she called after him.
"Nope."

With a mental shrug, she went inside. An oil lamp hung just inside the door, and a tin of matches waited on a shelf. She lit the lamp, then held it up and gazed around, wondering if she had been in this cabin before. She had been in many of the others, and they were all pretty much the same—practical, but with an eye toward comfort.

Bunk beds lined the back wall. Several more stuck out from another wall. A potbellied stove took the place of honor in the center. There was also a kitchenette and a bathroom. It was cozy, but also very cold.

The door blew open and snow swirled. Des stamped his feet free of snow and came in. "Here we go. This place will be warm in no time." He kicked the door shut behind him, then knelt in front of the stove and began feeding it wood. "Are you hungry?"

"I don't know. To tell the truth, food has been the last thing on my mind today." She positioned the lamp on the table.

"Well, think about it now. Without even looking in the cabinets, I can tell you there'll be a variety of soups, beans and no telling what else. Ranch hands have hearty appetites." He nodded toward the kitchen. "Do you see a cooler anywhere? Sometimes a truck will come out with ice and fresh food. We might luck out."

"I'll check," she said, basically to give herself

something to do. She was too keyed up to do nothing but sit around and wait.

"And I'll go out and bring some more wood in. We may be here a while."

"I'll light a few more lamps."

She settled on thickening up several cans of soup by adding beans and then ended their ad-libbed dinner with a freshly made pot of coffee. While it was perking, Des washed their few dishes and she put them away. But the tasks were soon done, and she couldn't think of any more work to keep her busy.

"Do you still want to wait?" he asked.

Reluctant to give up at this point and go home without seeing the men, she nodded. "I'm sure they're on the way back here."

"Okay, fine." He pulled up a chair to the potbellied stove and gestured for her to sit.

She shook her head. "Go ahead." She sank down on one of the bunks.

He took the chair. "This is nice." Without a trace of self-consciousness, he leaned back and stretched his long legs out to the warmth. "I've spent a lot of evenings in different cabins on different parts of the ranch doing nothing much more than this. Sometimes I'd play dominoes or maybe read." He looked over at her. "Most kids had television to keep them entertained. I had this ranch and the people on it."

She wished she felt as content as he looked, but eating hadn't calmed her a bit, and her nerves were still stretched to the breaking point. Unfortunately, though, it wasn't because of anything involving the

murder, but rather because of Des and the way just
looking at him made her think of things that could,
would, never be. "You obviously have a lot of good
memories from growing up here."

"You bet."

She envied that. The ranch and her work gave her
an incredible amount of satisfaction, but sometimes,
when she wasn't careful, her bad memories would
eclipse the good. "Tell me some of them."

He looked over at her. "Really?"

"Yeah. It'll be fun for me to hear a totally different
viewpoint than mine of growing up here." She also
needed something to distract her from the fact that
the two of them were alone in an isolated cabin during
a snowstorm.

"Okay, then. As it happens, I have several memories of you, and they happened in winter."

"Me?"

"That's right. Do you want to hear them?"

"Sure." The news that in the past she had managed
to capture Des's attention in some way, even once,
astounded her.

"Okay, well, let's see… Once I was driving along
and happened to see you." He slowly grinned.
"There you were, maybe twelve, thirteen years old,
skating all alone on that frozen pond out behind Barn
Twenty-six."

She blinked, trying to remember what occasion he
could be talking about, but the softness on his face
kept distracting her.

"You were wearing an old pair of jeans and a

faded green cable-knit sweater. And you had your hair pulled back into a ponytail.'' He chuckled. ''But as cute as that ponytail was, it couldn't begin to subdue that hair of yours.''

All at once she was intensely aware of how she looked. Jeans and a sweater was her normal uniform during the winter, and it was what she was wearing now. She reached up to push an unruly lock of hair off her face.

''Don't.'' The command was barely above a whisper, but she heard it and went still.

''Your hair is glorious. It always has been, and it always will be.''

The Des sitting across from her was one she didn't know how to cope with. Ignoring him was out of the question. And as for responding... Well, she had done that, and it had led her to a place she didn't trust herself to go again. ''Thank you,'' she murmured, wildly searching for some safe middle ground. Surely there had to be some.

He stared at her for several moments, his thoughts hidden, as they so often were. But there were his words....

Six

"**Y**our movements were utterly graceful as you skated," Des said, continuing. "And heaven above, but you were beautiful—all color and motion etched against a huge, slate gray sky. For the first time in my life, but not the last, I wished I was a painter so that I could capture you like that. But frankly, I can't think of an artist who could be that good. You were all about beauty and energy that day, just like you were today." He paused. "Just like you are now."

He left her breathless, and she honestly didn't have a clue how to respond. Or even how to help herself.

"And then there was another time, when you were about fifteen or sixteen. A young steer had wandered out onto one of the frozen ponds and onto a section of thin ice. He'd fallen in, of course, and was well on his way to drowning. Except you had found him and were doing your level best to save him.''

''What was I doing?''

''Somehow you'd managed to get a rope around his neck and had the other end tied off on the saddle horn. Your horse was backing up, doing his best to pull, but that wasn't good enough for you. You were down on the ice, tugging on that rope with all your might.''

There was no reason why she would have remembered that one incident, she reflected. Living and working on the ranch over the years had required her to do many things, and when she could, she had always tried to steal time away just for herself. Yet Des had remembered it.

''It looked to me as if you were about to go into the ice with the damn cow, so I slammed on the brakes and got out, intending to race over to help you. But you were fast. Before I had even gone a foot, you had wrestled that cow and yourself onto firm ground.'' He chuckled again. ''I'll never forget the look of complete and absolute determination on your face as you fought to save that animal. And I'll never forget the laugh you gave when he was safe.''

''You heard me?''

He rose and moved over to the bunk where she was. The mattress gave way as he came down beside her. ''If I had ever heard you laugh before, I couldn't remember it.'' He lifted his hand and touched her hair. "And the laugh itself—there was an elation in it that was…"

His nearness shouldn't affect her so much, but it did. It seemed it always had. She could feel the air backing up in her lungs. And she shouldn't care what he was about to say next, but she did. Desperately. "Was what?"

"Memorable."

"I—I don't remember you ever being around when I was doing anything like that."

"No, you wouldn't. Both times you were completely absorbed in what you were doing. I occasionally still see that same look of absorption and determination on your face today."

"But why didn't you let me know you were there?"

He shrugged. "I guess once I knew you were safe I got caught up in watching you. Plus, now that I think about it, I'm glad I didn't."

He was bewildering her, baffling her. "Why?"

"Because back then you had this tendency of turning shy whenever I was around. It would have spoiled the moment."

He was right. If she had known he was anywhere nearby, she would have turned extremely shy. And if she had known he was *watching* her, she most likely would have become paralyzed.

"But believe me when I say to you that both times you were absolutely wonderful." His hand slipped behind her neck, and he drew her toward him. "You were wonderful then, and you are wonderful now."

She barely managed to stifle a groan. He wasn't giving her a chance. "I can't believe that."

"I know you don't. It's part of why I find you charming."

"Des, I think—"

He pressed two fingers to her lips. "In this case, I can almost read your mind."

"I hope that's not true."

He smiled. "Okay, maybe I can only read part of your mind. The part that says things nearly got out of hand between us last night, and that now, suddenly, things are different than they were the day before."

He had guessed part of it. She cleared her throat. "To be accurate, there was nothing between us last night."

"Who are you trying to kid? I was there, remember? And there was definitely something. Admit it."

A warmth began to crawl through her veins. "Okay, there was something. There was…history."

"And what's so wrong about that? History's good. It gives two people something to build on."

Frantically she looked around, trying to find something to distract both of them. "You know, I—I'm sure the guys will be back any minute."

His mouth began to drop toward hers. "On the other hand, they could have decided to drive back to the homestead."

His breath caressed her lips. "I suppose."

"Or they could even have decided to camp out so they can be close to the herd."

"Uh-huh."

His mouth settled firmly on hers, and the heat was instant. It rushed to every part of her body. Like a wildfire, it consumed everything in its path.

It shouldn't be this easy, she thought vaguely. Just because he wanted to kiss her, that didn't mean she had to kiss him back. But of their own volition her lips opened beneath his, and, accepting the unspoken invitation, his tongue darted deep into her mouth. Welcoming the invasion, she twined her tongue around his, and whatever small amount of resistance that was remaining in her began to drain away.

Something in her stomach clenched. Something near her heart turned over. Fire filled her every pore. And when his arms slipped around her and he pulled her to him, she willingly went. Everything about this moment felt so good, so right.

What was the use? She couldn't fight her feelings for Des anymore. Why even try, when everything in her was shouting that exquisite passion was hers for the asking? She wanted it, she needed it, and so she allowed herself to take it.

She flattened her palm against his chest and felt the heavy pounding of his heart. Elation soared through her. He wanted her. The knowledge gave her a new confidence.

He skinned her sweater over her head. Her bra had covered very little of her, and soon it covered nothing. With a single flick of his fingers, the beige lace undergarment fell away, and in the next instant his hand was covering her breast.

In a distant part of her mind she heard a moan. It

took her a moment before she realized the sound was her own voice. It was a measure of how much he was affecting her that she hadn't recognized it more quickly.

"Are you all right?" Des muttered, kissing his way down her neck to her breast, leaving a wide trail of fire.

She nodded, unsure of her ability to speak.

His thumb found her nipple and flicked it back and forth. She hadn't know it could be the center of so much pleasure, but wondrous sensations radiated outward until there was no part of her left unaffected. Even her fingertips were singed.

Another moan escaped her, then another, as his mouth closed over the rigid tip and began to suck. Her fingers slid through his hair and pressed his head harder against her.

Over the years she had awakened with the memory of the dreams she had had in the night. They had been filled with a boy, a man, but she had never been able to tell who he was. Now she knew her dreams had been of Des. He was here, kissing her and touching her and driving her out of her mind. Her dreams had come to life.

"I want you."

Had she said it or had he?

"I want you," he said again.

A statement or a warning? Either way, it didn't matter. His voice was deeper and rougher than she had ever heard it, another sign that she was affecting him every bit as much as he was affecting her.

''Say you want me, too.'' His words came out on a hot breath that fanned over her breast.

''I want you.''

With a groan, he lifted his head and returned to her lips. Draining, possessive kisses followed. Deep, endless kisses.

He shifted so that more of his body was against her, and even through the layers of their clothes, she could feel how hard he was, and his body heat was positively scorching her.

She was almost overwhelmed. She had spent years fighting against her feelings for him, but no more. She wanted him inside her now, yet at the same time she knew she wanted this lovemaking to last forever. She wanted everything, and she was going to do her best to get it.

Gently she pushed against him until she had some maneuvering room. She wasn't sure what to say to him, but she knew what to do.

Her trembling hand went to the button of his jeans and undid it, then the zipper. With equally trembling hands, he began to help. Time slowed. Their surroundings receded; their circumstances were forgotten. Jeans, boots, sweaters, panties, briefs—they all came off. Then heated skin rubbed against heated skin. His hardened sex throbbed against her tummy. Her swollen breasts pressed against his chest, her nipples nestled into the curling dark hair. It was almost too much, yet deep down she knew it wasn't enough.

She was so glad she hadn't known how astonishing making love to him was going to be, she thought hazily. Because if she had, she never would have been able to stay away from him for so long.

He had said that he wished he could paint her on that long ago day. If she could somehow paint him, the canvas would portray strength and intensity. If she could paint what she was feeling now, it would be a canvas of bright, vivid colors swirled in a fury of passion.

She pulled him down on top of her, gladly accepting his weight. He positioned himself between her legs, then pulled back his hips and entered her with one smooth stroke. She gasped, and then, as if she had done it a million times before, arched up to meet his next thrust. She desperately needed him to fill her completely, to possess her absolutely.

As he moved in and out of her, she clung to him, rubbing her hands over his back and buttocks, delighting in the feel of his muscles shifting and rolling beneath the sleek, satinlike texture of his skin. She was consumed by the hunger she felt for him. Desire burned so hotly in her, she felt sure she would burst into flames at any moment.

It was as she had known all along— Des was a dangerous man to her.

She clutched at him, her fingers digging into his shoulders. "Des."

Des heard her whisper his name, heard the need and raw desire in her tone, and it was all the encouragement he needed. He pulled back his hips and drove as deeply as he could possibly manage into her tight velvet depths. Time and again he repeated the action, pounding into her until sweat sheened his body and his heart threatened to beat out of his chest. Caught up in the feral, heated rhythm, he was helpless to do anything else. Someone would have had to put a bullet in his head to stop him.

It was madness; it was ecstasy. He called her name over and over. Then heaven shuddered through him, followed by a thunderous, savage pleasure, and the world spun away, leaving only the two of them, clinging tightly to one another.

She loved Des.
Kit closed her eyes as the truth hit her with the force of a Texas tornado, stirring up a thousand thoughts and fears.

What was she going to do?

It was a beautiful, clear, cold day. The sun glinted off the pristine layer of snow that had fallen during the night, but the day's beauty barely registered with her. Des filled her thoughts. And his silence pounded against her ears as he guided his truck along the icy track toward NW Section 158.

In fact, he had said very little since they had left the cabin, but he didn't have to speak. As he had with her, she knew what was going on with him.

Earlier, before she had come fully awake, she had felt him enter her, and when the ultimate ecstasy had come, it had been even greater than what they had shared in the night.

Even amidst the passion, she had been aware that

it was much more than sex for her. But unfortunately, with the same sure feeling, she had also known it had been nothing more than sex to Des.

Now, in the bright light of day, Des no doubt was worried.

For years he had successfully navigated the minefields she and her sisters had attempted to lay for him. Then, during one snow-filled night, his resistance had crumbled.

But it wasn't his fault. Passion had flared in circumstances guaranteed to tempt even an angel, and he had given in to it. Now, though, he must be feeling monumental regret and wondering how he was going to back out of the trap he probably felt closing around him.

Besides the fact that it would be incredibly embarrassing to watch him try to gracefully maneuver back out of her life, she loved him too much to watch him try. She had to do something to help him. Later she would try to figure out how to help herself.

"You know, last night really meant nothing," she said in an attempt to reassure him, then inwardly flinched. She had spoken without thinking through what she was going to say and had phrased it very badly.

"Is that right?"

There was a touch of sarcasm in his tone that alerted her to the fact that he wasn't in the best of moods. She couldn't blame him.

She knew that another woman might see the night they had spent together as license to start making demands on him, perhaps even to plan a future for the two of them. But he had nothing to fear from her. If nothing else, she was a realist. She understood all too well that what had happened was a one-time-only event, a night of ecstasy she would remember the rest of her life, but a night never to be repeated.

As for Des, he was a man, and men were experts at compartmentalizing their lives and forgetting things that were too inconvenient to remember.

"It's just that I don't want you to worry that I'll read more into what happened last night than was really there."

"And I'm supposed to thank you for that?" His eyes glinted with dark anger.

She bent her head and gazed down at her tightly entwined fingers. "I'm sorry, Des."

"For *what?*"

"For a lot of things. For making you feel, however unintentionally, that you should help me find out who really killed Cody. But most of all I'm sorry for not listening to you when you said the weather was going to get worse."

He gave an impatient wave of his hand. "Don't worry about it."

"But I do. I—"

"Forget it. No one can predict Texas weather with any degree of accuracy. Not even professional weathermen. What makes you think you should have done it better?"

"You knew."

"It was an informed guess."

"And one I should have made, but I was too caught up in my problems."

"It's understandable."

"Still—"

"You *don't* owe me anything, Kit, much less an apology. There they are now." He pointed toward two men, who had stopped working on the fence and were watching them approach. He pulled the truck to a stop. "Are you okay about talking to them?"

"Of course."

"Then just signal me if you need any help."

"Okay." She hesitated, hating his abruptness. The knowledge that she loved him was so new it was throwing her. But she needed to regain her balance fast. Somehow she was going to have to find a way to deal with the fact that she loved him, and she was going to have to do it alone. But his continued bad mood bothered her, so much so that she tried again to reach out to him. "Des, maybe we should talk about it."

"You mean about what happened last night?"

He had known exactly what she was talking about—proof it was on his mind too. "Yes."

He gestured curtly. "It happened. It was great. There's nothing to talk about."

For a moment, she sat perfectly still, absorbing his brusque dismissal and searching for something to say that would ease the tension between them. She failed.

Then, because there was nothing else she could do, she climbed out of the truck and went to greet the two men who had worked on the ranch ever since she could remember. "Good morning, guys."

Burt greeted them with a wave. "Mornin', Kit, Des." He was tall and as thin as the toothpick that perpetually protruded from one corner of his mouth.

"Sure is nice to see you two," Red said, a grin plastered on his weathered face. He had been named after the color of his hair, though with age it had turned the shade of sand.

"You too. Did you all decide to camp out last night?"

Burt spat tobacco toward the fence post. "It was easier than fighting our way back in the storm."

"Figured we could have gotten lost if we weren't careful," Red added.

"But were you able to stay warm okay?"

"Shoot, yeah." Red pointed toward the roll tied at the back of his saddle. "We had all the comforts of home."

Burt repositioned his hat. "Fact is, I'd rather sleep outside. Don't cotton much to being cooped up. Never have."

Des smiled. "I never expected you to say anything else. Still, it's good to hear you made it through the night without getting cold."

Kit stuck her hands in the pockets of her jeans. "I agree." She had a sudden thought. If the men had returned to the cabin last night, she and Des wouldn't have made love.

If that hadn't happened, would she ever have admitted to herself that she loved him? Or would she have continued to go blindly through life without acknowledging how she felt? And in the end, which way would have been better?

Ultimately, though, it didn't matter. From now on, her life was going to be more difficult, but the fact remained that she would be forever grateful that she had had last night with Des.

"Listen, guys, I have a couple of things I'd like to ask you. It's about Cody Inman."

Red shook his head. "Heard about what happened."

Burt spat again. "Quite a shocker to know someone who got murdered."

"Right," Red said. "First time that ever happened."

Burt made a sound of agreement. "First time."

"That's the way we feel, too," Des said.

Kit shifted, trying to bank down her impatience with the men's chatty ways. "Does either of you know of anyone who might have fought with him or even wanted him dead?"

Red whistled. "Well, now, Kit, that's quite a question."

"You see, we really didn't know him all that well," Burt added.

Kit quietly sighed. She probably should have phrased the question more tactfully, but besides the murder, she now had Des and her love for him on her mind, and being diplomatic seemed beyond her. "Let me put it this way. Does either of you know anything about him that might help us figure out who killed him?''

Both men stared at her. With Burt and Red, one needed to pass the time of day for a while before getting to the real point. But time wasn't on her side.

''Anything at all?'' Des asked.

Red shrugged.

Burt looked at Kit. ''Rumor is you had some trouble with him.''

''That's right.''

Red nodded. ''He had a reputation with the ladies, that one did.''

Des's eyes narrowed. ''What do you mean?''

''He was somethin' of what you might call— excuse me for sayin' this in front of you, Kit— a womanizer.''

''There was sure that,'' Red said. ''From all accounts he was a real piece of work with women. Must have seen the main chance with you, Kit.''

''I suppose so.'' She just wished she had realized that truth sooner. ''Do you have any details that might back that up for us?'' *Us.* There was that word again. It was going to be a hard habit to break.

Burt shook his head. ''Not really.''

''Not exactly dates and times,'' Red said. ''But I did hear there was a married woman in El Paso who was on the verge of divorcing her husband for Inman. But Inman, he wasn't exactly what you'd call the marryin' kind, so he hightailed it out of town.''

Burt grinned. ''With her husband chasin' him every step of the way.''

Kit glanced up at Des, wondering if he was thinking the same thing as she. This was the first she had heard about Cody and other women. Was it possible he had been killed over one? And, if so, who?

"I suppose it was just a matter of time before someone took a tire iron to the son of a bitch," Red added.

"Tire iron?" Des fired out the question before she could. "You think he was killed with a tire iron?"

Red suddenly appeared uncomfortable. "Well, now, I can't really say. I was just talkin', you understand."

"Sure." Kit smiled, hoping it would soothe away some of his discomfort. "Thanks for your help, guys."

Once again Burt spat. "Don't seem like we did too much."

Red's forehead grooved with concern. "Hey, you're not in any real trouble, are you, Kit?"

She hesitated. "No, of course not."

"'Cause if you want us to do somethin' about that sheriff, we'd be mighty pleased to help out."

They were a throwback to another time, she realized with affection. However bad the idea was, she was touched at their offer to help. The truth was, she was rapidly becoming convinced that being in love with Des was going to give her far more trouble than the sheriff ever could. "I appreciate that, guys. Really I do. But I'm going to be okay."

"Okay, well, good, then." Burt spat.

* * *

The trip back to the homestead seemed to take twice as long as the trip out had taken, Des reflected darkly. But it was probably just him. From the start of the trip, Kit had been excruciatingly polite to him. Damn it, she had even apologized for saying she had wanted to stay at the cabin to wait for Burt and Red.

That had turned out to be the best part of the whole trip, which made it obvious as hell what she really wanted to apologize for was the fact that they had made love. That message was so clear, she might as well have yelled it at him.

Her attitude galled him. Where in the hell did she get off thinking there was any need to apologize? *He* had been the one who had started everything by telling her about his winter memories of her. And as he had, he had looked over at her and realized how much he wanted her. It had been just that simple, just that complicated. After that, it would have been impossible to keep his hands off her. And he had no intention of apologizing for that or for anything else.

He had also been the one who had started that kiss when she had been seventeen. His hands tightened on the steering wheel as he remembered that summer evening. She had looked so beautiful, with tears darkening her vivid green eyes and pieces of hay stuck in her tumbled red hair. His aching for her had hit bone, but he'd had to slam on the brakes. She had been only seventeen—way too young, way too innocent.

But last night had been different, and he had seen no reason to stop. She was older now, more experienced, and, if possible, even more beautiful. Plus, she had been completely willing.

In his mind, two consenting adults equaled a night of passion. However, always before he had known exactly what would happen the next morning. If he didn't want to see the woman again, he would simply bid her goodbye and make sure she got home safely. If he made the decision to see her a few more times, he would send her a bouquet of flowers, then follow them up with a phone call.

But in this case he had no idea what to do. Kit got to him like no other woman ever had before. And last night had been more than just another winter memory for his mental scrapbook. Last night had been branded into his flesh.

She was so damned independent, so damned wild. For all he knew, her apology meant she was trying to politely close the door against any further personal relationship between the two of them. But if that was the case, he was somehow going to have to change her mind.

When he had come home, he had initially intended to find out why she had started to avoid him since her sisters had married. He still didn't have that answer, but now it didn't seem to matter quite as much. Things had changed. The present circumstances had given him more than enough reason to be alone with her. For the time being, he planned to use those circumstances to his advantage.

Once Inman's murder was solved and no longer hanging over her head, that reason would be taken away. By then he hoped he wouldn't have to invent other reasons to be with her. But if he had to, he definitely would. Now that he'd had her, it was going to be impossible for him to get enough, at least as long as this clawing need for her lasted.

Seven

Des stopped his truck in front of Kit's house and nodded toward the familiar van. "Looks like Ada de la Garza is here again."

"Someone must have let her into the house." Kit stared at her front door. "A dictionary could use the woman's picture to define the words *rude* and *aggressive*."

"Just remember, you're under no obligation to tell her a thing, so don't let her hound you into it."

Kit smoothed her hair back from her face and reached for the door handle. "I understand that, but it looks as if the stigma of this murder is sticking to me whether it's deserved or not, so I should at least make an attempt to tell her my side of the story. Otherwise, who knows what she'll write?"

"Don't be stupid, Kit. She just wants the opportunity to put quotes around a few of your phrases. But I'll guarantee she'll take those phrases out of context and make you look as guilty as hell."

"Stupid?" She climbed down from the truck, but Des was there before she had taken two steps toward the house.

"Is stupid the only word you heard me say? Because, if so, let me rephrase it. *Don't* talk to that woman."

"I can handle this myself, Des." She couldn't believe she was once again arguing with him about basically the same thing as before. Now *there* was something that could rightfully be construed as stupid. But she didn't want to argue with him anymore. In fact, not ever again. With their lovemaking still so fresh in her mind, she just couldn't cope with it.

"Have you forgotten what happened the last time she was here? The things she accused you of?"

"No, I haven't. And that's exactly why I need to talk to her. Maybe I can sway her toward the truth, and if I can, even just a little, it's bound to help."

"Kit—"

"We're not going to argue about this, Des. Not again. Now please get out of my way."

Ada de la Garza wore the same camera-flattering red wool suit she had worn before, and this time, there *was* a camera. She had brought a photographer with her, and the man was currently walking around the living room, holding up a light meter.

"May I call you Ada?" Kit figured she might as well, since the woman called her Kit.

Ada smiled, revealing her perfectly capped teeth. "Of course you may. Now, Kit, tell me about your relationship with Cody, and please start from the beginning."

"That's just it, Ada. You need to understand that there was no relationship."

She glanced over at Des. He was leaning against the doorjamb, his moody gaze constantly moving from her to the reporter, to the photographer, then back to her again. And whenever he looked at her, she felt heat. She rubbed the skin of her forearm as if she could banish the feeling. It didn't work.

She remembered every detail of their lovemaking, and it seemed like only minutes since they'd been together at the cabin, wrapped tightly in each other's arms. It had been as if they were the only two people left on earth.

"But, Kit, you were with him the night before his murder. People *saw* you."

"That's true, but it was just a casual thing."

Ada shook her head. "No, that can't be right. People who saw you two together said it didn't look at all casual. In fact, they said it looked downright sizzling. You can do a lot with your money, Kit, but you can't rewrite history."

"If that's what you think I'm doing, then you're wrong."

Ada's left eyebrow rose in a dramatic peak. "I'm an excellent writer, but I'm at a loss to know exactly how to report this story so that my readers will believe what you're saying.''

''How about just writing the truth?''

''Which is?''

The woman was a certified bitch and definitely had it out for her. Still, she had to continue to try to get through to her. ''All we did was dance. Cody read much more than was there into the situation.''

''Really? My goodness, if all you did was dance, it doesn't make much sense that he would do that, does it?''

''No, it doesn't.''

For the first time since they had begun to talk, the woman wrote down something on her notepad. ''Then why do you think he would do that? I mean, if you didn't lead him on—''

''And I didn't.''

''But what about what other people saw?''

''They misinterpreted what they saw.''

''Gracious me,'' Ada said, writing something else. ''If I take what you're saying as gospel, it seems everyone is wrong about what happened that night but you.''

''Look, Ada, I'm afraid we've got a case here where the only other person who could tell you what really happened is dead. And even if he were alive, he might not tell you the truth. And I don't have much to say that won't cast Cody in a bad light. It's unfortunate, but that's the way it is.''

''If you don't mind my saying, you don't seem very sorry that he's dead.''

She minded a great deal, but she also knew it wasn't going to do any good. "Once again, you're wrong."

"And once again, you're the only one who's right. How fascinating." Her pen flew over the notebook as she wrote. "I guess it has to do with being so rich."

"No—"

A light flashed as the photographer clicked off a picture.

Kit flinched, and Ada's smile broadened. If it wouldn't add fuel to the woman's story, she would throw her out of the house, notebook and all.

"If you're not going to believe what I say, then why did you even bother to come out here?"

"Why, Kit, I'm surprised you have to ask. It's not my job to believe or disbelieve you. I'm completely neutral. As a reporter, it's my job to report both sides."

She rose. "Okay, then, you have the truth of what happened. Report it."

The photographer took another picture. Before Kit could react, Des had the photographer by his elbow and was ushering him out the door.

Ada gazed after the two men, her mouth momentarily agape. "Excuse me, but I *am* correct in believing this is *your* house, am I not? That should mean that Mr. Baron doesn't have the right to throw anyone out without your say."

Kit shrugged. "Oh, I don't know. He probably has as much right as the photographer had to take my picture."

"We're here for a story, Kit. What did you expect?"

"Professionalism."

"Mr. Baron's actions were very protective. Does that mean you're having an affair with him, too?"

"That's none of your business." She suddenly realized that a night without sleep had caught up to her and she was very tired.

"Right," Ada said, standing. "But Mr. Baron manhandled my photographer, and I'm pretty sure he hurt him."

"It's entirely possible. I suggest you go see about him. Oh, and don't forget to write about what happened, either."

"Believe me, my story will be a doozy." The woman left with a beaming smile.

Kit groaned and fell back onto the sofa.

"They're gone," Des said as he returned and sat down beside her.

"I hate to say this, but no matter how objectionable they were, throwing that guy out was a mistake."

Des shrugged. "So let him sue me."

"He may just do that."

"He'll lose." His voice was both confident and deadly.

She sighed. "This is my fault."

"There you go again, taking everything on yourself."

A day ago she might have snapped his head off, but a day ago she hadn't known the glory of his lovemaking. "Cody was a real jerk, and I didn't see it. Why?"

He slid his hand beneath her hair to her neck. "Lighten up on yourself. From what Burt and Red said, the guy was a charmer."

"Which I should have been able to recognize as false." Except that she had been too busy trying to avoid Des.

"Yeah, you probably should have."

"Thanks."

"You're the one who said it. I was only agreeing."

She sighed. "I know, but the fact that you're right doesn't make it any easier to hear."

"I understand. But now that the subject is out in the open…"

"Which subject?" His hand on her skin had begun to work its magic. When it came to him, her body was incredibly compliant.

"I asked you this once before, but you never really gave me an answer. Why did you go out with him in the first place?"

She shifted, changing her position so that his hand dropped away. "As I recall, I did answer you."

"No, actually we got sidetracked."

She believed him. They could become sidetracked with the greatest of ease. "Cody was just an opportunity to go dancing."

"And that was important to you? So important you'd go with just anyone?"

"He wasn't just anyone. He had always been very pleasant. He was a good dancer and good company.

Don't make this into the mystery of the century, Des. I went with him, and we had a good time until… Well, you know what happened.''

"It just doesn't seem like something you'd do, that's all.''

"How would you know what I would or wouldn't do? You don't know me. Not really." Actually, she was wrong, she reflected ruefully. In some ways he knew her better than was good for her peace of mind. He knew just where to touch her to make her come undone, just where to kiss her to make her forget everything….

But he didn't know she loved him yet, and she had to take care that he never did.

"I'm not being critical, Kit.'' He paused. "Well, maybe indirectly I am, but I don't mean to be. It's just that when it comes to the Double B and everything concerned with it, you're very conscientious. Always have been. And the night you went into town with Cody wasn't a weekend. Both of you had to work the next day.''

"What can I say? You're right.''

"Then why?''

She exhaled a long breath. "Haven't we gone over this?''

"In part, but it still bothers me.''

"Look, I shouldn't have gone, but…'' She couldn't tell him that she had gone in a knee-jerk reaction to his arrival, so she told him another truth. "My father made it a point never to socialize with anyone who worked for him. I think he felt it would undermine his position of authority if he let his guard down even once.''

''Now that you mention it, I don't think I ever saw him at any of the ranch's social occasions that involved the hands.''

''No, you didn't. In fact, he felt all social occasions were frivolous. He only tolerated them if they involved business and he knew he could gain something by attending.''

''Now I remember my dad saying something about that. Your father had a very narrow point of view about life, Kit. He should be pitied.''

''Pitied? What a remarkable and preposterous idea.''

His hand reached out to touch her again, and his thumb grazed up and down the side of her neck. He smiled. ''Okay, so that was a stretch. But did you just hear yourself? You basically said that you went out with Cody because your father never went out with people who worked for him.''

She had to wrench her gaze from his lips. ''I may have said that. It may even have been an underlying reason. But the main reason I like to socialize with Double B people is that I *like* them.'' It was another very real truth.

''And they like and respect you. But—''

''But the bottom line is that, in this case, I was a poor judge of character.''

''No, the bottom line is that there is no simple truth.'' He paused. ''You know, I never realized just how much your father has to answer for.''

"My father's been gone a long time, Des. The truth is, I should have known better. If I'd stopped to think for even *one* minute…" She rubbed her forehead.

"It's not your fault. Something must have happened. Maybe something about work was getting you down."

Now he was defending her. "No."

"Then what?"

"Let's just forget about it. There's no point in going over and over this." She pushed herself up from the sofa and began to pace. "I went out with Cody and now he's dead. The sheriff thinks I killed him, and so do a lot of other people. And you and I haven't found anything to prove otherwise."

He reached out and pulled her down on his lap. "But we will, Kit. We will."

Suddenly his arms were around her, and she felt totally engulfed by him. "How can you be so sure?"

"I just am."

She gave a nervous half-laugh. "Oh, a jury is going to buy that one for sure."

Another smile tugged at his lips. "I can be very convincing when I set out to be."

He was preaching to the choir. She was already a believer. "But if even one of them doesn't agree—"

"It's not going to happen. As a matter of fact, there's not even going to be a trial."

"But that first night you said—"

"I was just trying to anticipate what might happen. I was wrong."

"The great Des Baron wrong? That's hard for me to believe."

"It happens very seldom."

He was trying to make her laugh, and she appreciated his efforts, but she was frightened, and she didn't know how to handle the fear. Even more, she was in love and, because of it, off balance. It made thinking hard.

"Maybe my father was right in his belief that it was wrong to socialize with the people who work for you."

"He was wrong and you know it." His hand slid up to the side of her face and turned her so that she had no choice but to look at him. "I want to tell you something, and I want you to believe what I'm saying. In every way I can think of, you're far more successful than your father ever thought of being. Unfortunately, you're also incredibly vulnerable."

His words stunned her, and she didn't know how to reply.

"Looking back, I should have tried to get closer to you when you were growing up. Maybe I could have helped in some way."

"There's no reason for you to feel that I way. I did okay. Tess, Jill and I *all* did okay, and I don't know why you're bringing it up now." She needed to get away from him.

"I'm not really sure. Maybe because of what I said yesterday. That you were wonderful back then and you are wonderful now, and there's no reason for you to apologize for anything to anyone."

"Fine. I won't." She pushed against him, but his arm tightened around her.

"Don't go. Stay."

His arms were strong around her, and it would have been so easy to let herself relax into him. But unrequited love only brought pain. Why compound that pain? With superhuman effort, she broke free of his hold and slid off his lap to her feet.

"What's wrong, Kit?"

"Nothing."

He surged to his feet. "Then why are you trying to run away from me?"

"That's not what I'm doing at all. It's just that I don't think we should let ourselves get carried away. You said it yourself. Last night happened. It was great. There's nothing left to talk about."

"I was wrong when I said that. It wasn't just great, it was sensational."

She took a step backward. "There's a lot going on right now. Emotions are running high, and not just ours, either. But we need to remember that I'm suspected of murder and you're my lawyer."

"So far I agree with you," he said, his voice wooden.

"Good, because when you think about it, the stakes are enormous. It would be far better to keep our relationship on a purely business level."

"That's where I disagree."

"Then you're not thinking with your *brain*."

A muscle flexed along his jaw. "Once again, I agree with you."

As much as she ached for him, she couldn't let this dissolve into another night of lovemaking. Because if she did, somewhere in the midst of it, in some way, she would slip up and he would realize she loved him. If that happened, he would exit her life so fast, her head would spin.

And she wasn't only thinking of protecting *him* now. Pride she hadn't been aware of had come rushing into play. How could she ever face him if he knew she loved him? She couldn't.

Basically it had come down to the fact that she had to rescue herself.

"Last night was nothing more than a one-night stand, Des."

"And we were doing so well there." Beneath his mock regret, she heard a caustic tone so corrosive, she could feel it eating at her.

"It's true."

He reached out for her, but she managed to slip out of his way.

"Des, *listen* to me. I don't *want* to spend the night with you again."

His sudden stillness sent a chill through her. His eyes darkened until all light had vanished into black.

"I guess, when you put it like that, I can't argue with you."

Eight

"Good morning."

Kit nearly knocked over her coffee cup as Des strolled into her office the next day, wearing tight jeans and a leather vest over a navy blue flannel shirt. His inherent power and raw sexuality suddenly made her uncomfortably aware of everything that was feminine in her. One way or another, he was her undoing.

"What are you doing here?"

His lips quirked. "You need to work on your hospitality, Kit."

"You know what I mean. After last night, I didn't expect to see you—not so soon, anyway." She knew she was saying everything wrong, but at this point she had no clue how to stop. Perhaps she should simply say nothing.

"Did you really expect me to slink off and hide under a mesquite somewhere like a wounded animal?"

Saying nothing was not going to work. His anger was well earned, and he deserved a response. "No, of course not. It's just that when you left you seemed...upset."

"Angry, maybe. Confused definitely. Conflicting signals sometimes do that to me."

What could she say to that? This time she took her own advice and said nothing, which was apparently fine with him. He headed to the sideboard, where he poured himself a cup of coffee, leaving her time to try to regain her composure. Except it was extremely difficult.

She loved him and had shared a night of passion with him that she would never forget and never regret. But she had also done something else. She had made a decision to let him off the hook about their shared night together and, while she was at it, had safeguarded her pride and her heart. She had told him that what had happened had meant nothing, when in fact it had meant everything.

In retrospect, she had been neither logical nor rational when she had told him that. Then again, logical and rational were two words rarely associated with love.

"Why are you here, Des?"

Taking his time, he seated himself in front of her desk, crossed his long legs and took several sips of coffee. Then he gazed around the office, uncrossed his legs, eyed his coffee with interest and crossed his legs one more time. Just as her nerves were about to snap, he looked at her.

"Did you sleep well last night?"

"*That's* why you're here? To ask me that?"

"Did you?"

"Yes, I did." It was the truth. Despite the turbulent state of her emotions, she had managed to fall into a deep sleep. But she had dreamed. Oh, had she dreamed.

"I didn't."

"That's too bad." It was an automatic, courteous thing to say, but she couldn't come up with anything else.

"Don't you want to know why?"

"No." In his present mood, there was no telling what he would say. "*Why* are you here?"

"To see you." He paused, his intense dark gaze igniting warmth along her nerve endings. "No comeback, Kit?"

"No."

"That's a shame. I would have been extremely interested in what you could come up with."

"Disappointments are part of life."

"There now. That's a nice comeback. Congratulations."

"Des?"

"Yes, Kit?"

She drew a steadying breath. He was putting her through hell, and who was to say she didn't deserve it? Not her.

He held up a pacifying hand. "I'm also here because Bill Ridley called me early this morning."

"He called you?"

"I believe that's what I said."

If it had been anyone else who had addressed her in that cool, arrogant way, she would have verbally cut them down to size, then thrown them out. But it wasn't just anyone else. It was Des.

"It's just that Bill called me, too."

"Then you know that Scooter Garner and Johnny Don Galvez are back from Oklahoma City."

Now he was being all business, but she was as disconcerted as she had been before. "As a matter of fact, I asked Bill to send them over." She glanced at her watch. "I'm expecting them any minute."

"Then I'll wait."

"You don't have to."

"Yes, I do. Remember? I'm getting to see you. Plus, we've got a little matter of murder going on here, and I'm your lawyer. I know you haven't forgotten that, because you told me so just last night."

He smiled in the same way she had once seen a tiger smile on a *National Geographic* special. The tiger had smiled like that right before he pounced on his prey.

"Are those enough reasons, or do you want more?" he asked. "Because if you do, I'm sure I could—"

"Ms. Baron?"

Kit visibly jumped. She had been so wrapped up in Des and the tiger image that she hadn't even heard the two men arrive. "Scooter, Johnny Don—please come in and sit down."

Both men looked ill at ease, but nevertheless, they swept off their hats and chose chairs. They were in their late twenties and seasoned cowboys. Their browned skin attested to long hours spent in the sun, and their solid muscles spoke of the hard physical work they did every day.

"You both know Mr. Baron, right?" she asked, trying to put them at ease.

"Sure thing," Scooter said. "Morning, Mr. Baron."

Johnny Don nodded. "Morning."

"Please call me Des."

Kit pointed toward the sideboard. "Would either of you like some coffee?"

"No, thank you."

"No, thank you."

She inwardly sighed. She guessed she just needed to jump right into the subject. "Okay, then, the reason I asked you to come in this morning is because I'd like to ask you a few questions about Cody Inman."

"Shame about what happened to him," Scooter said.

"Damn shame," Johnny Don said.

All the men she had talked to had said pretty much the same thing, so she wasn't surprised to hear it from them. Plus, a murder where you worked would make anyone nervous.

"It *is* a shame, and I'm trying to help figure out who might have killed him."

Des cleared his throat.

"*We* are," she amended, with a glance at him.

Scooter shook his head. "I didn't see a thing."

"Me either," Johnny Don said, looking slightly alarmed.

"We didn't think you did, but we heard you were both at the same poker game as Cody was the night before he was murdered."

"That's right."

"Uh-huh."

"Did you see or hear anything that night that could help us find out who might have killed Cody?"

Scooter shook his head. "It was just a regular poker game."

Johnny Don tapped his hat against his knee. "It was already going by the time he got there. Nothing much was said except about what was happening with the game."

"By any chance did he win?" Des asked.

Scooter glanced around at him. "Not that I can remember."

"He didn't win," Johnny Don said with assurance. "Not a thing."

"Did that make him mad?"

"Naw." Scooter grinned. "When you play poker, you win sometimes and you lose sometimes. Everyone knows that. And if you don't, you don't belong in the game."

She felt as if she were pounding her head against a brick wall. In fact, it might feel better than this.

"Do you know anyone, anyone at all, who might have wanted him dead?"

Surprisingly, neither of them answered right away.

Scooter looked over at Johnny Don, then back at her. "I guess he had his faults, but then, I don't know any angels."

"None of us do," Des murmured. "But unfortunately, Cody's murder has thrown the spotlight on him, and we're having to look for a reason why someone was so angry with him that they killed him."

Scooter shrugged. "Putting it that way, I suppose there could have been a few."

"Women, mainly," Johnny Don said. "He had a way of getting women to fall for him, then leaving them."

There it was again, the suggestion that a woman somehow could have been involved in the murder, and it was completely plausible. There were plenty of women who worked on the Double B, or who were wives and daughters of men who did. And from what Burt and Red had said, she couldn't rule out married women, either.

She edged up in her chair. "Is there some specific situation you're referring to?" she asked.

"Not really. Actually, none of us were too happy with Cody that night."

"Why's that?" Des asked.

In the other interviews he had let her do most of the questioning, but now he must feel, as she did, that they were getting close to the truth.

Johnny Don gazed at his hat as if it was the most

fascinating thing he had ever seen. "He was doin' some bragging."

"About being out with me, you mean?"

"Uh-huh."

He had just confirmed what she had previously suspected. The first person she had interviewed, Scott McKee, had told them that Cody had mentioned he had been out with her, and she had guessed Cody had probably bragged about it.

"Fact of the matter is," Scooter said, "no one at that game was real happy with Cody. It was a work night, and there he was, getting drunk and shooting off his mouth. It wasn't right."

"Mike wasn't happy with him, either."

"Mike? Mike Stillwell?"

"Mike Stillwell," Johnny Don confirmed.

Without realizing what she was doing, she looked at Des. "He's the one who's at his sister's funeral, isn't he?"

Des nodded at her. "That's right."

Johnny Don gazed at Des. "I never heard Mike say much about his sister before, but he was sure upset when he took off for the funeral."

"I think they were close," Scooter said. "He once told me he had raised her. Seems like I recall her name was Angie. I remember thinking it was a nice name."

"Then his parents must be dead?"

"Yep."

Kit hoped there was nothing in her manner that was giving away how tense she felt. If such a thing were truly possible, she was certain she would jump right out of her skin. "Is there anything else you can tell us about Cody?"

Johnny Don shook his head.

"Can't think of a thing," Scooter said.

Des stood and extended his hand, and both men followed suit. "Thank you for your time. We really appreciate you coming. And if you think of anything else that might be relevant, please call either Ms. Baron or me."

"Will do."

"Sure thing."

The men left to go back to work, and Des turned to her. "What do you think?"

"It's got something to do with a woman."

"I agree. Unfortunately, we still don't know whether that means a woman killed him, or whether he was killed over a woman."

"But jealousy seems a likely motive."

"Maybe."

She frowned. "Is there something I'm not getting?"

"No. It's just that I've been involved in a lot of murder cases, and if there's one thing I've learned, it's to not be surprised when something that seems clear turns out to be muddy as hell."

"Well, for now, everything looks clear. We've talked to everyone who was at that poker game except Mike Stillwell, and I think we need to talk to him next.'' She heard the *we* and changed it. "*I* need to talk to him.''

A slight smile graced his mouth, though he didn't comment on her change of *we* to *I*. ''You know, Kit, the murderer might not even have been at that poker game.''

She stood. ''Quit raining on my parade, Des. I'm going to follow the clues until I run out of them.''

''And you're doing the right thing—the *only* thing you can do at this point. I just don't want you to be disappointed if you run into a dead end, that's all.''

''Don't worry about it.'' She quietly sighed. She would give anything if the atmosphere between them weren't as strained as it was. But she accepted the full blame. It would be so much easier if she didn't love him....

''Kit—'' His head swung toward the door. ''Someone else is coming. Who are you expecting?''

''No one.''

Sheriff Moreno walked in, the men close behind. ''Sorry to interrupt your, uh—'' his eyes narrowed on Des ''—business meeting, Ms. Baron, but I brought some men to search your house.''

''You *what?*''

Des surged to his feet. ''You can't do that.''

''Ah, yes, I can.'' With a smirk, he flourished a legal-looking document. ''See for yourself.''

Des took it from him, snapped it open and read. ''He's got a search warrant, Kit.''

Kit felt the room begin to tilt around her, and she quickly sat. ''There must be some mistake. The homestead has *never* been searched.'' To her it was inconceivable. In her mind, the homestead had always been and would always be inviolate.

''There's no mistake.'' His gaze held steady on the sheriff. ''What are you looking for?''

''Anything that can help us find out who killed Cody Inman. In addition, we still haven't found the murder weapon. And since Ms. Baron hasn't come in yet to be fingerprinted, I decided to keep the investigation moving forward in this way.''

''What's your plan?''

''I've borrowed men from a couple of counties so we can search all the homestead buildings and the barns at the same time.'' He walked out into the hall and called, *''Get started.''*

Kit watched in horror as strangers spread out through her house. The rest of the cars took off toward the barns.

''Just a minute, Moreno,'' Des said. ''I want your promise that your people will be careful in the search.''

''The men I brought today are the best.''

''That's not the issue. I've seen well-trained men destroy a place, and I'm telling you now, they better handle everything they touch with kid gloves.''

''I'm sure they will.'' His smile was entirely unpleasant. ''In the meantime, you and Ms. Baron wait here while the process is being carried out.''

''We'll wait. Just remember what I said.''

The sheriff didn't even pretend to smile this time.

''Not even you, Baron, are powerful enough to get in the way of justice.''

''There's justice, and then there is justice.''

''You're a high-priced lawyer, Baron, and I know you could stand there and argue with me all day long and never cover the same subject twice. So there's no way I'm going to waste my time arguing with you. Stay here with Ms. Baron, and I'll be back in a few minutes.''

Des stared after the sheriff, fighting the urge to go after him. He would gain an immeasurable amount of personal satisfaction if he could just beat the hell out of the man. But in the end, he knew he would accomplish nothing.

He turned back into the room. Kit had lost all color in her face. Lord, he needed to help her, and he didn't know how. There had been very few times in his life when he had felt as frustrated and as helpless as he did at this moment. But now all he could really do was wait with Kit.

She might not realize it, but he knew exactly how much this house meant to her. She had worked hard to make it into a home she could call her own. She had opened it up, allowed light into it, and decorated it with impeccable taste. She had personalized it in the most basic way and in the process wiped out all memories of her father from it.

Damn the sheriff.

While he had been with Kit at the cabin, the man had been working on the search warrant. Normally he thought several steps ahead of his opponent, but he had been so wrapped up in his need for Kit that he hadn't seen this coming.

Now what was he going to do?

"It'll be all right, Kit. They know that if they damage anything, I'll sue them to hell and back."

She wrapped her arms around herself and numbly nodded. "I'm sure you're right."

He would rather she rant and rail at him than mutely accept what was happening in this quiet, almost fragile way. He thrust stiffened fingers through his hair. "This is all my fault. I'm sorry. I should have anticipated that Moreno would do this."

"It's not anyone's fault. You're not a psychic."

"No, but I'm a lawyer, and I know damn well how things work."

She shrugged. "It's okay." A loud thud sounded somewhere on the second floor and drew her gaze to the ceiling.

It was too much for him. He moved purposefully toward the door.

"Don't, Des." Her quiet, calm voice halted him. "Let them work. The sooner they do what they came to do, the sooner they'll leave."

Her composure was shattering his. "You need some hot coffee."

The truth was, he needed to do something, anything. He poured a cup, then liberally dosed it with brandy. When he turned to her, he found her watching him with a calm, green-eyed gaze.

"You're pale," he said, explaining away the brandy.

She took the steaming cup from him. "You could use some, too."

"You're right." He helped himself and had downed about a third of it when the sheriff returned. "Find anything yet?"

"No, but then, we're not through, either."

"If you haven't found the murder weapon by now, I doubt you will anytime soon. It could have been thrown in one of the stock ponds or buried underneath that new snow we had."

Moreno shrugged. "We'll find it. It may take a while, but you can be sure we'll find it."

Kit spoke up. "Would you like a cup of coffee, sheriff?"

Moreno's face creased with brief surprise. "No thanks."

Des thought quickly. Maybe it would slow the sheriff down if he appeared to cooperate. He gestured to one of the chairs in front of Kit's desk. "Sit down, sheriff, and I'll bring you up to speed on our investigation."

"*Your* investigation?"

"Sit. Please."

In an unnecessary move, Moreno shifted his gun out of the way, then sat down. "Look, Baron, you're an experienced litigator, but I doubt you know anything about proper investigative technique."

"I know something about it." With a glance at Kit to make sure she was still all right, he took the other chair.

"I doubt it. Common sense tells me that you're too busy to do any investigating. You hire it out."

"Common sense," Kit repeated softly. "Now there's an idea."

A glance at the sheriff assured Des that her ironic comment had gone over the man's head.

The sheriff leaned forward. "You're not experienced in investigations, and I want you to leave it to me, Baron. Too many people tramping around over the same ground can make a big mess."

Des nodded. "I see your point. Then why don't you tell us what you've found out so far?"

"I'm not ready to disclose that information just yet." Moreno looked at Kit. "I want you to come back to town with me this afternoon and be finger-printed."

Des spoke before she could. "Then you've found *hard* evidence that points to Ms. Baron?"

"I've got enough."

"What you have is circumstantial, and you know it, and I don't want Ms. Baron subjected to finger-printing until you have something concrete."

Moreno's eyes narrowed. "I could have you charged with obstructing justice."

"Try it."

A vein pounded in the sheriff's forehead. "If Ms. Baron doesn't get herself into town within the next few days to be fingerprinted, I'll have a warrant issued for her arrest."

"You know you can't do that."

"I can do anything I want."

"Only for a limited period of time, and we both know it. So let me just caution you that arresting Ms. Baron wouldn't be advisable."

"You don't *advise* me."

The two men glared at each other.

Kit cleared her throat. "I assure you, Sheriff Moreno, the last thing Mr. Baron and I want to do is obstruct justice. Since I did *not* kill Cody Inman, we are rooting for you to find the person who did. As for not coming in to be fingerprinted, that's my fault. Business obligations." She said the two words as if they explained everything. "As for my seeing the men in question, in the course of running the ranch and on any given day, I naturally talk with quite a few of my hands."

With a certain amount of resignation, the sheriff pulled out his notebook and flipped to a certain page. "Who have you talked to?"

"A few of the people who were at the poker game the night before Cody was killed."

"Who?"

"Scott McKee."

Moreno nodded. "I talked with him."

"Get anything?" Des asked innocently.

The sheriff ignored him.

She continued. "Red Tinsdall and Burt Salatore."

"I have their names, but I haven't been able to locate them. Some manager told me they were working in a southern section and gave me directions. Took me nearly half a day to get out there, and when I did, no one was there."

She hid a smile. He had been told to go in the exact opposite direction of where the men actually were. "Our hands are trained to go where the work is, and that can change hourly. They must have been needed elsewhere."

"Damn inefficient way to run a business if you ask me."

"We've managed to have some success."

Her mild reply drew a sharp glance from him. "I plan to find those men today."

"I'm sure you will. In fact, I don't know which of my managers you saw, but I'll have Bill Ridley talk to you. He can tell you exactly where the men are."

"Good." Her cooperation seemed to pacify him.

"Sheriff, no one wants this case wrapped up quicker than I do."

"I'm sure." He checked his notebook again. "What about the other three? I was told Mike Stillwell was attending a funeral, and the other two were in Oklahoma getting supplies? Let's see... Scooter Garner and Johnny Don Galvez."

"Scooter and Johnny Don are back now. Again, Bill Ridley can tell you where to find them."

Moreno stood. "Then as soon as my men are finished here in the house, I'll go find this Bill Ridley."

"Fine."

She rose and held out her hand. "I know you're doing your best, Sheriff, and I appreciate it."

He paused and looked down at Des. "I understand Ada de la Garza paid you a visit and that there was a bit of a problem with her photographer."

Des casually lifted his shoulders. "No problem that I can think of."

"Both Ada and the photographer said you roughed him up."

"I merely showed him the door."

"They both used the term *roughly*."

"I like the term *firmly* better."

"I don't have time to play word games with you, Baron." Moreno nodded to her. "I'll be getting back to you."

"I'll be here."

As soon as he walked out of the office, Kit sank into her chair and took a drink of her spiked coffee. It tasted so good, she had another.

Des began to applaud. "You were superb with him. You handled him much better than I would have."

"That's because your temper gets the best of you whenever he's around."

"You've seen me angry, but you've never seen me lose my temper. Neither has he."

If that was the case, she hoped she never did. "I figured I didn't have anything to lose by going along with him."

"You were right."

In this case, being right didn't make her feel any better. It also didn't help her.

"But you're *not* going in to be fingerprinted."

"Whatever you say."

He paused. "You have quite a talent there, managing to humor both me and the sheriff."

"Is it working?"

"I'll let you know."

She smiled. No matter what the circumstances were, she was becoming accustomed to having Des around all the time. When the person who actually committed the murder was found, that would end. How was she going to stand the pain? "I better call Bill Ridley."

He nodded. "That's just what I was going to suggest."

She picked up the phone and punched in the number. "Bill, this is Kit. I've sent the sheriff your way."

On the other end of the line, Bill cursed. "He's going to be wasting his time."

"Don't perjure yourself for me. Just answer the questions as best you can."

"Sure thing, but, you know, I don't have a very good memory these days. Old age, I reckon."

"I appreciate your loyalty, Bill, but the truth is, I don't have anything to hide."

"Shoot fire, I never thought you did. It's just that from what I hear, this man is a donkey's hind end."

She took another drink of her brandy and coffee. "I'd have to agree with you there, but I just want to get this whole thing over with. Listen, the main reason I called is to ask how long you think Mike Stillwell is going to be gone for his sister's funeral?"

"I don't know. In cases like a death in the immediate family, the time off is open-ended."

Even though Bill couldn't see her, she nodded out of habit. "That's what I thought. Do you know where the funeral is being held?"

"I know the name of the town, because I notified the business manager's office so that the ranch could send flowers." She heard a shuffling of papers. "Here it is." He read off the name.

"Thanks, Bill. And by the way, I wouldn't mind if you didn't tell the sheriff about this."

"I can handle the man. Don't you worry about a thing."

"Thanks again, Bill." Such good advice. Too bad she couldn't follow it.

Next she dialed the business office and requested the name and location of the funeral home. When she hung up from them, she looked at Des. "I don't think it would hurt anything if I got to Mike before the sheriff does."

"I agree. Let's go."

She automatically started to tell him that she could go by herself, but ultimately she was too much in love with him to deprive herself of spending even a little more time with him.

"I'll order the helicopter."

Nine

Des.

Kit fell back onto the hotel bed, still dressed in the forest green cashmere sweater and matching suede skirt she had worn for the trip.

She looked up at the ceiling. It had been a long day. By rights she should be tired, but she had never felt more awake, more wired. The blame, if you could call it that, was her close proximity to Des, who was in the adjoining room.

Earlier, she and Des had landed in Oklahoma, rented a car and driven straight to the funeral home. It had taken only a moment's inquiry to find that the funeral had already been held. But when Des had inquired about any next of kin information, the funeral director had refused to tell him, stating that fraudulent practices were all too common and easy against those still mourning for departed loved ones. They'd had no choice but to check into a hotel. It was a long way from the five-star hotels they were both used to, but it was clean and had everything they needed for one night.

A lock clicked on the door to the adjoining room, and she heard the door open. A moment of silence was followed by a knock.

Des.

Though they hadn't asked for adjoining rooms, the clerk who had checked them in had arranged them. She went to open the door.

"Would you like to go down for dinner? I saw a coffee shop off the lobby. They may have some chili or something. Or we could go somewhere else."

His light blue shirt was open at the collar, revealing the column of his brown throat, and the long sleeves had been rolled up his strong forearms. Kit turned away and returned to sit on the bed. "No, thanks. I'm not hungry, but you can go if you like."

Their night of reckless lovemaking had reduced them to excruciating politeness, she reflected dully. When she glanced at the door again, she saw that he had disappeared. She could only imagine how much he disliked her now that she had told him their night together had meant nothing. Though her intentions had been the best, she couldn't find it in her to like herself very much, either. Surely there was a kinder way she could have said the same thing.

She briefly closed her eyes against the pain that knifed through her heart. Even though she had been trying to protect both of them, she now had a sickening feeling that she had acted precipitously. He was so close....

He reappeared with a phone book. "I've looked up the name Stillwell and have found quite a few. Why don't we divide them up and start calling? Who knows? Maybe we'll get lucky and Mike will answer."

"Good idea." It would at least give them something to do. She pulled her room's phone book from the built-in nightstand, and flipped to the correct page.

"I'll take the first half," he said. "You take the last."

She nodded and began calling. It took a while to get through the names, since several of the people turned out to be quite chatty and insisted on giving her the history of their family tree. However, none of them were able to tell her anything about a Mike or Angie Stillwell.

Next door, she heard a receiver drop onto its cradle; then Des strolled into her room and settled onto the bed next to her. "No luck?"

"No luck."

"Me either, but I've had another idea."

He looked at her. "What?"

"We require our prospective employees to give references. Mike might have given his sister as one. If he did, it will list her address and phone number. If not, maybe one of the references will be able to tell us where we can find him.''

''Great idea.''

In the light from the nightstand lamp, his eyes gleamed, and she found herself caught up in them. ''I—I don't know why I didn't think of it before now. It was such an obvious thing for me to do.''

''I said it earlier. You've had a lot on your mind. Plus, you don't handle the personnel end of the business.''

So what was his excuse for not thinking of it?

''There's just one problem. The personnel office at the ranch closes at 6:00 p.m. If I was home, I could probably track down someone who works there, but as it is, I left home without any of my numbers.''

''Don't worry about it. We're settled in for the night now. You can give them a call in the morning.''

She nodded, wondering what else she could say to keep the conversation going. She had tried earlier to bring up what had happened in the cabin, and he had cut her off. She felt she owed him apologies on so many levels, but he wouldn't want to hear them. And she was positive he was still angry about her comment that their night together had meant nothing. No doubt he was used to making that decision.

Then she thought of something. ''Remember when you told me about the memories you had of me when I was a young girl?''

''That's not something I'd forget.''

''Okay, well, I have some of you.'' He looked so surprised she almost laughed. ''I remember when you were about sixteen or so. There was this wild horse that no one could get close to. But one afternoon you went out to that corral and spent hours with him, talking to him, gentling him. You were amazing with him.''

''Just like you are with Dia.''

She shrugged off the compliment. ''You were very special with that horse.''

''I was just doing what I had learned from some of the older guys.''

''Maybe, but with this particular horse, no one was having any luck until you came along. By the time the afternoon was over, that horse was literally eating out of your hand. By the next day you were riding him.''

''Where you at the corral?''

''Not at the corral, no, but I was nearby.''

''In one of the barns?''

''Yes. I was up in the hay door.''

His lips quirked. ''I had no idea.''

Her gaze fixed on his lips, then returned to his eyes. ''There was no reason why you should notice me.''

He grinned. ''In retrospect, I don't know how I could *not* notice you. I must have been blind.''

''Not at all. You forget, I wasn't even a teenager at that point. Plus, at that age, the difference in our ages seemed larger than it actually was.''

''If I was sixteen, you must have been around eleven.''

''Right.'' She hesitated. ''I remember the girls, too.''

"Girls?"

This time she did laugh at his surprised look. "Don't act so innocent. Let's see, there were Donna, Melissa and Jennifer, just to name three. Don't you remember them?"

"Now that you said their names I do."

"I remember Donna, in particular, because you brought her to a wiener roast that, amazingly enough, I happened to get to go to, thanks to your dad. Somehow he managed to talk my father into letting me and my sisters go, though I'll never know how he did it. I was thrilled, though."

"A wiener roast? I don't remember. Seems like I went to a lot of wiener roasts, along with hay rides, barn dances, that sort of thing."

The way his forehead creased whenever he was thinking fascinated her. The way the crinkles beside his eyes became more pronounced when he smiled enchanted her. In fact, at this moment she couldn't think of a thing she didn't enjoy about him. "I'm sure you did, but I didn't. Being able to go was a big, big deal for me, so I remember this one very well. You were with Donna. And that night, as I recall, I experienced jealousy for the first time."

He grinned. "*You* jealous? I just can't imagine that. You've always seemed so self-contained."

"Ah, but you see, Donna was something I could never imagine being at that time—*sophisticated.*"

He laughed. "Donna? No, honey, I don't think so. If I was sixteen, then she was sixteen."

Honey. Warmth flooded her, an outsized reaction

to an offhand remark. She was beyond hope. "Let me assure you that in comparison to me she was definitely sophisticated. And there was more. She was on an actual *date* with you. I couldn't even imagine such an exotic thing. And she seemed so comfortable with you."

He slid his hand up through her hair. "But you're comfortable with me now, right?"

She hadn't anticipated his move. She waited a moment until her equilibrium returned. It didn't. "Uh, no, not when you do things like you're doing now."

"What? Touching you? But we've spent the night together. You remember that, don't you?"

Did he seriously think she could forget? "Of course I do, but it doesn't mean that I'm, um, actually accustomed to having you touch me."

His fingers moved restlessly in her hair. "Why not? Didn't I do it enough?"

"Yes, but—"

His other hand found the rapidly beating pulse at the base of her neck. "I remember that I kissed this spot right here." He bent his head and pressed his mouth to the spot. "And then I remember kissing you right here." He kissed the same place behind her other ear.

She closed her eyes as warmth rivered through her. "This isn't fair."

"Who said it was?"

His lips smoothed up her throat and stopped at the sensitive area behind her ear.

"And then I distinctly remember touching you here."

His hand closed over her breast, and she smothered a moan.

"I also did this a lot," he said huskily as he caressed her breast, lightly massaging and rubbing her until she was fearful for her mind.

"Des…" The word *stop* stuck in her throat. Even though she knew all the reasons why she should say it, she couldn't. What he was doing felt too good for her to say anything.

"I also remember unhooking your bra and doing this."

Magically her bra was unhooked; then his palm lightly pushed against her rigid nipple and rolled it round and round until she had to reach out for him to stay upright.

"What are you doing?" she asked, gasping for breath.

He leaned his body weight into her and pressed her down to the bed. "Why don't you just consider this an extension of our one-night stand?"

There it was, proof that he was still angry with her. But he also still wanted her.

"Oh, Des…" She heard the surrender in her voice. If it were possible, she wanted him even more than she had wanted him that night.

She was his.

Whether he liked it or not. Whether she liked it or not.

They could be in the hayloft of a barn or a faraway cabin, even in an Oklahoma hotel room. Forever and always, she would be his.

Her inhibitions evaporated. Her clothes disappeared. One by one, she felt her bones melt. Then his fingers stroked up her thigh to between her legs and, incredibly, his lips followed. Unerringly, he found her center.

White-hot bolts of heat began to devour her. Reality slipped away, leaving only ecstatic sensations and an unearthly sensuality. An intolerable urgency took her over. If she had ever had any patience, it deserted her. Their time together was ticking away.

"Please, Des. *Now*."

He straightened over her, and with one strong stroke, he entered her. A pleasure so hot and intense flashed through her that she could only call his name again and again.

As if they had been lovers for years instead of hours, their bodies moved together in an astounding synchronicity. A molten pressure began to build within her. It grew, expanded and stretched until there was nothing left of her but that. She became need.

Hours later, minutes later, seconds later—she couldn't tell—it burst apart inside her with a volcanic force, taking her into another dimension where only love and passion existed. Dimly something occurred to her. They hadn't used protection, not last night, not now. She could be pregnant.

She prayed she was.

Des drew the covers over Kit and pulled her sleeping body closer. Soon it would be a new day and they would once again be occupied with finding out who really killed Cody Inman. But for now he could concentrate on the amazing woman who lay in his arms.

She presented a big problem to him.

He loved helping her, protecting her, and despite the circumstances of the murder, he had loved this time they were having together. Most of all, he loved spending the night together with her. And he loved the many ways he had come to know her.

He loved watching her think, so much so that he often forgot to. He loved the way she came apart in his arms, and the fact that she could make him come apart, too.

In her sleep, she stirred against him, and for no particular reason, he smiled. Silly, he supposed, but there it was. He loved everything about her that he could think of.

Hell, he even loved her independence and stubbornness. But he could feel her constantly trying to put an emotional distance between them. It was obvious she didn't want to be close to him, and that was the problem.

He couldn't think of anything that would make him happier than to be close to her for a long, long time.

He loved her.

He *loved* her.

He went still.

His big problem had just become gigantic. How was he ever going to have her completely? How was he going to keep her by his side day in and day out for the rest of their lives?

He didn't know, but he would definitely have to figure out a way. He had never been in love before, never known this aching need to make a woman part of him and his life. And with Kit, his logical, problem-solving abilities went right out the window.

She stirred against him again. This time, he did what seemed so natural. He shifted over her and pushed into her. And as if she had been made just for him, her velvet sweetness welcomed and tightly sheathed him. At that moment he wasn't entirely sure she *hadn't* been made just for him. They fit together so perfectly, he could stay that way forever.

In the next instant he knew he couldn't. He wanted her too damn much.

He gritted his teeth, trying to hold himself back from his release until she was fully awake and could enjoy their lovemaking as much as he did. But it was hopeless.

Slowly and surely he thrust in and out of her, and little by little she began to respond, lifting her hips to receive him in a perfect harmony that made the blood sing and race in his veins.

Her eyes drifted open, and she smiled up at him. He smiled back. In this one way he could make her his, if only for this small space of time. And he proceeded to do just that.

"What time is it?" Kit asked, snuggling in a contented way against him.

Des automatically reached for his watch on the

nightstand, then realized he had taken it off in his room. "It's morning."

She chuckled, and he softly kissed her. When he pulled back from her, he saw a look of amazement on her face.

"What was that for?"

"It was a reward for laughing. You don't do it enough."

She smiled. "Gee, you're easy. Did Donna know that?"

He grimaced in mock pain. "Will you please get off the subject of Donna? I'm in bed with you, not her."

"It's not good enough. I won't be happy until she *knows* you're in bed with me not her. I want her to be as jealous of me as I was that night of her."

"Even without knowing about us spending our nights together, I imagine she's plenty jealous of you already. As a matter of fact, none of the girls I dated have even come close to accomplishing all that you have."

"You mean running the ranch?"

"The Double B is not just a ranch, Kit. Under your guidance, it's become one of the most successful ranches in the world."

She was silent for several moments, but he could see her thinking and wondered what she was going to say next. Before her, he had never even cared what a woman might say next. But Kit had broken the mold. No other woman would ever again do for him.

"I heard that Donna became a lawyer."

"That's right."

"And you still don't think she has accomplished what I have?"

"Not even close."

"I also heard she married and now has two children. Sorry, but any way you look at it, *that* is a wonderful accomplishment."

"I have to agree with you there."

She looked up at him, a frown on her face, laughter in her eyes. "You should have continued to disagree with me."

"Sorry. Next time I will."

"Really? Okay, I'll test you. Let's see... Back when you and Donna were both sixteen, you didn't really like her all that much, did you?"

Thankful for whatever had put her in a good mood, he threw back his head and laughed. "I was *sixteen,* Kit. My hormones were raging. Of course I liked her."

"You just failed the test miserably."

"Sorry, but I'll repeat it again. *You're* in this bed with me and she's not. Plus, I seem to recall that I dated Donna only a few months before someone else came along."

"How few?"

He rubbed his face. "I don't know. That was a long time ago. And besides, I can't think of any reason why I should remember."

"Okay," she said, sounding partly pacified. "So who was the girl who came along after Donna?"

"I'm hungry. Let's get dressed and go find some breakfast."

"You're changing the subject."

"Because I don't like to take on subjects I can see no way of winning." He patted her bottom lip with a finger, emphasizing each word.

She kissed the pad of his finger. "I never would have thought it, but you're a cowardly man, Des Baron."

"What I am is a *smart* man."

She laughed, and he felt his heart swell. Kit looked relaxed and happy. More importantly, she wasn't trying to put emotional distance between them now. He felt as if he had won at least a small victory.

"It was Melissa, wasn't it?"

"What?"

"Your next girlfriend was Melissa, wasn't it?"

He groaned. "You know this isn't fair."

"I think I said something like that not too long ago and it didn't do me a bit of good."

"But you didn't have any boyfriends when you were growing up, which gives you the distinct upper hand in this type of conversation."

She smiled. "I know. Tell me about Melissa."

"No."

"I heard she became a pediatrician."

"You seem to hear a lot."

Her green eyes glittering with mischief, she nonchalantly lifted one bare shoulder. "I manage."

A sudden thought struck him, a *hope*. "So do you want to have children someday?"

Without moving a muscle, she withdrew from him. "Now that you mention it, I'm hungry, too. I'll take a quick shower and then we can go eat." She slid out of his hold and off the bed. Belatedly, she seemed to remember she was naked. Hastily she reached for the bulky bedspread and wrapped it around herself.

"You didn't answer my question."

"You'll get over it."

He came up on one elbow. "I'm sorry I didn't use protection, Kit. I wasn't prepared."

"Don't worry about it. And you didn't answer *my* question, either."

"The one about Melissa? They're not even in the same category."

"They were both questions."

"Do you want to have children, Kit?"

She looked away. "More than anything in the world." Before he could respond, she vanished through the bathroom door. Soon afterwards, he heard her turn on the shower.

Once again she had withdrawn from him, but this time it was okay. He had gotten the answer he wanted. She wanted children. He did, too. Maybe that was the leverage he needed.

Kit sat in the tub and allowed the water from the shower to rain down over her. She didn't know what had gotten into her, teasing Des as she had, but it had been fun, and she had thoroughly enjoyed herself. She was also bone-deep happy that they had made love again.

Besides, Des had seemed to forget that he should

be angry with her. In fact, he might even feel that in some sort of odd way they were even now. After all, his lovemaking had driven her right over the edge of sanity. Some time in the night, she could even remember pleading with him to put her out of her agony of need.

He had. He had driven into her hard and fast, taking her to the precipice of ecstasy and then beyond. And then he had followed her, making it absolutely perfect.

It would be another memory for her when Des decided to go his separate way from her. But ultimately she now knew that her memories would be cold comfort. They could never even come close to the reality of Des and this time they had spent together.

The fact that she would probably see him around the ranch from time to time was going to make it even harder on her. How was she going to remain carefree and casual when her heart and body would be crying out for him?

Lost in thought, she remained where she was for a while, until she realized that she was wasting time thinking about the gloomy future when the present was waiting for her.

But when she hastily toweled off and returned to her room, she found that Des had gone to his. It was just as well, she told herself, and wished for more conviction. Still, they had to find Mike today, and the sooner they could get started the better it would be.

She picked up the phone and called the Double B's business office. Luckily Mike had given his sister's name as next of kin, and her address was on file, too.

Ten

At the restaurant, Kit and Des placed their breakfast order, then she went to call the apartment of Mike's sister to make sure he was there. He was.

"Mike?"

"Yes?" He sounded tired.

"This is Kit Baron. I need to talk with you."

"Ms. Baron?"

"That's right. I'm sorry to bother you at a time like this, but I'm in town and would like to come over and talk with you if I may."

Mike was quiet for several seconds. She could imagine how surprised he was to hear from her.

"What about?"

"I'd rather not say until I get there." Cody's murder was not news to be broken over the telephone.

"I don't understand what this is about."

"We'll tell you all about it when we get there."

"We?"

"Des Baron is with me."

His stunned silence filled her ears. "If you've come all this way to fire me, you could have saved yourself the trouble. I quit."

"I'm sorry to hear that, but listen, please don't worry about your job right now. Now is not the time for you to be making major decisions. And you're not in any trouble with us. I have no intention of firing you."

"Then what is it?"

"There's just something we'd like to discuss with you."

"Okay, then. Uh, do you need directions over here?"

"We'll get a map. Oh, and we'll be there in about an hour, if that's all right."

"I guess. See you then."

Back at the booth, Kit sent a troubled look at Des. "I hope he's going to be able to help us, because if he can't…"

Des reached over and trailed his fingers down her cheek in an extraordinarily tender way. "If he can't help us, we'll find another way. The main thing for now is that we're doing something to help you, rather than sitting around, waiting for that laughingstock of a sheriff to decide to arrest you. So for now, try not to worry."

She *was* worried and fervently hoped Mike would

be able to give them at least one piece of information that would help her. But what was worrying her even more was the challenge she faced of living without Des once he grew tired of her.

Angie Stillwell's apartment was small and consisted of a kitchen that was separated from the tiny living area by a bar. Through a doorway, she could also see a bedroom and bath. Empty cardboard boxes littered the floor. A framed photograph of Mike with his arm around a beautiful teenaged girl held place of honor on a side table. The young girl—Angie, she guessed—was staring adoringly up at him.

"Thank you for seeing us, Mike," Kit said as a way of starting off. "First of all, I want to tell you how sorry we were to hear of your sister's death. You have our deepest sympathy."

"Thank you." His tone was flat, wooden, as if he had spent all his emotions and had none left. Then, as if it were too much effort to continue standing, he dropped down into the chair opposite them.

She glanced at Des. He nodded at her encouragingly. "Mike, I'm afraid I have some more bad news. The morning you left the Double B, Cody Inman was killed."

Mike stared at her blankly; then his face crumbled into utter sadness.

"I'm sorry to have to be the one to break the news to you. Were you close?"

"No."

"Still, I know it's a shock. It has been for all of

us.'' She paused. ''Mike, the reason we're here is because we were told you were at the poker game that took place the night before Cody was killed. And we were wondering if anything happened during the game, or if anything was said, that might help us figure out who would want him dead.''

He glanced at the photograph she had noticed before. ''I don't know about anyone else, but…I did.''

''Excuse me?'' She exchanged a quick look with Des.

''I wanted him dead, though when I left the ranch that morning, I wasn't sure he was.''

Des's dark brows rose. ''I'm afraid I'm not sure what you're saying, Mike.''

Mike exhaled a long weary breath, then gazed down at his palms. The calluses there spoke of hard, physical work. ''Right before I left the ranch to come up here to bury my sister, I found Cody in the barn and had a hell'uva argument with him. Then I picked up a shovel and gave him a good whack in the head.''

''But why?'' Kit asked incredulously. She could hardly believe that Mike was actually confessing.

''A while back, Cody came up here with me on a visit. He was kind'a friendly with Angie, but at the time I didn't notice anything unusual. I was just glad they seemed to hit it off. Later I learned that he had come up here several times to see her.'' His voice broke. ''It was my fault. I should have paid more attention. Angie was a bit slow, you see. And when any man paid attention to her, she just opened up like a flower. And I *knew* that.'' He rubbed the heels of his hands against his eyes, then slowly shook his head. "I can't believe she kept his visits from me. She always told me everything, but she must have known I would try to stop it."

"Why would you have?"

He met her gaze. "Cody was okay to hang out with now and then, but he wasn't someone you would want your sister seeing on a regular basis."

"So you're saying Cody dated her?"

"I'm saying he got her pregnant, then told her he didn't believe he was the father and she was on her own." A tear trickled down his cheek. "The *bastard*. She was a good girl and believed everyone was good. And when he dumped her like he did…" Another tear spilled unnoticed down his cheek. "I guess by then she was too ashamed to tell me, but a friend of hers who worked with her called me and told me the story."

"When was that?" Des asked.

"The evening of the poker game. So when Cody showed up for the game, I was madder than hell at him. Except I didn't want to say anything to him with all the guys around." He spread out his hands. "I was trying to protect her, just like I'd done all her life." A sob broke from him. He paused to compose himself and wiped his face. "So anyway, I waited until after the game was over with. I confronted him and told him he damn well would make it right by Angie, but the son of a bitch just laughed and went off to drink some more." The tears started again. "I didn't sleep much that night, and by the next morning,

I'd made the decision that I would quit the Double B, move up here and try to help Angie. But the next thing I knew, the police called and told me she had committed suicide.'' More tears flooded down his face.

"So you went looking for Cody?"

"Right." Mike wiped away the tears and gazed at Kit. "I was standing outside the barn when you two had your argument."

She shook her head uncomprehendingly. "But Tio was outside the barn when I went out."

"I was at the back door. I waited until you left, then went in and confronted him. Things got out of hand. First thing I knew, I picked up a shovel and hit him upside the head."

"Was that the fatal blow?" Des asked.

"It was the only blow. He went down, but still it didn't occur to me then that I might have killed him. I don't know why—it just didn't. Maybe I was just too busy thinking about what I had to do when I got up here." He shrugged. "But somewhere in the back of my mind I think I did know it. I just wouldn't let myself think about it too much, you know?"

Kit nodded. "I know."

"That's the whole story."

"One more thing. What did you do with the shovel? It hasn't been found."

"I don't know. I guess I threw it down before I left."

"Where?"

He shrugged again. "I wasn't paying attention."

Des cleared his throat. "Mike, are you willing to tell the sheriff what you just told us?"

Bleakly Mike nodded.

Kit barely resisted the urge to reach out to Mike and comfort him. Oddly enough, she felt nothing but compassion for him. "Will you come back with us now?"

With a visible effort, he roused himself out of the lethargic stupor into which he had fallen. "First I've got to finish packing up Angie's things, though there's not really much. But I can't think what to do with a lot of this stuff. Guess I'll give her clothes away."

"I'll help you," Kit said impulsively. "You pick out the things you'd like to keep, then we'll pack them up and put them in storage. After that I'll arrange for the rest of her things to be given to charity."

"All right." He clasped his hands together between his legs and bowed his head. "Ms. Baron, I'm real sorry for the trouble I've caused you. It wasn't on purpose. None of it was."

"I know that, Mike. I know."

Des.

Where was he tonight?

Kit was curled up in her cashmere robe on the corner of the sofa in her living room. A small lamp shining in a corner provided light, along with the fire that crackled warmly in the nearby fireplace.

She should feel contentment, she reflected sadly. The hunt for the real killer was over. Mike had been arrested and would be charged with manslaughter. Des was pretty sure that with his help, and once Mike's story was heard, he would draw a light sentence. But all she felt was an aching emptiness. She had never really had Des, yet it felt as if she had lost him.

She had fought hard for her independence and had always been proud of it. And even in the middle of those two blazing nights when Des had held her and made love to her, she had never considered giving up her independence.

Yet she had become accustomed to his arms, to his company, to his good-humored moods and his bad. She had become accustomed to *Des*. And now that she thought about it, accustomed was too mild a word. Addicted was more accurate.

"Hi."

She jumped at the soft deep voice and looked around. "Des?"

"Sorry," he said, walking slowly over to her. "I didn't mean to frighten you."

"You didn't. It's just that…my mind was somewhere else. What are you doing here?"

He sat down beside her on the sofa, leaving a cushion between them. "I came to see how you were."

"Oh, I'm fine, just fine. I've already called Tess and Jill. They were thrilled."

"That's good." He tilted his head to one side. "You must be tired. It's been a gruelling few days."

"I guess so."

"You don't sound too sure."

"No, you're right. It has been gruelling."

"You must also be glad it's all over."

She wrapped her arms around herself. "It was like a weight on me to have even one person think I could kill a man."

"Trust me. No one who really knows you could ever think you would be capable of that."

Her lips quirked. "Which of course leaves out the sheriff."

"Definitely. You know, if there's one thing I've learned listening to Mike's story, I suppose it's that you don't know what you're capable of until it comes right down to it, what you'll do in any given situation, especially if your reason is strong enough."

"That's right."

"I don't suppose the sheriff apologized to you?"

She chuckled. "I won't hold my breath."

"I can get him to apologize if you'd like."

She didn't doubt for a minute that he could. "The man is vermin. Not worth another second of my life."

"That's a good attitude to have."

Something in his expression caught her attention. "You plan to do something to him, don't you?"

Des nodded. "Let's just say I'm going to do something *about* him. As it happens, the state's attorney general is a friend of mine, and I'm going to have a talk with him. The only reason I haven't contacted him before now is because I didn't want anyone to be able to say you got out of this mess because of favoritism. But now all bets are off."

"Des, don't go out on a limb because of me."

His eyes softened as they rested on her. "I can't think of a better reason."

"No. I don't want you to risk anything."

"Risk won't even come into it. And there's no limb. You said it yourself. The man is vermin. In addition, he's a rotten sheriff. He didn't look at anyone else besides you as the potential killer. He needs to be relieved of any type of position where he can destroy someone's life because he sees something in it for himself."

"When you put it like that, I can't disagree with you. I wouldn't like to think of any innocent person's life being ruined."

"And what about Ada de la Garza? I thought I'd leave her to you."

She grinned. "I haven't forgotten about her, and, as it happens, I've decided she *is* worth a few more seconds of my life."

"I can't wait to hear *this*. What have you planned and do you need any help?"

She chuckled. "No. I don't need or want any help on this one, thank you. I'm going to call the editor of her paper and make sure the true story of what happened to Cody, Mike and Angie is told...by *another* reporter. That request alone should put the brakes on any advancement she might have been hoping for."

"If you didn't, I was going to."

"There's more. When I tell the editor how she acted, he might just show her the door. In fact, from now on I'm going to keep an eye on her career. I know that type of journalism is what is selling today, but it doesn't belong in any respectable newspaper."

He smiled. "Perfect."

His mouth... Beneath her robe she felt her nipples harden. She remembered every detail of how his mouth had felt on her lips, on her breasts, on her entire body. "So how about you? You must be relieved, as well. Now that you're no longer going to do trial work, you can have that luxury of...time. Isn't that what you said?"

"And I said I was going to be *home*."

"Home." She repeated the word.

"I'm glad you brought that up."

"You've changed your mind?" She didn't want him to, she suddenly realized. She had dithered over which situation would be less painful for her. She still didn't know, but her indecision was over. She wanted him near her.

"No, but I've discovered something very important in the last few days. Or rather, I should have said I've discovered *someone*."

"S-someone? What are you talking about?" An unthinking fear clutched at her.

"You, Kit. I've discovered *you*."

She stared at him, quite sure her mind had played a trick on her. She couldn't have heard right. And if she had, she had to be misinterpreting what she was hearing. "What?"

With extreme tenderness, he took her hand in his. "Marry me, Kit. I know I'm doing this badly, but I've never done it before."

She felt the blood drain from her face. ''What are you doing?''

''I'm asking you to marry me.''

''No.'' Her answer was spoken before she had time to think about it, but once it was out, she knew she had given the right one.

Silence ricocheted around the room. It hit the walls with an awful percussion. It was horrible, and she rushed to stop it. ''I—I can't marry you, Des. Please understand.''

''I'm sorry, but I don't. Frankly, I thought you'd jump at the chance. I remember a time when you were throwing yourself at me.''

''I never did that.'' Now he had her on the defensive, a place where she didn't want to be. How could she have forgotten his stellar reputation as an attorney who could tear the opposition to shreds?

''Yes, you did.''

''You're talking about the time when my sisters and I went after you because of our father's will. That's a totally different situation.''

''Not really. The will still stands.''

''But the circumstances have changed. Tess and Jill are happily married now, and they've learned there are more important things in the world than to have controlling interest in a company.''

''I agree they're happy and have learned that, but don't kid yourself. If somehow they were handed control, they would take it so fast your head would spin.''

It was true, she thought morosely. But she no

longer cared who got what percentage. He would never believe her, though, nor would he understand.

"*But* if you and I married," he said, persisting, "*you* would have the advantage over your sisters."

"You would still vote your shares."

If there was one thing she now knew Des had in spades, it was integrity. No matter what anyone else said, he would always do what he thought was best. And she was positive he would think keeping control of his fifty percent was best. Besides, what man wouldn't want to have voting control of one of the richest companies in the world?

"My wife's opinion would be very important to me. I would consult her on all decisions."

His wife. She could barely stand to think about it. A surge of jealousy nearly brought her to her knees. The mere idea of another woman lying in his arms at night, eating breakfast with him each morning, made her almost sick. "I'm sure you would," she said in the most noncommittal voice she could manage.

What irony. He was offering her everything she had ever thought she wanted on a silver platter, and she was turning him down because he wasn't offering her his love. She had to be mad.

"The idea of that control doesn't tempt you even a little bit?"

Briefly she thought about lying and saying yes, but that would only give him more fuel for his argument. Plus, she needed to be as truthful as she could. She could get caught up in a web of lies. As long as he didn't ask her point-blank if she loved him, she would be fine. But love was the one word he hadn't used. "No. Not at all."

He raked his hands through his hair. "Then what is it, for Lord's sake?"

"There's no point in talking about this anymore."

"There's every point, because I don't understand. We have so much in common. We both love the ranch and the memories of it. We even both want children."

"Children? *That's* what this is about? You want children, and I happen to be handy, with all the necessary equipment to have them for you?"

Frustration creased his face. "Sure, why not?"

Now it all made sense to her. Des had accomplished a great deal in his life. He had left a positive mark on his chosen profession, and he was financially secure. But most of all, he had reached that age when a man started to think of children to carry on his name, his genes.

"How much of this has to do with the fact that we didn't use protection?"

"I hadn't even thought about it."

"I'm not pregnant, Des. I know it for a fact." She wished with all her heart she could be, but she had started her period a couple of hours ago.

"That's too bad. But after we're married, you could get pregnant. Why not, Kit? Think about it. Wouldn't you love to have a little girl with curly red hair and sparkling green eyes running free over the Double B?"

Truthfully, she wanted a child so badly she could almost taste it, a child she would raise in love rather

than fear. A little girl, as he'd said. Or perhaps a little
boy with the quick intelligence and dark good looks
of his father.

"Think about how happy she would be when we
gave her her first pony," he said, his deep voice continuing to hammer away at her. "Think about the
wonder she would feel when she saw her first calf
being born. Think about a little girl who would love
this land as much as you and I do."

She could feel her strength beginning to crumble.
"You're talking about a marriage of convenience,"
she said desperately. "No child should be brought
into a loveless marriage."

"Our child would be loved."

"Of course it would. But he or she would know,
Des. She would be able to *feel* that something was
wrong between us. She might not know what she was
feeling at first. But later, when she was older, she
would realize that there was no love between us, and
believe me, it would make her desperately unhappy."

"Not if we were the best of friends, and, Kit, I do
consider you my friend."

She couldn't stand one more second of his badger-
ing. Any second she was going to crack. "Can't you
just take *no* for an answer, Des? *Just take no.*"

He looked at her for several moments, his expression shuttered. "When you put it like that, I guess I
have to."

Kit couldn't sleep. Des wouldn't stay out of her
mind. Every word he had ever said to her came back

to her, as did every stroke of his hand on her skin. But most of all, the memory of the way he had made love to her burned in her brain, in her body.

She tossed and turned for hours, reliving every moment of his marriage proposal. Had she done the right thing by turning him down?

If she married him, the pain would be enormous, because she would always know he didn't love her. And she didn't think she was strong enough to live with him day in and day out for the rest of her life knowing that.

Yet there would also be tremendous pain trying to live without him, and her only comfort would be in knowing he wouldn't wake up one day and feel trapped. He would be free in case he ever truly fell in love.

The question was, which pain would be worse?

She paced the night away, and just before dawn, she took Dia out for a ride. He relished the run, his blond mane and tail streaming out behind him, his long legs easily eating up the distance.

The last time she had ridden him, she reflected sadly, she had been another person. In comparison to the way she felt now, she had been immature then. She hadn't truly understood what love was all about. She hadn't even begun to imagine the ecstasies and the heartbreak it could hold. She had considered herself in complete control of her life. She had felt young and strong.

Now she only felt old.

The wind whipped through her hair, and the cold

air bit at her skin. But no matter how far or how fast
she rode, she couldn't resolve her question.

There was only one thing she knew. No matter
what had happened between them, Des had remained
an honorable man. And by turning down his proposal
of marriage, she had hurt his male pride. If nothing
else, she owed him the truth.

She turned Dia back toward the homestead.

"Kit?"

She glanced over her shoulder, then went back to
brushing Dia down, trying to build up her courage to
go see Des. "Hi, Tio."

Tio had come to the ranch years before she was
born and had made it his home. He was one of those
men who seemed ageless, but his dark brown skin
was as tough as leather. "How are you this morning?"

"Fine, just fine." He ambled up to her, took off
his hat, then put it back on again. "Congratulations
on finding out who killed Cody."

"Thanks."

"'Course we all knew you didn't do it."

She threw the brush into a bucket, then patted Dia's
neck. "Thanks for your faith in me, Tio. It really
means a lot to me."

"Oh, I wasn't the only one. I hope you know that.
Most of us knew you were innocent. It was just
that…"

Tio obviously wasn't just passing the time of day
as she had originally thought. He had something he

definitely wanted to say to her. She closed Dia in his stall. "Just what?"

Tio gave a shake of his head. "Just that *damn* sheriff. I have to say, I don't take a quick dislike to many men, but I shore did him."

She smiled. "I know what you mean."

"Uh-huh." He glanced away, then back at her. "So I did something."

"What?"

"Well, you know, I was just outside the barn when you rode out after fightin' with Cody. Then, later, when I went in and I found Cody..." His lips came together, and he gave another shake of his head. "Well, I tell you right now, I was downright shocked just about out of my boots at finding him dead like that."

"I can well imagine," she said with sincere sympathy. At the same time, she was having a hard time figuring out what he was trying to tell her.

"And there that shovel lay, big as you please, with his blood all over it."

"You *saw* the murder weapon?"

"Oh, yeah. It wasn't that far away from him."

"But, Tio, no one has been able to find it."

"Yeah, I know. See, now and again, I'll read a mystery, and I sure do enjoy 'em. So when I saw that shovel, I decided it wouldn't hurt a thing in the world to hide it until I saw which way the wind was gonna blow."

Her mouth dropped open. "You *hid* it?"

He adjusted his hat. "Shore did. See, I remembered

your argument with Cody, and I got to thinkin' how you're always in and out of the barn, doin' stuff, and the like. And, well, I wasn't shore just exactly what had happened, but my thinkin' was that mornin' that it might be best to just hide the damn thing for a while. So I just up and took it out and buried it under some rocks in a ravine. When that sheriff came huffin' and a puffin' around, trying to make you out as guilty, I knew I'd done the right thing.'' He shrugged. ''Then it snowed.''

She stared at him, speechless.

''Don't see no point in diggin' it up now,'' he added.

''Tio, don't you realize that if the sheriff had found it, you could have gotten in big trouble?''

''Never gave it no mind at all.''

''I would have been really upset if that had happened.''

''Didn't.''

Impulsively she went over and hugged him. To her surprise, his face turned beet red. ''I can't tell you how much I appreciate your loyalty.''

With a great big grin on his face, he stepped back from her and touched the brim of his hat. ''Anytime.''

Still reeling from the information Tio had given her, Kit rang Des's doorbell. The last time she had visited this house, she reflected, it had been right before the death of Des's father. Thankfully, after her own father had died, she'd had the opportunity to grow close to her Uncle William. He had been so dear to her, so kind. She supposed that if she needed another reason to tell Des the truth, it would be to honor Uncle William. But she didn't need another reason. She only needed courage.

Des opened the door dressed only in a pair of jeans. She had lived all her life on a ranch where jeans were the norm, but Des looked better in jeans than any man she had ever seen. Her courage threatened to desert her.

Des frowned down at her. "Is something wrong?"

"No. May I come in?"

"Why?"

"I have a couple of things to tell you, one of them being about an amazing encounter I just had with Tio."

"And I would be interested in this because...?"

He definitely wasn't making this easy. "Because it concerns the murder."

He immediately stepped out of the way and gestured toward a door midway down the hall. "Go into the office."

She repressed a sigh. Obviously he wanted to keep things strictly business between them.

As soon as she walked into the office, she was immediately enveloped by a warm familiarity. Uncle William's big desk still sat in the same place as it had when he was alive. Large picture windows overlooked the snow-covered landscape and allowed in a flood of morning sunlight. A worn leather chair beckoned by a blazing fire. A nearby table held a rack of pipes and a humidor. Everything about the room soothed her.

"I see you haven't changed anything."

"I haven't seen any need to."

"I wouldn't, either."

"You mentioned Tio?"

He wanted her to get right to the point. This time she couldn't repress her sigh. "Yes. When I got back from my ride, Tio sought me out and told me that he hid the shovel Mike hit Cody with."

"You're kidding."

"No."

"Did he say why?"

"Out of loyalty to me."

He rubbed the side of his clean-shaven face. "I didn't even think of that possibility, but now that I do, it makes perfect sense."

"Tio also said he didn't think much of the sheriff."

"He's got good taste."

She smiled. "He's a good man."

"So where's the shovel?"

"In some ravine somewhere. I doubt we'll ever find it, and I don't see any reason to even go looking for it."

"I don't either." His gaze turned brooding. "So you have something else to tell me?"

She nodded. It was now or never. "It's about you asking me to marry you last night."

"You've said everything you need to."

"I didn't tell you the entire reason I turned you down."

He folded his arms across his bare chest. "You don't need to. You said no. That's more than enough."

"You don't understand."

"Oh, I understand *no* perfectly. Granted, I did try to change your mind at first, but you finally convinced me. I don't need further convincing."

"Okay, let me put it this way—I didn't tell you the entire *truth,* and I think you deserve it."

"If there's one thing I've learned by practicing law, it's that what a person deserves and what a person gets are two entirely different things."

One way or the other, she was determined he was going to listen to her. "Des, I *love* you."

Every muscle in his body stilled. "Would you repeat that?"

"I love you—too much to agree to a loveless marriage. It would end up being a trap for you. One day you'd fall in love with someone and end up resenting me and our marriage and maybe even our children."

He threw back his head and laughed.

Of all the reactions she had expected, that was the last. "Des?" she asked quietly. "Why are you laughing?"

"Honey, everyone should have the problems you and I have."

"I don't understand."

"You're smart. Figure it out."

She had never felt more stupid in her life. "Tell me."

"I love you, Kit. I love you irrevocably, completely and madly."

It couldn't be possible. Tears sprang into her eyes and hope trickled into her heart, but she had taught herself to be cautious. "Are you sure?"

"Did I leave out positively?" He drew her to him and spoke huskily. "I love you, Kit Baron. Our marriage won't change your last name, but it will change the rest of our lives for the better. Will you marry me?"

She began to laugh with pure happiness and threw her arms around him. "I may be slow, but I'm not a complete idiot. Of *course* I'll marry you."

He kissed her, and she returned the kiss with all her heart and soul.

Epilogue

Spring arrived at the Double B with a profusion of color. A gentle breeze rippled through colorful stands of Indian Blanket and Paintbrush. Newly planted tulips and daffodils held their pretty heads high. A just-built gazebo decorated with garlands of wild daisies stood in a freshly mowed meadow not far from the homestead.

As if she were also planted, Kit stood rooted before the cheval mirror in a corner of her bedroom. She had worn her hair down as Des had requested, but unsatisfied with what she saw, she flicked at the red curls, tugged at the ivory satin skirt of her tea-length wedding gown and readjusted the garland of spring flowers on her head.

Tess glided up behind her. "Stop fussing, Kit. I've never seen you look more beautiful."

"Or radiant," Jill added, coming up on her other side.

Kit smiled at the image of her two pregnant sisters in the mirror. Tess had just discovered she was pregnant and Jill was due in a month.

She couldn't wait to be an aunt, or for that matter a mother. She and Des planned to start on that project tonight. For their honeymoon, they were going to the island of *Serenity,* which Des owned with Jill's husband, Colin Wynne, and she couldn't wait.

"Considering that 'beautiful and radiant' is the way I would describe you two, I consider those great compliments."

Tess laughed. "The only way you can describe me these days is green with morning sickness."

"Green looks good on you." Kit held out her hand, palm down. "Look at this—I'm actually trembling."

"You've got nothing to be nervous about," Jill said. "Des is madly in love with you."

Tess smoothed her hand over her blond French twist. "He's also one of the world's truly great guys."

"I know. I know. It's just that I never thought I'd ever marry."

Tess grinned. "The only important thing now is that you had the good sense to say *yes.*"

Jill turned Kit around to face the two of them. "We brought you something."

"Oh, you shouldn't have done that. I'm just glad you're here."

"No more than we are." Tess left the room, then quickly reappeared carrying a long box that contained a gorgeous profusion of purple irises that had been tied with an ivory satin ribbon. "Jill and I would truly love it if you would carry these today as your bouquet."

A smile glinted in Jill's bourbon-colored eyes. "Half of them are from my garden, and half of them are from Tess's."

Kit gasped with surprise. "This is so *sweet* of you."

"It's from our hearts," Tess said. "Nick's grandmother gave me my start from her garden. When Jill married, I gave her a start from mine."

"And I've enjoyed them more than I ever thought possible," Jill said. "And, amazingly enough to me, they've actually thrived and multiplied."

"Now we want to give *you* a start, and we thought it would be nice if half came from each of our gardens."

"I'm very touched. Thank you."

A knock on the bedroom door sounded. "Kit?" Des called. "May I come in?"

"No," all three sisters answered in unison.

Jill walked over to the door and spoke through the wood. "What's wrong with you, Des? You know perfectly well that the groom is not supposed to see the bride until the wedding begins. It's bad luck."

"I don't believe in superstitions," he answered. "Besides, Kit and I are going to make our own luck."

Kit placed the bouquet on her bed. Just the sound of his voice had her pulse racing. She was still having a hard time believing that she was actually about to become his wife. But it was true. When she had agreed to marry him, she had entrusted her heart to him, and now she had complete faith that he would always treat it gently.

Jill glanced over her shoulder at Tess. "It's up to you."

She laughed, because she couldn't believe they were actually standing there, debating whether she was going to see Des now or see him in fifteen minutes. Besides, truthfully, she couldn't deny him anything. "I think he's right about our luck."

"Maybe he's got a point," Tess admitted to her. "I mean, after all, how many people are lucky enough to find their true soul mates the first time around? And not only have you and Des managed to do it, but Jill and Colin have done it, and so have Nick and I. *All* of us are incredibly lucky."

Kit gestured at the door. "So open the door."

Des walked in, and she felt her heart melt. He was wearing a hand-tailored black suit with a blazingly white shirt. She didn't think she had ever seen him look sexier or more handsome, nor had she ever been more in love with him than she was at that moment.

He immediately crossed to her. "You look beautiful, Kit."

Tears of pure happiness misted her eyes. "So do you."

He laughed, and the sound created a flood of joy in her.

Tess planted her hands on her hips and eyed him sternly. "Okay, Des, now you've seen her. So *go*. You'll see her again at the gazebo."

With obvious reluctance, Des stepped away from Kit. "Actually, as much as I wanted to see my bride-to-be, that's not the only reason I'm here. I want to conduct a short business meeting before the wedding begins, and I promise it won't take long at all."

"What?" Tess exclaimed. "Are you out of that amazing mind of yours? Get a grip. This is your *wedding* day."

"She's right," Jill said firmly. "We're *not* having a business meeting today, nor are we having one until you two get back from your honeymoon."

Kit put her hand on his arm. "Is this really that important, Des?"

He smiled down at her. "Besides asking you to marry me, I consider this one of the most important things I've ever done."

Jill's dark brows lifted. "Good grief, what is it?"

He reached into his jacket and retrieved three folded legal documents from its inner pocket. "I have a wedding gift I'd like to present to each of you."

"The *three* of us?" Tess asked. "I don't know what etiquette book you read, but it sounds interesting."

"My own." He patted the documents against his

palm. "I've divided up my fifty percent of Baron International into thirds, one for each of you."

Kit glanced at her two sisters and saw that they were as speechless as she was.

"I won't bore you with the details right now. Just know that as of noon yesterday, when our corporate lawyer officially filed the original documents, you each have full and equal rights in the company, with the stipulation that you'll will your portion to your children in equal parts. That same stipulation will apply to them, and so on and so on into perpetuity."

"*Des.*" Tears flooded Kit's eyes. "What a wonderful thing for you to do."

Jill and Tess stared at him, stupefied.

Jill was the first one to find her voice. "I can't believe you've done this."

He handed her a copy, then did the same for Kit and Tess. "Look for yourselves."

None of them could tear their astonished gaze from him.

"But what about you?" Jill asked.

He chuckled. "Don't worry about me. I've managed to make quite a few valuable investments over the years." He grinned at Kit. "Besides, if I ever go broke, I can live off my wife."

Jill shook her head. "That's not what I meant. Uncle William intended for you to have his share of the company or he never would have willed it to you in the first place."

"The most important thing my father ever taught me was to do what was right. He not only would have approved, but if he's looking down on us right now, he's giving a good old Texas yell.''

Kit leaned over and lightly kissed his cheek. ''Thank you, Des. It's the best gift you could ever have given us.''

His dark eyes glinted with love. ''You couldn't be more welcome, my darling, and it was my pleasure. See you at the altar?''

''I'll be there.''

''You better be,'' he whispered. Then, louder, ''I'll be the one with a bluebonnet in my lapel.'' He shot a grin at Tess and Jill, then left with a quiet click of the door behind him.

''I didn't think I could be any happier than I was before he came in,'' Kit said, brushing the tears from her eyes, ''but I am.''

''Good, because you deserve all the happiness in the world,'' Tess said. ''In fact, we all do.''

She took her sisters' hands in hers. ''We've done it. We've come through the fire our father created for us and we have survived. More than that, we're actually thriving. We deserve to be extremely proud of ourselves.''

Tess sniffed back her own tears. ''You're right.''

''Yes, you are.'' Jill blinked the moisture from her own eyes, reached for the bouquet of irises and handed it to Kit. ''So let's go. Colin and Nick are waiting for Tess and I, and you've got the most important date of your life at the gazebo.''

Letting out a peal of laughter, Kit cradled the flowers in her arms and headed out the door. Her future was waiting, and she didn't want to keep it waiting one more second.

Des.

*   *   *   *   *

SILHOUETTE®
DESIRE™

AVAILABLE FROM 16TH AUGUST 2002

TAMING HER MAN

THE TAMING OF JACKSON CADE BJ James
Men of Belle Terre
Haley Garrett knew she wanted Jackson Cade from the moment she
saw him. But despite their searing attraction Jackson fought and
resisted her. Could Haley penetrate his heart's defences?

COWBOY FOR KEEPS Kristi Gold
Dana Landry was mesmerised by Will Baker but his eyes showed he
was one hundred per cent male...and zero per cent husband! Dana
longed for the fairytale—but how to get Will to agree?

SURPRISE BABY

SINCLAIR'S SURPRISE BABY Barbara McCauley
Secrets!
Amnesia meant Lucian Sinclair couldn't remember his passionate
night with Raina Sarbanes. But one look into the eyes of Raina's
baby daughter and Lucian realised this child was *his*.

HIS BABY SURPRISE Kathie DeNosky
After just one sweet night with Lexi Hatfield, Dr Tyler Braden
discovered that Lexi was pregnant! Ty didn't want a wife...or a son,
so why was he fantasising about a lifetime of loving?

HIS BRIDE AT LAST

THE BRIDAL ARRANGEMENT Cindy Gerard
A marriage-of-convenience to naïve virgin Ellie Shiloh meant that
Lee Savage could claim his ranch. Lee wouldn't admit to needing his
bride but was his promise really made out of duty...or love?

A COWBOY, A BRIDE & A WEDDING VOW
Shirley Rogers
Jake McCall and Catherine St John had been lovers. Time had
hardened Catie's heart to Jake but, once he knew he had a son, he
vowed to keep the boy, and to have Catie—in his bed and as his bride!

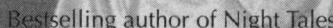

THE
COLTONS

FAMILY   PRIVILEGE   POWER

*Look out for our fabulous brand
new limited continuity series*
THE COLTONS,
*where the secrets of California's
most glamorous and talked about
dynasty are revealed!*

Available from 16th August

On Sale
16th August 2002
Beloved Wolf *by Kasey Michaels*

20th September 2002
The Virgin Mistress *by Linda Turner*

I Married a Sheikh *by Sharon De Vita*

18th October 2002
The Doctor Delivers *by Judy Christenberry*

From Boss to Bridegroom *by Victoria Pade*

15th November 2002
Passion's Law *by Ruth Langan*

The Housekeeper's Daughter *by Laurie Paige*

20th December 2002
Taking on Twins *by Carolyn Zane*

Wed to the Witness *by Karen Hughes*

17th January 2003
The Trophy Wife *by Sandra Steffen*

Pregnant in Prosperino *by Carla Cassidy*

21st February 2003
The Hopechest Bride *by Kasey Michaels*

SHERRYL WOODS

about that man

It was going to be a long, hot summer...

On sale 18th October 2002

Available at most branches of WH Smith,
Tesco, Martins, Borders, Eason, Sainsbury's
and most good paperback bookshops.

1002/136/SH35

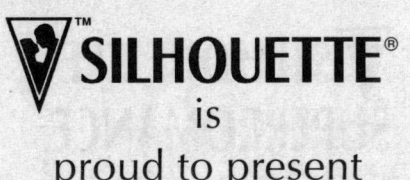**SILHOUETTE®**

is

proud to present

CHILDFINDERS, INC.

by

Marie Ferrarella

**When a child is missing
and a heart needs mending,
it's time to call CHILDFINDERS, INC.**

HERO FOR HIRE - *June*
Silhouette Sensation

AN UNCOMMON HERO - *July*
in *DANGEROUS TO LOVE*

A HERO IN HER EYES - *August*
Silhouette Sensation

HEART OF A HERO - *September*
Silhouette Sensation

0602/SH/LC30

FREE!
1 Book
and a surprise gift!

We would like to take this opportunity to thank you for reading this Silhouette® book by offering you the chance to take another specially selected title from the Desire™ series absolutely FREE! We're also making this offer to introduce you to the benefits of the Reader Service™—

- ★ FREE home delivery
- ★ FREE gifts and competitions
- ★ FREE monthly Newsletter
- ★ Books available before they're in the shops
- ★ Exclusive Reader Service discount offer

Accepting this FREE book and gift places you under no obligation to buy; you may cancel at any time, even after receiving your free shipment. Simply complete your details below and return the entire page to the address below. *You don't even need a stamp!*

YES! Please send me 1 free Desire book and a surprise gift. I understand that unless you hear from me, I will receive 2 superb new titles every month for just £4.99 each, postage and packing free. I am under no obligation to purchase any books and may cancel my subscription at any time. The free books and gift will be mine to keep in any case.

D2ZEB

Ms/Mrs/Miss/Mr ....Initials ....
BLOCK CAPITALS PLEASE

Surname ....

Address ....

....

....Postcode ....

Send this whole page to:
UK: The Reader Service, FREEPOST CN81, Croydon, CR9 3WZ
EIRE: The Reader Service, PO Box 4546, Kilcock, County Kildare (stamp required)